WHERE NO MAN PURSUETH

WHERE NO MAN PURSUETH

a novel

MICHEAL E. JIMERSON

atmosphere press

Published by Atmosphere Press

Cover design by Nick Courtright

Where No Man Pursueth
2020, Micheal E. Jimerson

10 9 8 7 6 5 4 3 2 1

atmospherepress.com

This novel is dedicated to the people of East Texas. I have witnessed your courage, resiliency, and Christian values throughout my career as your County and District Attorney. Wickedness preys on all of us. Our measure is not that evil befell us, rather it is how we respond. Our rich history inspired the events depicted; however, the characters are fictional.

Proverbs 28:1 (King James Version)

The wicked flee when no man pursueth, but the righteous are bold as a lion.

PROLOGUE

Warm syrup filled the little boy's cheeks, flooding the corners of his mouth. He closed his mouth in time to catch most of the warm nectar. The rest of the viscous liquid dripped down his dirty face like honey. He bit into the squishy peach slice before flaking loose the golden fried crust with his tongue.

His eyes rolled back into his head, savoring the gooey treat. He looked at the treasure near his hand. Should he try the apple, the pear, or the sugar and cocoa powder? Soon gritty sweet granules of chocolate displaced the peach syrup. Each grain exploded with flavor as they passed over his lips.

His head jerked forward as he heard his mom call his full name. It was always bad when she included his middle name. He ran then stopped, turning back around. The board holding the pies was behind the trunk of an enormous magnolia tree. All he saw were limbs, trunk, and the slick, glossy-green long leaves covering each branch. He took comfort in the sight and began running again.

His short legs were in full gait as he swung around the corner of the sun-bleached batten-board house. The house stood on brick piers and he almost slid under it, his tiny heart was beating so strong. It banged in his head and throat like a drum. He looked up at his mother. He swung his head up and back from the hem of her long violet dress to her stern face. Then he darted his gaze away. She stood above him on the top step of the porch. Behind her his father stepped into the doorway.

Again, she called him by his full name. She had to know it was him. She was looking right at him. Then she asked, “Where are the pies? I had them cooling on the window sill.”

He opened his mouth, yet words didn’t form on his tongue. He shook his head from side to side.

She said, “You know you nail Jesus to the cross every time you lie.”

The man behind her placed a huge hand on her shoulder. “The boy didn’t do it. I told you it’s the no-account bum you keep feeding. You never should have let him do odd jobs around here. Told you it won’t do. Looks bad.”

The mother looked through the child, and then turned to her husband. The man’s black eyes were cold. He slouched from a full day dragging logs with his mule team. The indebted farm needed the extra income. She had so wanted to reward his hard work and lift his spirits with his favorite dessert.

The boy peered at her out of the corner of his eye. Her downcast countenance revealed nothing but anger to the boy. A more sophisticated viewer might have seen in her hazel eyes the raging debate to determine the lesser of two evils.

The man’s gruff voice spoke. “I’m going to lie down before Thatcher and his boys bring the dogs. Instead of coons, we’ll hunt us your little pet tonight.” He turned, disappearing into the house.

She descended the porch steps. The boy looked at his toes in the dirt. He moved to give his mother room to pass and then felt the stemmy Bahia grass stub his bare feet.

She reached around his back pulling his hands around to her. They were sticky, coated in gooey peach resin. The realization overcame the boy like a vibration riding down a current into his feet. She knew. There was no fooling momma. Why hadn't he told her the truth?

He might get punished, though it wouldn't be a hard spanking, not like if his father caught him. He would have to find her a switch. After it was over, she might ease his stomach pain.

She folded onto her knees, sitting in the grass so she was eye level with the boy. "Can you find the church?"

"Yes, ma'am."

"You remember Tob? The old man. Remember, you asked me why he had no hair and only one arm."

The boy nodded.

"Preacher lets him live in a shed behind the church. You're gonna tell him I said, 'Run.'"

The boy continued looking at his feet, nodding.

"What did I say to tell him?"

"Run."

"Tell him the truth and tell him I said, 'Run.' Now go, and when you get back put my board back on the window sill."

The boy hesitated. She turned him around and smacked his backside enough to put his small body in motion.

He ran. His belly cramped, yet still he ran over rocky gravel digging into his bare feet, and still he ran. The boy raised his hands to keep from striking the door of the shed. The shed held yard tools and the occasional church decoration.

The builder had made a door using unfinished two-bysixes braced by two-by-fours. Bark remained on the edges of the lumber. The door swung inward revealing a thin man.

Tob smiled, "Boy, what you doin here?"

The child spoke in a series of snorts, drawing breath, and yelling at the same time. After a moment, drawing his breath, he recited his message. "Momma say run, run now."

"Can't run, boy. Promised the preacher-man I would get those flower beds weeded and ready for fall." He looked in the boy's eyes placing his one good hand on his knee for balance.

"Run. I ate the pies. Pa thinks you did it. Momma says run."

"So, your momma thinks your Pa will beat on me some."

The boy hadn't put it together, though he nodded his head forward and backward.

"Done nothing. I ain't gonna run. Promised the preacher man. Man's only as good as his word, boy."

The child shook his head from side to side, tears streaming down his cheeks. "I'll tell Pa the truth."

The old man slid his leg back, moving down to one knee. He put his thumb on the boy's cheek, sliding the full tear from the mix of dirt, sweat, and peach elixir. His voice moved in a sentence rising from tender to firm. "No sense in that. Done's done. No lookin back. Won't be the first time I been beat on."

Tob lifted the child's head. "You promise me boy. Anybody ever say anything bad about your momma, you don't believe it. Lady's like Jesus with skin on."

The boy nodded and Tob released him with a shout.

"Get."

He ran past the front of the church back to the road. As his foot touched the road, he felt a fear so strong it shook his shoulders. Why had his mother been so insistent Tob run? What would his father do? Why would his father hurt Tob? Tob had never done anything to anybody.

Looking up behind him he saw the steeple. The preacher never locked the church and older children had already shown him how to reach the bell in the steeple. He folded himself into a corner from where he could see Tob's shed. He leaned his head against a wall of the church spire, and he slept.

Little wonder his mind filled with nightmares. His insides were a mish-mash of golden, warm, sweet, flaky, jelly filled pies. He knew he hadn't fooled his mother. Still, instead of being mad her voice had trembled with fear.

Was the barking of the dogs real or part of the dream? Other than the dogs no noise reached the spire. The boy looked down. Tob rolled on the ground trying to protect his body from punches and kicks. His father stood to the side, neither taking part nor trying to stop the beating.

They were beating Tob over what the child had done, though the boy didn't understand why the pies brought down so much wrath. He wanted to tell his father the truth. He knew what Tob said was true, "Done's done. No lookin back." There was no way to make them stop. No way to help Tob. No way to fix the mess he had made.

The sour taste of bile invaded his throat. He was vomiting onto the bell. He scurried down. All the way home, his head pounded and his belly ached. The boy couldn't look at his momma. He wrapped his arms around her legs. Her long dress caught his tears.

PART I

There'll Be No Lynching, No Burning, and No Skinning

CHAPTER 1: THE MURDER

Pine forest weave through the hills of East Texas before such trees give way to ancient oaks rising from sloughs and anchored by cypresses encased in Spanish moss. No trace marks the years, centuries, and eons. Only delving beneath the surface reveals the product of an imponderable chronology, crushing pressure, and massive heat. Oil is not the real treasure of East Texas. Her true gift to the world is a heritage handed down by generations who have proven racism, corruption, and greed don't define the human condition. Rather, it is an unwavering belief that the image of divine justice within our souls is both our heritage and our future.

Young Ray Elliott was standing in the lobby of the Halten bank in Nacogdoches, Texas. Soon, events would occur, driving the remainder of his life. In fact, he held no appreciation for the power of the crucible before him. He had meandered through adolescence without expectation for his life.

Ray Elliott had heard racial slurs yelled out in anger. Although he didn't use such language, it was commonplace. Why did the words take him aback today? It was the source. The source seemed so unlikely.

The offending speaker was a handsome man wearing a blue suit and a high starched collar with a matching tie. Everyone in Nacogdoches was acquainted with the man. He was the bank owner's son-in-law. Even while yelling, the man spoke with no perceptible accent, a rare sound in the Deep South. Moreover, because of his father-in-law's wealth and standing, this man was akin to a celebrity.

Ray Elliott shook his head, pondering the inexplicable incongruence. Such open bigotry from a man the accepted gossip claimed was carrying on an affair with a young black girl. Yet here stood Richard Watersong, disparaging another man in a vile manner for the color of the person's skin. Richard Watersong added to his considerable tirade of racism, "... you have to satisfy your debts."

Ray Elliott interjected, "Always heard tell Lukas Halten built his banks on Christian values. Figured it was a bunch of lies." He gestured to the man bearing the brunt of Richard Watersong's yelling.

Richard Watersong's face indicated he was beyond perturbed by the insolence of young Ray Elliott. Richard Watersong reached his left hand out in front of him like he was catching some part of himself for fear he would leap upon the boy. "I am not doing this. I am not arguing with a white trash scrap of a boy over a colored who can't pay his debts, so take your chickens and your eggs and whatever else you are going around selling and tell your momma and daddy they won't be doing any more business with this bank. Tell them they better look to their own note."

Ray Elliott scanned the long wood counter topped by parallel iron bars extending to the ceiling. His eyes met the hired clerk, and he stole a glimpse of the young black woman who was the topic of gossip throughout the community. Ray Elliott's family would face ruin, for what? Because he irritated the wealthiest man in town? Why had he made such an impetuous and stupid decision?

Grappling with self-pity regarding the unfairness of

the universe only led to more guilt in the end. As his father had said, "He was old enough to know how the world worked."

The middle-aged black man was dressed similar to Ray Elliott. They were both wearing the uniform of a poor farmer. The black man begged for his home. "Mr. Richard, I paid the money back. That's what I rode all the way from London to tell you. Please don't take my land. It's all my family has."

Richard Watersong said, "No receipt is no payment. I am sure you were told the same at the home bank in Henderson."

Richard Watersong appeared to be drawing a deep breath to complete the castigation of the debtor when the thud-dinging sound of a hammer hitting wood resonated from the back of the store. Richard Watersong turned toward the back of the bank. "Dock, stop tearing out the wall."

Ray Elliott looked toward the back of the store. He couldn't see past the start of a narrow hallway. Then he turned his slumped shoulders in the other direction, toward the door, looking for fresh air. Ray Elliott decided somehow money must rot because banks always smelled musty.

Richard Watersong swung back around, directing a long finger at the black farmer. "You get out of here before I have the sheriff arrest you."

Before Ray Elliott reached the door, it swung open, revealing an elegant lady dressed in a flowing series of emerald green ruffles which were set off by black embroidery. Her red hair was in a tall bun held in place by heavy dark comb. The dress drew out the green in her hazel eyes. Perfume like fresh-cut flowers divided the humid morning air. Behind her was a well-dressed elderly man in a dark suit.

Ray Elliott recognized the old man. He was bank owner, Lukas Halten, and this must be his daughter, Richard Watersong's wife. She was the second most talked about woman in town these days. Ray Elliott had to compare the two women. Everyone else did. He wondered whether Mrs. Watersong even knew she had a rival. Then he answered his own question. Of course she didn't know.

The younger woman, really a girl, busied herself in a corner with a broom. She was a vastly different kind of beauty. A petite and dark-skinned doll with a heart-shaped face appearing as if she were molded from chocolate, like she would melt at the touch. The rumors claimed she hadn't melted at Richard Watersong's touch. Her flower sack dress couldn't diminish her.

Lukas Halten's voice boomed from the entryway. "Richard, we need to talk. Now, in the back." The tone was in stark contrast to his frail appearance.

"Queeny, get a cup of coffee and bring it to Mr. Halten." Richard Watersong bellowed as he turned for the hallway.

Ray Elliott looked at the large raised letters over the door. *A heart at peace gives life to the body, but envy rots the bones, Proverbs 14:30.* He stepped through the door, surveying the intersection of Pecan and Main Street. The square was crammed with wagons and mules. Across the traditional Spanish style square, he could see the Old Stone Fort decaying on the opposite corner.

His mind was racing. What was he going to do? He heard the voice from over his shoulder and turned toward the sound.

"I appreciate you trying to do right. I'm Cecil Grant and I paid him back once."

"I don't doubt you, Mr. Grant."

The big man's dark eyes were pleading. "My father got the land from the Freedman's Bureau. I am grateful he has been called to glory and didn't live to see me lose it."

Ray Elliott gave the man some space. He looked out over a square crowded with wagons and mule teams. "I reckon you got a family."

"Four kids and a wife." Cecil Grant offered his hand. "I want to thank you again for trying. Not many white folks would, especially not a young man like yourself. It's odd, downright curious of you, but thanks."

Ray Elliott moved the plucked broilers from his right hand to join the basket of eggs in his left before shaking the man's hand. "I will pray for you." Ray Elliott really wasn't much of a praying person, but it seemed like the thing to say. Besides, the man's compliment was kind of a strange compliment, though the look in the Cecil Grant's face conveyed sincerity.

The tall man turned and walked toward a swayback horse. The old horse was a flea-bitten gray with a saddle, which looked like it might have served a conquistador on an expedition of conquest in an earlier century. The bridle was braided horse hair made in a style no longer in use. Cecil Grant's tall gaunt frame echoed the announcement of poverty his horse and saddle made.

Ray Elliott had the answer to why he had crossed a powerful man and put his family at risk with no thought as to the consequences. Cecil Grant had nothing material in this world, yet his head was high and his demeanor firm. Debtor or small-town king, black or white, young or old, man or woman, Richard Watersong had no right to any person's dignity.

Ray Elliott looked all around the square. There were shops, businesses, and residences in every direction. Still, there was nowhere presenting any better prospect of selling his wares than any other direction. His mother was trying to raise money to take one of his little sisters to the doctor. His youngest sister was born sickly and never seemed to get much better. Liza Jane was the most affectionate of his siblings, and the one to whom he was most attached. How was he going to tell his parents he had failed again?

The square and the town looked the same as it had when he was fourteen, when he was ten, the same as long as he could remember: small, stifling, and mind numbing. There was no opportunity, no future, and no escape. His father let him plant his own patch of tomatoes this year. They had gotten the blight early in the season and rotted on the vine. The saggy skin of the tomatoes covering the slippery unformed pulp fell into a black decomposition. He looked down at his feet, half expecting to see the dark rot overtaking him too.

His head snapped back at the sudden swoosh of the door behind him. A blur slammed into his chest. It twisted him sprawling onto the street with the chicken and eggs flying into the air. A boot landed next to his head in the warm mud and then it was up and gone.

Ray Elliott looked toward the bank and caught the sunlight reflecting from Richard Watersong's cuff links. He was hollering something. He was yelling, "Murderer."

"Stop him. He killed Lukas Halten." Richard

Watersong's fine suit was covered in a wide spatter pattern of blood.

Ray Elliott strained his head to look between wagons and mules. He glimpsed a black man wearing a pair of light-colored overalls and a tan shirt running frantically. The man knocked over an old farmer and kept running.

Ray Elliott jumped to his feet. He easily passed Richard Watersong, weaving through the crowded square. He continued chasing the man in overalls south onto Fredonia Street. He crossed the footbridge over Banita Creek.

Ray Elliott put the route together in his head. He began running for Auggie's livery as if he knew where the man must be going.

A gunshot echoed through the street. Ray Elliot ran toward the sound. He crashed into the barn and caught movement past him in the corral. There was another gunshot and Ray Elliott looked himself over, surprising himself with the absurdity of his reaction. He was looking to see if he was shot. There was no blood, no holes.

Ray Elliott saw the proprietor, the man he knew to be old Auggie. He wasn't hit, though he was stumbling. "Smacked my head against the wall and beat me with my own pistol. Strong fellow, dark as night."

Ray Elliott towered over old Auggie, so it was easy to see the trickle of blood above the elderly man's left ear. "Auggie, we need to get you to a doctor."

Old Auggie shook his head. "No, the scoundrel has the horse I just bought. He's only green broke. Going to be the best with a little work. You got to get him for me or I'm done, cleaned out."

There was a loud voice from the street. "No one is going to 'get' anyone. It's foolishness, nothing but a good way to get yourselves killed. I will probably telephone and wire the surrounding sheriffs and marshals, then the rangers. Someone will stop him along the way."

The voice belonged to a man wearing a shiny star on his dark waistcoat who was making his way through the street. He was pulling a small crowd of townsfolk behind him. His attire seemed more appropriate for a stage production. He wore stove-pipe boots with 'Sheriff' embroidered on the tops in grey, matching the wide brimmed Stetson hat. Ray Elliott's attention was drawn to a large white tie pin made to mimic a diamond with the initials, I&GN in black letters.

Old Auggie turned to the sheriff. "Take days to get lawmen here. He'll be long gone. We got to go now." Old Auggie was a tiny framed man who walked stooped, even when he hadn't been injured.

The sheriff shook his head with deliberation and then grimaced. "The man is well mounted, armed, and desperate. It is too late for Lukas Halten. A stolen horse and a pistol are not worth getting killed over. We got no good men to go chasing him. Even if he gets a little further down the road, we are not going to lose a crop over it."

Ray Elliott looked at Old Auggie. He couldn't remember not knowing the man. Auggie had been old all Ray Elliott's life. Despite an ever-increasing stoop to his shoulder and the obvious damage inflicted to his twisted hands by arthritis, Old Auggie never complained. So, for Old Auggie, the ask was akin to begging. Ray Elliott said, "I'll go." The crowd looked at the youth, and his words surprised him, too.

The sheriff's face tightened, and his mustache seemed to twitch. He waved a gauntlet encased finger at Ray

Elliott. "You are not going, boy."

Richard Watersong arrived, looking disheveled. He was out of breath. "The sheriff is right, boy. He is a cold-blooded murderer."

The sheriff asked, "What is the killer's name?"

Richard Watersong answered, "Dock Baxter. He was remodeling my office. He stole some cash from the vault room but couldn't get in the safe. I suspect Lukas Halten walked in on him."

While the sheriff continued to interview Richard Watersong, Old Auggie slipped to the back of the barn and saddled a blue roan.

Ray Elliott put his hand over Old Auggie's shoulder and stepped in front him. Ray Elliott found the stirrup and squeezed his legs. He was out the back door before the sheriff could yell at him.

The powerful horse was loping in the general direction the murderer appeared to be headed. Ray Elliott had no experience chasing murderers. He had read a few dime novels. Actually, he read the same few until the covers wore off and the bindings broke. The long strides of the gelding were taking him further and further from town, further and further from the life he knew. Later, he would look back realizing he cast himself on the sea of a dangerous life without thought to the ramifications.

CHAPTER 2: THE PROMISE

Would a murderer use the road or try his luck across country fields or deep woods? He sat back on the horse, slowing the spirited animal until he made a stop, turning the big blue's head back toward him.

Ray Elliott leaned down and patted the horse's neck. "Never rode a blue horse before. Blue, where would we go if we had killed a man? We're on a green broke, stolen stallion. The horse has got to be a handful. Now, if I'm no horseman with a powerful lot of horseflesh under me and I want to go fast. I reckon I would just ride without much thought, likely in some panic after killing a man. Maybe a water crossing might unhorse a man who is hanging on more than riding."

Ray Elliott patted the big horse then continued pondering his options. The murderer was traveling generally northwest, which after many days of traveling might get him to Dallas or Ft. Worth. Good places for a man to get lost, but north meant he had to cross the Angelina River. There it was; a choke point, because this Dock Baxter having his hands full with an untrained horse would likely take the easiest crossing.

Ray Elliott touched the saddle gun tied by the ring and scabbard to the saddle. He recalled an elevation overlooking the most likely crossing on the Angelina River. It was a fine spot to set up with a long gun.

The blue roan began galloping over gradual hills, then onto a road. Soon Ray Elliott saw the oak trees denoting the bottom land country. He was approaching the river.

The water was probably about normal height, judging from the level on the oak trees along the creek bank. Ray Elliot hid the horse in a dense motte of pin oaks not far east off the road and pulled the rifle Auggie had placed in a scabbard tied to the saddle. Then he waited behind a big post oak.

Ray Elliott had plenty of time to reflect on the words of the sheriff and Richard Watersong, mocking his ability to catch the killer. The sun was hot even in the shade. There was some relief here on the river bank. Ray Elliott's hands were soaked with sweat. There was little to do except ponder whether Dock Baxter had passed a different way, taken another crossing, or changed directions altogether. For all Ray Elliott knew, the green horse had claimed the green rider and Dock Baxter was laying somewhere with a broken back.

Ray Elliott had every tree and bush in the landscape memorized. His eye was drawn immediately to movement to his south. In the distance, he could make out a rider. As the rider gradually closed the distance, Ray Elliott could see the dark horse was lathered in foamy sweat. He concluded the murderer had ridden the horse as hard as the mount could gallop. There was no way to know how many times Dock Baxter had changed directions and then thought better of it before finally choosing this road.

Ray Elliott stepped out from behind the tree and fired into the air. As he anticipated, the skittish horse raised straight up and dumped the rider on his back side. "Let me see your hands."

Dock Baxter was trembling in fear. Ray Elliott instinctively looked at his own hands. There was a strange calm to them.

Dock Baxter sat up, leaning back on his palms. "I am no murderer. Mr. Richard killed Lukas Halten."

"You going to have to work on your lying. It don't even make sense."

Dock Baxter was soaked with sweat and more than shaking; he was vibrating in fear. "Look mister, all I know is he called me into the storeroom and there he was, bigger than Dallas, Mr. Richard Watersong standing over Lukas Halten."

"You're lying."

The whites of Dock Baxter's eyes were all the brighter under the shade of the oaks. He was unarmed and covered in dust. What had looked like a mountain of a man was now cowering in the muck near a narrow crossing.

Dock Baxter clasped his hands together in a prayer. "Mister, just shoot me now. I watched a man get lynched when I was a boy. They got tired of holding him up and he slipped down, then they pulled him up again. Kicking and swinging and thrashing, losing control of his self, messing himself. I can't die being lynched. You got to promise I won't die being lynched or burnt up."

Dock Baxter was on his knees. His posture was even more of a prayer kneel. "I will never get a trial, not even a three-hour Jim Buchannan trial. Mr. Lukas Halten was a rich man. Richard Watersong is too. People will lynch me as soon as I get back. You won't even try to stop them. It's a strangling death where a man lives as long as he can bow his neck." Tears were rolling down his cheeks.

Ray Elliott held the gun with his right hand and raised his left hand in an effort to stop what had become outright wailing.

Dock Baxter slowed his tears enough to speak. “You know he’s sporting the young black gal, Queeny, and still he would lead the white cappers to lynch me tonight. I could hear you. I was in one of the back offices. You stood up to Mr. Richard and tried to help a black man. Why I started hammering louder; I was mad.”

Dock Baxter placed his head against the end of the rifle barrel. The action took Ray Elliott by surprise, and he reasserted his two-handed grip. The crying had ended. Ray Elliott heard the gentle swish of the slow-moving river. He felt the pressure on the end of the old Winchester seventy-three. After so many sudden events, time slowed, almost running backwards.

Dock Baxter looked up at his captor. Ray Elliott could only see two huge dark orbs set in pools of white.

Dock Baxter yelled, “Promise me or I will make you kill me here and now.”

Ray Elliott shook his head and looked above Dock Baxter, out over the muddy river and into the jungle-like vegetation on the bank. “You are going to make me kill you, unless I agree to kill you before you can ever be lynched. I mean, I might only be saving you to get you lawfully hung by the judge.”

Dock Baxter pushed his forehead further into the barrel. “A real hanging breaks a man’s neck and he is graveyard dead in a heartbeat. A real hanging ain’t like skinning a man alive for talking to white women or setting a man on fire and watching him run. No kind of right and you know it.”

Ray Elliott struck a fateful bargain which would drive him for much of his life. “I give you my word, there’ll be no lynching, no burning, no skinning. I’ll put a bullet through your head myself first. I expect if you have any honor then you will help me collect your horse and ride back to Nacogdoches."

The ride to Nacogdoches was uneventful. Ray Elliott wanted to believe Dock Baxter's honor compelled the man not to attempt escape. However, his gut told him the old Winchester carbine served as powerful persuasion. Ray Elliott remained silent, often looking at the gun in his hand like he was living someone else's life.

Dock Baxter chattered the story of his earlier escape from town, including the harrowing ride. He bragged about his skill as a horseman, despite holding onto the mount by whatever providence provided whether saddle horn, cantle, mane, or tail.

It was near dusk, and the streets were full of townspeople. The promise consumed Ray Elliott's thoughts now. He looked at the townspeople. If necessary, could he fire into a crowd of people he had known all his life? His gaze tuned to Dock Baxter. Could he kill an unarmed man in cold blood? The all-encompassing promise pushed all other thoughts from his mind. What an absurd idea? Dock Baxter chose him because he was not a racist, yet if he kept the promise, he might kill a defenseless man for the color of the man's skin. He boiled with anger at the bigot known for his affair with a person of another race. All Southerners knew such a relationship was forbidden, miscegenation. Ray Elliott had heard the huge word hurled like a grenade at the non-prejudiced.

Then there was the incredible promise. He would shoot Dock Baxter in the head prior to permitting the man to be tortured. Ray Elliott knew it was possible many of his friends and neighbors would take justice into their own hands, regardless of the accused's race, but so much more if he were black. This man asked him to do more than simply try to stop the vigilantism. Such an attempt was likely futile, anyway. This man, this Dock Baxter, asked Ray Elliott to terminate his life in a humane manner. It was both an infinitesimally small request and an unfathomable demand all at the same time.

The crowd looked at them like they had never seen a murderer, but on the other hand, neither had Ray Elliott before today. There was no norm for how they were supposed to react.

When they finally reached the sheriff's office, the sheriff was no more genial than when Ray Elliot had left town. His greeting gave no inkling of welcome. "You are lucky he didn't shoot your fool head off. Tenderfoot pup chasing a killer, but there with no more sense than God gave a Billy goat."

Ray Elliott defended himself against the verbal lambast. "I reckon he dropped Old Auggie's gun trying to ride the green broke stallion."

The sheriff turned and faced the crowd more than Ray Elliott. "All the same it was a fool thing to do."

Someone yelled out from the crowd. "Sheriff, you might as well pin your star on the boy. You'll have to do it after the next election, anyway."

Another said, "It took a boy to make a lawman with some sand."

The sheriff's face went pale and his mustache twitched as he stepped backward. The fine tie pin caught the light, and Ray Elliott was again drawn to the lettering. "Hold on now. Boy, what is your name, anyway?"

"Ray Elliott."

Sheriff said, still addressing himself to the crowd, "Boy, I may have judged you a mite too harsh. You got a knack for this business. I am going write a letter to the adjutant general in Austin and get you on with the rangers." The sheriff was smiling. "Likely they will send a good hand like you to the frontier battalion, bringing order to the border country. I will do all I can to see to it you get there. Now you come in here and take a rest while I lock up this outlaw."

On the porch standing over the sheriff's shoulder stood Richard Watersong. Ray Elliott raised the other matter plaguing him on the ride back to town. "Dock Baxter didn't have a dollar on him. Odd, ain't it?" This time it was Ray Elliot who turned his voice to the crowd as the sheriff had done so earlier. "So, he killed Lukas Halten because he caught him stealing. Where is the money, Richard?"

Richard Watersong looked around as if he had rehearsed his response and the cue had been given. "Farm boy, don't call me Richard. Don't seem odd to me, farm boy. If he can't hold on to a gun riding a big stallion, then I don't see how he could hold the money. Equally likely he hid it somewhere along the trail or even lost the money altogether while he was riding for his life." Richard Watersong was smugly reminding Ray Elliott of stories about how Richard Watersong had purportedly had some acting courses in the fancy Eastern college he attended.

Ray Elliott looked to Dock Baxter, expecting at any moment the man would protest his innocence and point the finger at Richard Watersong. He didn't. He just came over the horse, head down and bent over at the waist as he walked into the jail. Was he guilty or was he scared blaming a town pillar would get his neck stretched even quicker?

The promise didn't include providing an adequate defense, yet Ray Elliott couldn't help but question Richard Watersong's smugness. "How much did he take, anyway?"

"Farm boy, I didn't stop to count it. I got a balling wife and two little boys who lost Grandpa. Sheriff, I don't see any point in putting my family through a trial or waiting for a district judge and lawyers to take these good folks' tax dollars. I am first to say a man should have a trial, but not when he is guilty."

The crowd raised a shout, cheering the assertion. Ray Elliott didn't have a response for such horsesense. It was imminently reasonable; after all, a trial made no difference to a guilty man. The crowd shared the sentiment. A roar of agreement went up, then a hand arose from inside the jail and pushed Dock Baxter into the street.

Ray Elliott had given his word. Southern culture instilled the value of honoring his word, regardless to whom it was given. He must honor the commitment. Still, Ray Elliott felt betrayed. Dock Baxter had assumed a guilty posture when he should have repeated his accusations against Richard Watersong. Didn't these developments work to release Ray Elliott's obligation? No, and he couldn't ponder longer on the moral quandary presented to him.

Ray Elliott pulled the trigger, and the Winchester barked into the air as he pulled hard left on the reins and steadied the jumpy blue roan horse. "I gave my word there would be no lynching. I don't aim to be made a liar over a few days and a judge's time."

The sheriff pulled his pistol. "Boy, you're not the law

here."

The pistol was leveled at Ray Elliott while the younger man's saddle gun was pointing to the tin star. Ray Elliott looked into the grey eyes of a tired and aging sheriff. He knew the sheriff wasn't going to pull the trigger. This was the only thing the cheap novels had right. A person doesn't look at the gun or to the gun hand which has the drop on him. Neither the question nor the answer resides there. Ray Elliott's investment in outhouse literature was paying off. The sheriff was a dandy man who enjoyed living too much to die today.

Ray Elliott recognized a sometime-stable worker from Auggie's Livery. "Charlie Portis, go get me two fresh saddled mounts with any provisions Auggie might have for a trip. Let him know I will get his horses back to him."

Someone from the crowd yelled, "We'll have to get us a bigger rendering pot, we got two of them to scald the skin off of now."

Richard Watersong stepped forward. "Where can you go, south to Lufkin, east to Timpson or Louisiana? It's all timber country and your colored stole the payroll for some of the largest outfits in the business."

The two men stared at each other. Richard Watersong's dark blue eyes held no trepidation. They were cold and deep, like calm pools hiding a vicious riptide.

Richard Watersong broke the silence. "I know what you are thinking, boy. You can turn north to Henderson, maybe the Henderson Rifles, and the militia unit from the Jim Buchannan trial will save you. Well, let me remind you of a little fact; Lukas Halten was raised in Henderson and it is still the home bank."

Ray Elliott transferred to the new horse and nodded

for Dock Baxter to do the same. After the barrel of the lever gun swung toward the sheriff again, he moved for Dock Baxter to reach the horse. Ray Elliott motioned for the sheriff to tie Dock Baxter's hands to the cantle.

Ray Elliott spoke under his breath in a hushed tone to Richard Watersong "God help you if you tried to kill an innocent man."

Richard Watersong retorted in the same hushed tone. "Nobody is innocent, boy. We come in this world guilty and progress worse from there; even you, boy."

Ray Elliott fired into the air and in one smooth motion he took the reins of Dock Baxter's horse, spurred his own and both mounts were in a gallop.

In addition to the mob suffering from a lack of courage, there was a lack of effective leadership. The deficits combined to prohibit action. The sheriff muttered something about phoning and telegraphing as many places as possible. Then he seemed to fix on a realization. Perhaps he did not want all of East Texas to know he had lost a prisoner. The sheriff had thus painted himself into a corner. The hothead who had made the rendering pot remark was useless without a white cap and a bottle of liquid courage.

Richard Watersong said, "If you hens are done clucking, then let me tell you I refuse to let the murderer of Lukas Halten by a colored stand. Lukas Halten dedicated his life to the negroes. He started a bank not to turn a dollar, but to give all people opportunity and peace of mind. This was treachery, pure and wicked. More proof you can't do enough for the lesser races; Lukas Halten is dead. I, for one, leave tonight and I won't return until Lukas Halten has been avenged, as God is my witness."

CHAPTER 3:
INTO THE CAVE

"You going to try to hide out in a cave. Man, I knew you was crazy." Dock Baxter was gazing up at a small wood facade cut out of the side of the hill. There was a door and a few rough-cut pine boards on each side with narrower batten boards placed over the seams. There was nothing square or even cut to the same length. The early dawn revealed the yard consisted of pine and sweet gum saplings, barely distinguishing it from the surrounding wilderness.

Ray Elliott and Dock Baxter stepped off their horses. Ray Elliott kept the rifle trained on Dock Baxter and yelled at the house. "I am looking for William Preston Henry, the lawman."

The door wouldn't have been sufficient for a chicken coop, much less a house. There was a loud boom like a stick of dynamite had been ignited and the chicken coop door exploded open, as well as into pieces.

Ray Elliott and Dock Baxter hit the ground. Ray Elliott's ears were ringing and his head felt like it was cracked open. He was able to gather enough of his wits to realize a substantial load of something, probably buckshot, had destroyed the door from the inside. Out of the smoky dark interior stepped a half dressed, long bearded man in boots and a tall, crestfallen cowboy hat. The hat looked like it hadn't been taken off his head in twenty years. The long beard was white, except for dark tobacco juice stains. He was thin as a rail and holding a gun with the largest barrel

Ray Elliott had ever seen.

The man's voice was harsh and loud, easily breaking through the ringing in Ray Elliott's ears. "Put your rifle on the ground and back away where I can see your hands.

Ray Elliott complied. Dock Baxter raised his hands to show they were tied, and he was unarmed.

Ray Elliott yelled, "Why did you shoot at us? I'm only looking for William Preston Henry."

"I been called W.P. Henry, Preston Henry, or Will Henry, but nobody has ever called me William Preston Henry. Tells me you are a stranger and strangers aren't welcome. Now you best talk quick because I reloaded."

"My name's Ray Elliott. You are my mother's brother. I knew you used to be a lawman and I need your help."

"Are you Rebecca's boy?"

Ray Elliott began to rise but left his hands out and open where they could be seen. "I am Jacie's oldest, Ray Elliott. You didn't know she married and had children, did you?"

William Preston Henry said, "She has not spoke to me in better than twenty years."

"Why?" Dock Baxter looked as if he surprised himself with the question.

"Why? Why, I have just been enjoying the silence. Never occurred to me to ask, why? What did you do anyway?" William Preston Henry placed the big Sharps rifle barrel on the chest of Dock Baxter.

Ray Elliott answered, "Richard Watersong claims this man killed Lukas Halten—"

William Preston Henry responded, "You brung him to me to shoot?"

"He didn't do it. What I am trying to tell you is Richard Watersong murdered his own father-in-law and blamed

Dock Baxter." The absurdity of the situation poured over Ray Elliott like a cold shower. He was defending a man he didn't know. Worse, the defendant's dark skin made him near indefensible in society. Ray Elliott's desperation had driven him to a long-lost relative whose primary qualification was what some called a contrary nature. Others claimed a contrary nature was something more noble, an immeasurable amount of what was known as 'sand' among country people.

William Preston Henry shook his head. The white hair blended unnoticeably into the beard draping to his waist. He opened his mouth to speak, then took a long pause, evidencing he was pondering on the situation. "This here man, as you want to call him, is accused by one of the wealthiest bankers in these parts of killing another one of the wealthiest bankers in these parts. Then, looks like you bust him out of jail and find me because the two of you want company getting hung."

Ray Elliott protested, "You don't understand. He is innocent."

William Preston Henry had a sharper tone, still mocking the much younger man. "There ain't no innocent. You the one who don't understand; innocent is like complaining about a horse being lame after he's dead. This man is dead. You got a chance to live on the run. Take it."

Ray Elliott was crushed. He fought back tears of desperation. This was the only plan he had formulated, and it had failed before it started. He yelled at the ancient looking man. "I heard tell you was married to a colored woman, gave up being sheriff in Panola County for her. They say even the white cappers stepped aside when Will Henry walked past. Figured you'd think a black man should get a fair trial?"

"Well, I also rode with Quantrill and owned slaves. Being one don't make me any more or less the other. The best thing you can do is put a bullet in this man's brain pan right now."

He swung the big long gun to Dock Baxter's forehead. "This is a Sharps 45-110, shoots better than a 500-grain soft lead bullet. I seen it blow out the innards of a man's head like a rotten pumpkin. If you killed Lukas Halten, tell me now. I will put you on a fast horse before you get my nephew killed. If you are 'innocent' then I will make it quick and save you torture like you can't imagine."

For the first time, Dock Baxter looked William Preston Henry in the eye. Dock Baxter spoke in a deliberate almost calm tone. "I didn't kill anyone."

William Preston Henry eased the hammer down on the heavy rifle and turned to face Ray Elliott. "You have wasted your advantage. You should have ridden for the state penitentiary at Rusk. Held them off long enough for the governor to send a company of rangers."

The weight lifted off Ray Elliott's shoulders. His reaction was immediate. "Then we need to ride for Rusk."

William Preston Henry said, "No. You're getting on a train. I'll get your friend to Rusk. Come on in the house so you can tell me everything."

Ray Elliott looked at Dock Baxter. 'Friend.' This man wasn't his friend and yet, look at what he'd risked. His mother and father had likely heard by now. How were they going to face the community? Could his mother stand up to the shame? There was no one there to tell the truth, and he knew the local newspaperman. There would be a whole series of scathing articles about the killing of the great Lukas Halten and the miscreant youth who helped the murderer escape. He had read similar articles. The only question would be the motive ascribed to him for taking up with Dock Baxter over his own family and people. His shoulders shuddered thinking about all the possible small town lies and insinuations.

William Preston Henry and Dock Baxter were walking through the shack-like entrance while Ray Elliott stared at the cave. For a moment, his mind saw the white frame house of his parents. He was there only yesterday, yet he might never see it again. He could see the wash on the line and smell the scent of soap. It hadn't occurred to him until William Preston Henry had stated what should have been obvious.

As much as Ray Elliott had mocked the mundane farmer's life, he had always taken a strange comfort in knowing he would live his entire life outside of Nacogdoches in the Douglas community. He would be buried in line with his mother and father before joining the rest of his people in heaven.

Why hadn't he thought before he took Dock Baxter out of town? For him, anticipating consequences wasn't an option, likely no more than any of the decisions which rendered William Preston Henry a hermit. Ray Elliott explored the possible results of his actions only after the fact, in the aftermath of action. He nodded his head thinking they were two of a kind. He might as well walk into the cave and see what his future held.

The lighting was poor. Ray Elliott had to cover his nose from the smell of mold and body odor. There was an oil lamp on a spindle. The spindle must have held some kind of large roll of cable at one time. The chairs seemed far too small for a man. The floors were clay, almost as hard as brick. The walls were covered in paper from newspaper and catalog to heavy packing paper. In a corner was a rope bed with a thin mattress. There was a small brick mantle and fireplace with cooking pots and a grill. The cave wasn't really a true cave. It was carved by hand, hewn from the side of an enormous clay hill.

Dock Baxter helped himself to soda crackers and a tin of sardines on the table while William Preston Henry interviewed Ray Elliott. From time to time, the interview was suspended and William Preston Henry told a story about Lukas Halten. The men had been friends in their youth.

Dock Baxter asked for the outhouse.

William Preston Henry laughed. "The whole world is my facilities. Just walk outside the door, but now you remember the only thing keeping you alive is my nephew here. You walk too far... Just as well to me. You will end up lynched and he won't have to die with you."

Dock Baxter ducked his head as he walked through the cave entrance.

Ray Elliott asked the question consuming him. "Would you have really shot him if he had killed Lukas Halten?"

William Preston Henry retorted, "You don't know he didn't kill Lukas Halten."

"He said he didn't do it."

William Preston Henry nodded. "And there may be some truth in him. Eleanor broke her daddy's heart when she married that fop, Richard Watersong. Everyone has heard he was stealing from her father's banks, both the one in Henderson and Nacogdoches."

Ray Elliott rose up. The sudden epiphany surprised

him. "It all makes sense. Lukas Halten probably was on to Richard Watersong, so Watersong kills him and blames Dock Baxter, reckoning the man would get lynched before anyone could find the truth."

William Preston Henry laughed, "The truth, right." He swung an old homemade cotton shirt into the air. He was obviously trying to sling the dirt out of the garment but the attempt was futile. No matter how much dust filled the air, the garment remained saturated with filth.

Ray Elliot agreed, not appreciating the sarcastic nature of the comment.

William Preston Henry shook his head. "I have seen people all over God's creation get murdered by all kind of folks. Killing a man is a curious thing and the more you study on it, the curiouser it gets. I never seen one make tight neat sense like this one."

"But you believe him too?"

William Preston Henry answered, "Nope, yet not knowing, I can't rightly say, least not enough to kill a man. Always wanted to be fair about taking a life, especially in cold blood."

Ray Elliott almost laughed at what he thought must be a joke. He stopped because something about the strange old man's countenance revealed he was deadly serious. How many men had William Preston Henry killed? He wanted to ask but thought better of it. Instead he asked a more innocuous question. "How long will it take to ride to Rusk?"

"I'm taking you to Overton for the International and Great Northern Railroad. Once you are on the I&GN, you can go west to Laredo. When this storm blows itself out, maybe you can come home. If not, it's a short ride to

Mexico."

Ray Elliott asked, "Mexico?"

William Preston Henry said, "Man can make a good life in Mexico; spent some time there myself after the war."

"I don't want to go to Mexico."

"What do you want? Did you want to go to jail or be shunned by decent folks and have to live like a hermit like me?"

William Preston Henry had stepped close enough his breath was hot and rancid in Ray Elliott's face. Ray Elliott wanted to step away, to look away, except he couldn't. It was a test and he was failing.

Ray Elliott was near tears, yet somehow, he steeled himself and stared back at William Preston Henry. "I want things to be right. Truth is, I don't know what I want."

"You chose death." William Preston Henry released the tension with laughter and stepped back. "I would ask you what you were thinking, but not knowing, I don't reckon you can rightly say."

Ray Elliott was shaking his head, coming to terms with the idea he might live the rest of his days in a foreign country when Dock Baxter walked back into the cave. Ray Elliott asked, "Why don't all of us take the I&GN to Palestine and then Rusk. Be a lot quicker."

"The fancy sheriff you mentioned; I know of him. He beat one of my old friends in the last election. He's an arrogant coward. An arrogant coward with lots of friends of his own. I expect he didn't put out a bulletin on you two. Won't admit a kid and this here colored man bested him, but like as not, he has sent word to his friends." William Preston Henry paused long enough for Ray Elliott to nod in agreement.

William Preston Henry pointed at Dock Baxter. "You can't hide your friend. Sheriff Fancy's men are looking for the two of you. We'll draw less attention if Baxter and I ride the back roads to Rusk."

Ray Elliott wanted to protest. He had orchestrated this odd combination; it never occurred to him he wouldn't see it out. He thought about telling William Preston Henry about the promise, but it seemed he had suffered enough over it. This wasn't an outhouse novel, and he wasn't a lawman. William Preston Henry was a legend, a real-life legend. The small old man's demeanor made 'no' an impossible response.

There wasn't much for William Preston Henry to pack. Down the hill, he had a horse tied to a shanty house. He went in the shanty and returned with a saddle and a bundle he described as hot water bread and jerked beef. When Ray Elliott had pressed William Preston Henry about his threadbare clothing, broken-heeled boot, and grimy formless hat, the elder man remarked, "A confederate pension will buy a bottle of whiskey and a binder of tobacco a month; no more, not even a bag of beans."

Yet, there was an incredible contradiction. To this point, everything the old man owned would have been near worthless. However, this horse was magnificent. She was tall, maybe a true seventeen hands and the distinctive salt and pepper most folks called steel. William Preston Henry mounted with some difficulty. Ray Elliott saw an old Colt below the long white beard. Ray Elliott determined the pistol was a black powder conversion in a cross-draw holster. He looked at Dock Baxter. The glance exchanged denoted a shared appreciation for the transformation. Minutes previous, William Preston Henry could have passed for a poverty-stricken farmer, but no longer.

Dock Baxter asked, "Why are we turning east? Overton is west and north of here?"

William Preston Henry said, "I ain't going to explain myself to you."

Dock Baxter said, "Can't talk to a black man, huh?" He looked at Ray Elliott and added, "Y'all all alike."

William Preston Henry pointed to the little shanty. "Those folks there are black and I call them kin. Not you though. I call you a murderer until I know better. Don't forget your place again, prisoner." He turned to Ray Elliott and said, "We're gonna swing back to the north outside of town then follow the Henderson Overton line. I thought about riding to the courthouse right through the center of town. I figure this county's sheriff and militia, the Henderson Rifles, are good folks, but I can't be certain. Lukas Halten wasn't only a rich banker. He was a good man and you couldn't fill a Mexican *jacal* with all the good men in this world."

Ray Elliott had never heard the Mexican term. He wasn't going to question the man. Besides, William Preston Henry conveyed his meaning by pointing to the little shed house.

It took most of the morning to make an arc reaching around Henderson, turning to the rails and arriving at a little depot outside of the small community of London. There were a number of men loading tomatoes from wagons into two railway cars. Ray Elliott thought he saw Cecil Grant, but he wasn't sure and he wasn't going to draw attention to himself. If he could have just shut up while Richard Watersong treated Cecil Grant in such a poor manner then maybe he would not have chased Dock Baxter or made the fool promise which he had let ruin his life.

Ray Elliott pondered the irony of his situation. He had lived his entire life as a farm boy, devoid of anything he considered real excitement. He had formed no plans, no dreams; rather, his life would be farming like his father and everyone they knew. Through a series of events which he struggled to unravel in his mind, he was now on an adventure comparable to any latrine literature quest. He reasoned away doubts and justified his quest as he rode.

They stopped on the outskirts of Overton, a little railway-stop town. William Preston Henry motioned toward the small depot for the I.G.N.R.R.

Dock Baxter broke the silence. "You can't leave me. This man don't like my kind. He will turn me over to the mob first chance he gets."

William Preston Henry said, "Your kind being murderers?"

The two men exchanged a stare and Dock Baxter looked away, back to Ray Elliott.

William Preston Henry said, "I told you, I'll get him to the state penitentiary in Rusk and see he gets a fair trial. Too old to start breaking my word now."

Ray Elliott nodded but didn't move his horse. There was something about the way the little elderly man set his jaw after the statement. It had the quality of a warning Ray Elliott had never witnessed. He might as well have told Ray Elliott, 'Don't question me, boy.'

Dock Baxter's eyes were intent on Ray Elliott. The huge dark saucers were highlighted against white backgrounds.

William Preston Henry shook his head. "You bit off more than a company of good men can chew. I'll give you some sand for making a fool decision and sticking with it, but your only chance is to take a fast train to Laredo and wait for me to wire you to come home or go into Mexico. We are betting hard this fancy fellow sheriff didn't already get a warrant and bulletin out for you because he's too embarrassed." He motioned the huge rifle at Dock Baxter. "I won't kill your friend here, unless I decide he is for sure guilty." Cocking the big hammer on the Sharps made a noise like cracking an axe handle over a rock.

CHAPTER 4: ELLIE

Eleanor walked past people she had known all her life. Was sympathy in their eyes or the contentment generated by watching the mighty fall? Whatever was in their eyes, she didn't know. She struggled to lift her head up while avoiding eye contact.

Worse than the embarrassment and the shame was the self-loathing. Eleanor was staying up late at night reading her Bible, but the peace she had always found in Scripture was eluding her.

Her sainted father murdered. Not the exceptional death the great hero deserved, rather a vulgar killing over a few dollars. Combined with the concerns her husband caused her, she was suffering a tragedy like those she had grown up reading in the Old Testament. How had she failed God to deserve such wrath?

She was lost in thought, looking down at her father's body, then pulled back into the moment by the expressions of sympathy from the line of mourners. Friends and acquaintances pledged their love for her and her family. Did they love her, or were their assertions only the required etiquette of Southern society? The same society which held miscegenation as an unforgiveable sin. It was what was really pulling her head inexplicably to the ground.

Had her husband Richard Watersong truly set out to capture her father's killer? Then why was Queen, the young black maid, gone too? The hush about her marital woes was something she could literally feel when the mourners neared the front of the line, like the air was pulled out of the room into a storm moving toward her. They were even gossiping about her on the way to her beloved father's visitation. She wanted to die.

Eleanor drifted back into the moment and realized the sheriff was standing before her.

"Your daddy was a big man, Eleanor."

Eleanor looked up the bright red shirt to the large diamond stickpin before reaching the sheriff's grey eyes. "Why aren't you out there finding Dock Baxter?"

"Now, Eleanor. I came to pay my respects, not to be treated like a field hand." The sheriff raised his arm in an obvious attempt to hush her. "Sure, I could go chasing all over creation like your husband chose. Don't make any sense, though. I got feelers out all-over East Texas—"

"So, all the sheriffs have been alerted?" Eleanor blurted in a tone denoting she really didn't care who heard her.

"Ellie, there are other ways to put out a bulletin." The sheriff motioned his hand to quiet her and then gently slid his hand over her own. She pulled away, but he forcefully grabbed the top of her hand. He whispered, "I am running for the legislature next year when R.E. retires. It wouldn't do to brag about a darkie killing a war hero and banker in broad daylight. All you need to know is I have friends and I will find him. Then I'll let these good ole boys' skin him alive while you watch if you want."

Eleanor looked around the room and forced a smile. She looked in the sheriff's pale grey eyes and whispered through clenched teeth. "The days when you called me Ellie have long passed. You will address me as Mrs.

Watersong."

The sheriff made a public performance by shouting his condolences before turning for the door and promising to capture the low murderer who robbed Eleanor of her father.

Eleanor greeted the next person to offer their sympathies, and out of the corner of her eye she saw Mrs. Ramey, her old piano teacher. The two women hugged while Eleanor's head filled with questions. Was Mrs. Ramey genuine when she offered to pray for the success of her husband, Richard Watersong, as he chased her father's killer? Was she truly crying because of Eleanor's loss of her father, or did Mrs. Ramey believe Eleanor's husband had absconded with the young black snip of a woman, leaving Eleanor to raise two children in shame? They must all be wondering why her husband chose Queen. Was Eleanor such a failure as a wife? Of course, she was a failure. She felt worthless, as if everyone saw her secret shame laid bare in front of the only people she had ever known.

The last to leave was her pastor. She prayed with him. The prayer brought her no comfort. She kept debating whether the preacher knew about Richard's affair. What must he think?

Eleanor longed for the only company offering her any respite, her children. The boys didn't appear to be awake. What time was it? She found her housekeeper Yolonda in the kitchen.

"I saved you some egg bread and peas, Ms. Ellie." 'Housekeeper' didn't really describe Yolonda. She had more raised Eleanor than worked for the family.

"How are the boys?"

Yolonda avoided the gaze and tried to avoid the question. "They are as well as can be, I expect."

Eleanor picked up on the awkwardness of the answer. "What does 'well as can be' mean?"

"Little Master Richard got into a tussle. He got his eye dotted some."

Eleanor turned to the door. "Got his eye dotted some? You didn't come get me?" Eleanor was running, lifting her long dress as she bounded up the stairs. She flew into Richie's room.

The little boy squinted, his eyes adjusting to the gas light. His eye was beginning to darken.

She asked, "Didn't Yolonda get you some ice for your eye?"

"It was too cold." The six-year-old lifted a soaking handkerchief from the nightstand.

"Let's not put the ice on the furniture. How did this happen?"

"Billy said my daddy married Queen and took her away. I told him to take it back—"

Eleanor added, "He wouldn't take it back, would he?"

"I popped him."

"Looks like he popped you back, too."

Eleanor tried to stop the tears, but it was too late. A day of holding back the anguish and the relief of seeing her son safe, absent the hint of a shiner, was too much. The dam broke loose.

Richie asked, "Momma, is Queeny going to be my new mommy?"

"No son. I am forever your mommy." Eleanor held the boy until he fell asleep, then she made sure her toddler was asleep. The tears were past. She was erupting like a long dormant volcano, spraying more ash than lava. She believed she had condemned herself to a life without passion, a loveless marriage. She told herself romance was passing while love was a choice, not a feeling. She had been a good and dutiful wife, yet her husband had betrayed her, anyway.

Truth poured over her. She wasn't a bad wife. Richard Watersong was a faithless scoundrel. A disservice to all humanity. Why would anyone feel loyalty to a person so undeserving? As soon as she formed the thought in her mind, she became convicted of her own failing, her own faithlessness.

Yolonda had been the closest thing she had ever known to a mother, and yet she had never treated the woman with the respect of a mother. Yolonda was born a slave to Eleanor's mother and father. Even after Juneteenth, Yolonda chose to stay and help a widower raise his daughter, a widower who had held her family in bondage and fought with such ferocity for the confederacy that he had won the respect of his comrades on both sides.

Had her father appreciated Yolonda's devotion? Were the lessons taught by her and others the impetus to build a bank to lift all people, black and white? The bank; the bank was sinking in a sea of debt. She knew enough about business to know the precarious situation, despite the best efforts of her father. She also knew her husband was suspected of stealing by the board. Protesting his innocence seemed so stupid now. Would she even be able to pay Yolonda this month?

She found Yolonda still in the kitchen. It was difficult to come up with a way to say what needed to be said. There was no way to preface it, so she didn't. "Yolonda, I am sorry. You are all the mother I have ever known and I have never treated you decent." Tears stopped Eleanor from blurting more out.

Yolonda defied arthritis to cross the kitchen in a step. "Ellie, you always been one of my children." She held Eleanor with hands which were near permanently bent. "What is wrong with you, Baby?"

Eleanor recited the litany of misery between gasping, tear-filled breaths.

Yolonda said, "Your father knew the Lord and the older he got, going home was all he talked about. As for Richard, you better off, and your children better off growing up without him. He broke your father's heart, my heart. Everybody who loved you knew he was trash. We need to pray right now and thank Jesus the man is gone and took his little trollop with him."

Eleanor pulled back, and the tears stopped. "I didn't know you knew."

Yolonda said, "You knew, even though you weren't going to admit it. Queen is my niece. My sister fell on hard times and your father helped her out by hiring Queeny. I blame Queeny because she was raised better."

Yolonda dropped to her knees. "Get on this floor and give praise to God. He sent wicked Richard Watersong away before it cost you or your children more than you could bear."

Eleanor did as commanded. She was ambivalent. Yolonda was so adamant, her faith so strong, and her prayer so vehement. Eleanor did take some comfort and such enabled a certain clarity of purpose. "I have to go out for a little while."

Yolonda answered, "Don't go doing nothing stupid

Baby."

Eleanor stepped one foot in front of the other, lamenting each step, past the kitchen, the house, and into the street. She dreaded the final step, suffering almost as much angst as when she knocked on the door.

The sheriff smiled. "Ellie, come right on in, my dear." He was wearing a bath robe accented with an ascot and his customary tie pin.

Eleanor walked through the door before responding. "We both know my husband has run off with Queeny. I will hire you to bring him back."

The sheriff offered her a seat and took one himself. "Awfully Christian of you to take him back—"

Eleanor raised her voice to interject, "I have no intention of taking him back. He has been stealing from my father for years. I intend to discover where the money is hidden and then see him jailed. If there is any money left."

The sheriff moved his hand over Eleanor's fingers. "There is still money, all right. Knowing Richard, I expect he has it hid from here to New York. You got to give me a reason to help you. You know what I mean."

"You are helping yourself. You think R.E. Saunders got elected by himself. My father put him in the legislature just like I can put you—"

The sheriff interrupted her, "Your daddy backed Spradley for sheriff. I already beat your machine."

Eleanor no longer attempted to emulate the speech pattern of her husband. She spoke in her natural, deeper Southern accent, reminiscent of her father. Scotch-Irish had traversed an Ocean and the Appalachian mountain range before ultimately leaving their mark on East Texas.

"As daddy used to say, 'Tell yourself whatever you need to hear and throw in a good-sized dollop extra to make yourself feel better. Think hard, would you rather run with the machine or against the machine?'"

The sheriff smiled. "I always want things easy. You're asking me to find somebody who don't want to be found. I figure he is well on his way to South America." The words were slurred and slung together.

"You're a drunk. One of the reasons my father backed Spradley."

The sheriff shook his head. "We both know Spradley was too close to the darkies, the way he tried to stop Buchannan's lynching. He didn't stop it. He only kept himself from being re-elected." He smiled again. "Not stupid."

"I never thought you were stupid. I expect you have a good idea where my husband is holed up and where he is going. Scoundrels think alike."

The sheriff moved his hand up Eleanor's arm until she pulled back. "Not so much alike. I would never choose a little darkie girl over a fine-looking woman like you. I am ashamed to even know him."

Eleanor had pulled one hand over the other, and she responded to the comment by mock clapping a few solemn times. "Well said. Now, tell me where you would go."

The sheriff's broad grin returned and the gas light reflected off his grey eyes. "I wouldn't take a fast train to Houston and then a boat to South America. I couldn't be sure I had sold the whole 'I am going to avenge my father-in-law,' bull. I mean, everybody knew Richard hated your father, and the directors were starting to catch onto the embezzlement. I bet he could barely keep a straight face. I know I had trouble doing it while I watched his little performance."

The sheriff was impressed with his own analysis, so Eleanor hid her horror at how obvious her husband's motives had been to others. She had seen a flawed, but good man. In truth, Richard Watersong had never been a good man.

The sheriff continued, "I would be cautious, stay off the main roads and avoid railroads altogether. So, what is the most unlikely way to the coast?"

Eleanor looked lost. She tried to smile, thinking the sheriff wanted her to appreciate his genius, but she was suffering at the cold math Richard must have also calculated.

The sheriff shook his head. "Ever since they cleared the log jam, you can barely get a steamer up to Jefferson. A few cotton haulers still run, though. I mean, nobody is looking for him to the north. Ride fast at night, stay off the main roads, then catch a steamer from Jefferson. I mean, the last thing you want riding with a black girl is attention. He makes it to New Orleans where he puts together all the money he had hid in secret accounts all these years. Besides, a white man and young black girl won't draw a lot of attention in New Orleans. Then, he takes a ship anywhere in the world."

Eleanor fought back her tears and stiffened her spine, remembering why she found Sheriff Ralph Kingfisher so repugnant. He was an unemptied chamber pot clothed in fine fabric and perfume. She said, "Then Richard Watersong may not have left Texas yet."

The sheriff added, "He may not have even reached Jefferson. Even if he has, the steamers are few now, what with the log jam having been cleared. The water is too low most of the time."

"My father kept the truth hidden. There was already a warrant for Richard where he stole from the home bank in Henderson. I will give you the authority to draw whatever funds you need, pay you a thousand dollars on his capture, and put you in the legislature."

The sheriff pushed his bare foot up Eleanor's stocking leg. She said, "No. Not part of the deal."

He retorted, "I remember a time at the lake when you weren't so eager to turn me away."

"Ralphie, the difference between us is I don't remember. Five hundred up front, all expenses, the legislature, and a five percent finder's fee on anything you recover. My best offer."

The sheriff looked around, then reached back toward Eleanor's hand. "Well, it is not your best offer."

CHAPTER 5: WHEN THE WORLD WENT DARK

Ray Elliott had never traveled outside Nacogdoches County. Now he was waiting for a train to take him almost to Mexico. It was surreal. Thoughts of Mexico, the family he was abandoning, and guilt over his promise to Dock Baxter made him oblivious to his surroundings.

He debated whether he should have so completely trusted William Preston Henry. Dock Baxter had been terrified the old gnome of a man would kill him, but Dock Baxter didn't know William Preston Henry's story. The truth of it was Ray Elliott didn't know much. As a small boy, he'd overheard enough of his parents' conversation to know William Preston Henry gave up his wife, children, and career to live with a negro woman in a cave. Ray Elliott's parents mocked the decision, like probably most of the world. As for a young Ray Elliott, a romantic mystique arose around the uncle he had never known. The man had grown up in times of slavery, and yet he had rejected all comforts of civilization to follow his heart regardless of color.

The man, William Preston Henry, struck Ray Elliott as a far cry from the romantic hero he envisioned. The man was coarse, downright mean, and what happened to the woman? Did she die, leave him, or did he leave her? William Preston Henry wasn't telling, and no one had the courage to ask the man; at least, Ray Elliott was certain he did not possess the necessary fortitude to pose the question.

The clerk for the I.G.N.R.R. disappeared from the depot for long periods of time. Upon one of his returns, Ray Elliott bought a sliver of red rind cheese and a stack of stale crackers. The evening wasn't as hot as recent days, so Ray Elliott chose to step outside to continue waiting on the train.

It had been a long summer. The East Texas countryside was still largely green past the handful of businesses making up Commerce Street. As he wandered through the edge of the depot building, he caught sight of the sun. The orange ball was falling into the green-leafed hardwoods and pines along an irregular horizon of hills. For a moment the frantic thoughts ceased. He enjoyed the view. How many times the sun had risen and fallen in his life, yet he never really saw it?

Ray Elliott was asleep when he heard the boarding call. William Preston Henry had provided the money for the fare. For such a poverty-stricken man, he seemed to have a good-sized roll of cash. He had been generous with his nephew. Ray Elliott might have to live on the run for some time.

There were rows of benches on the left side while the other side had two chairs joined to make a row to the right, running the length of the railway car. There were already passengers, so Ray Elliott sat near the back on one of the few empty benches.

He was pleased to have a bench to himself because it offered the opportunity to spread out and sleep. In an instant, two men joined him. He noticed most of the remaining seats in the coach were filled in short order. The man next to him politely nudged him, making him move closer to the window. The man was big, and it was fairly dark but his tie pin shown like a diamond, I&GN. He noticed many of the other men had them as well. Ray Elliott reasoned these men did something for the railroad. They weren't engineers or trainmen of any sort; maybe they were clerks. He couldn't make a lot out in the dark.

Ray Elliott realized the big man was wearing a coat of some kind. It wasn't cold. There wasn't much fall in Texas. Summer moved into a less hot summer then into winter. Ray Elliott was no longer lost in thought, pitying himself. He recalled what William Preston Henry told him about how a wanted man has to always be ready to move. Moving one way or the other might be the difference between Mexico and a noose.

Ray Elliott debated his options. This situation wasn't right. He couldn't explain why it was wrong. If he got up and left, then he would be stuck here another day, every minute risking alarm from the Nacogdoches County sheriff. He remembered where he had seen the tie pin. The image clicked in his mind and he succumbed again to his propensity for decisiveness. Ray Elliott moved. He was rising as quick as he could. He felt something solid drive into his chest. It was a shotgun. Even as an issue of first impression, the press of the two saw-off barrels was unique and unmistakable. The man had hidden it in the coat.

"Sit back down, friend." The voice was gruff.

"We are not friends."

The man made a cold chuckle, chilling Ray Elliott's spine. Then the voice said, "We all going to get very friendly before this is over, friend."

Ray Elliott felt the train get underway. He had rarely ridden a train, and the sensation was still a novelty, adding to the surreal nature of the moment. He couldn't be sure how many other men were allied with the shotgun man. Still, Ray Elliott figured he was dead if he didn't come up with something fast. Would the man fire the shotgun in close quarters, risking the lives of innocents or his own men? Killing innocents probably wasn't good for the railroad business. The man wouldn't fire.

Ray Elliott was wrong. He shoved the end of the shotgun away as the barrels exploded, discharging into the railway car. Ray Elliott leaped upright. His boot caught the edge of the door face. He went sprawling forward. His head crashed into the connection of the railcar and bounced. Ray Elliott rolled off the edge of the railcar, hitting his head again, this time on the cross ties.

There was a boom of light exploding in Ray Elliott's mind. He wobbled, rolled over, and laid back next to the cross tie. He reached up and felt the blood pouring from his head. He didn't know if they would stop the train or send men out from Overton. One thought was in his head. These tracks weren't safe.

He couldn't be sure if he had been out a minute or an hour. All Ray Elliott knew was he had to move to stay alive. His head was pounding like a red-hot piece of steel being slammed by a heavy hammer. Ray Elliott dragged himself until he could crawl. He slipped down a small rise and rolled under the edge of a cedar tree. In normal times, he would have avoided the prickly needles of the cedar tree, but instead he rolled under the limbs. He could move no further, not even to save his own life.

Ray Elliott almost chuckled at his own demise, but

couldn't expend the effort. He was done, or rather undone, by the flashy dressing sheriff. The dandily dressed dude must have been well connected with the railroad, probably a former I.G.N.R.R. detective. Detective was generally considered a kind word for thugs. The sheriff could have put the word out among his old friends. Maybe it was more. Perhaps he had been outguessing Ray Elliott all along. A realization came over Ray Elliott like a powerful cramp. William Preston Henry was likely riding into a trap. The sheriff would have guessed Ray Elliott's real goal was trying to protect his prisoner. It was where William Preston Henry suggested, so surely another lawman would come up with the Rusk State Penitentiary on a short list of safe places.

He had to warn them. He had to move. If he could just start with his foot, perhaps wiggling his toe. What could he do? He was alone, hidden in the dark. He hurt so badly he couldn't move, couldn't cry, and couldn't yell or even whisper. He no longer saw stars. The world went dark.

CHAPTER 6: Marie Laveau and the Caddo Queen

No one saw Richard Watersong turn back to Nacogdoches later and collect Queen. The couple stayed off the main roads as much as possible. A white man and young black lady would attract attention traveling together. It made more sense to be cautious, at least while still close to Nacogdoches.

They moved through the tall, seemingly unbroken pine forest of East Texas toward Jefferson. For many years Jefferson had been the gateway into Texas through the natural wonder of Caddo Lake. Lake Caddo emptied into the navigable portion of the Red River. The Red River flowed into the mighty Mississippi River to the port of New Orleans. Jefferson had once been a jewel of the Antebellum South. The clearing of the great log jam rendered Jefferson too shallow for the big river side-wheelers. In fact, only a handful of smaller paddle steamers made the journey now.

Richard Watersong prided himself on how unlikely his choice of escape route had been. He was also thoroughly impressed with his acting skills. He was going to avenge his father-in-law alright. He was going to enjoy the old fool's money.

Queen sat in a grand hotel room in Jefferson. She was watching the tiny bubbles in the champagne. Each one was destined to reach the top before it popped. The bank had kept liquor for customers, but never had champagne, nor had she ever stayed in a hotel.

Richard Watersong had the meal brought to the room. Another new experience for Queen. Even for Richard Watersong, it was a feast compared to the poor meals along the road. There was steak, sweet potatoes, then shrimp and grits, followed by a desert of fried apple pies.

Richard Watersong said, "Queen, you think there is something here you can eat?" Then he laughed.

Queen laughed too. "It all looks so good."

"I have been worried about you. You have been getting sick nearly every day."

Queen said, "It is probably just missing my family. I will never see my father, mother, or my sisters again."

Richard Watersong took her hand in his own. "We have both given up our families. I will never see my sons again. We are a family, Queen, you and I. Maybe we should get married on the way. I was going to wait until we were in Cuba, but maybe we should get married sooner."

Queen leaned forward and kissed him. "I love you, Richard.

Richard Watersong said, "I am going to find you a doctor. I don't want you getting sick on the boat to Cuba."

"I don't want to go to a doctor."

"It will be alright. I will take you tomorrow."

Tomorrow's light didn't find Richard Watersong and Queen until nearly noon. Richard Watersong rose, dressed, and left Queen at the hotel for several hours.

When Richard Watersong returned, he had a coach and a driver. He avoided Queen's inquiries during the ride. Queen had never seen anything in her life like Caddo Lake. It didn't look like a lake at all. She was surrounded by sloughs of murky dark water under a canopy of enormous cypress trees. The rust-colored foliage of the cypress trees was draped in Spanish moss, creating a vast jungle over the standing water as far as the eye could see.

It was as if the buggy was taking them back in time to a place where the world was newer, more primitive. She could smell the moisture in the air. They stopped at the edge of the water and the driver pushed a canoe into the water. The dark-skinned driver called the canoe a pirogue as he slid it into the dense looking water.

Queen blurted out. "Richard, I don't want to go."

She questioned getting into a canoe. Richard Watersong doubled down on the ruse with his best acting skills. "I can't have you getting sick on the boat. We can't be married or start our life if you don't get in the boat."

Queen asked, "What kind of doctor could be out here."

He grabbed her by the arm hard enough to move her tiny frame.

Queen complied, and the driver became an oarsman. The pirogue was moving through the water, making only a narrow wake. The Cyprus trees were even more imposing in the water.

The sun was falling down into a palette of infinite oranges and purples. The canoe was pushing into open water. After some time, there was a cabin on a long finger resembling an island in the distance.

The driver pulled the pirogue onto the bank. Richard Watersong and Queen stepped onto the narrow peninsula. The cabin sported a porch partially extending over the water.

They stepped inside where dim candlelight illuminated a large black woman seated at a table, alone. A series of red flat circles lay on the table. Queen looked at the circles.

"Eat one Missy. Clay pies, keep your insides together." The whites of the old woman's eyes were reflecting the weak lamp light.

Richard Watersong said, "I was told you are the best doctor in these parts and my wife needs attention."

The big woman snapped at him. "The girl's not your wife and you already know what I am. Do you have my fee?" She was old and dressed in a long purple dress with what looked like a matching turban covering her head.

Richard Watersong handed the woman a flat brown envelope. She held it close to the light for a moment.

The woman spoke with a raspy voice. "Now you go back out in the lake. *Galeux* tell you when it is time to come back if he don't fall asleep."

Queen tried to follow Richard Watersong out the door, but he shut it quickly.

"Come have a seat child. I won't eat you. I'm full of clay pies." The big woman laughed.

Queen was shaking. "Who are you? What are you? Are you a witch?"

"Your fool man thinks I am Marie Laveau? He doesn't know she has been dead for years. She never got this far north, anyway."

Queen asked, "Who is Marie Laveau?"

"Voodoo queen in New Orleans."

"Voodoo queen?"

The old woman chuckled. "No child, I am a healer. I make a few dollars off foolish white folks who want their future told. I never really tell them their future. Dangerous to read the future."

"Did Richard leave me to get my future told?"

"No. Sit down girl."

Queen sat on a stool near the small table in the cramped little one-room cabin. Her legs were shaking, and she put both hands on them to try to stop the movement. She couldn't see much around the room. The light barely illuminated the woman.

Queen focused on long ropes hanging from the ceiling. She near leaped backwards when she realized they were snakes.

The old woman chuckled deeper. "They're dead, child. Gifts to the saints, the special spirits who serve God. We have to feed the spirits to get their help. Ran out of snake, so I made clay pies."

The old woman motioned to the girl. "I am called *Chouette*. I been paid to heal you."

Queen said, "I'm not really sick."

"You are with child. I could smell it on your breath when you came through the door. Man calls it your sickness. I call it stupid. There is no future for a baby with a white man."

Queen rose from the stool and backed to the door. "I won't let you hurt my baby."

The old woman raised her hand. "Stop child. I said he paid me. I didn't say I was going to do it. Now sit back down."

Chouette continued, "It's a crime to mix the races. Most are scared of losing their wife or going to jail, but not this man. This man is bad; maybe he's evil. He doesn't love you. If you stay with him, he will kill you or you will have to kill him. Do you understand?"

Queen swallowed and kept looking at the dark floor. If snakes covered the ceiling what might be on the floor? A more pressing question weighed on her heart. "Will he ever really love me?"

"The day you die, the man will love you." The old woman smiled with a broad grin, which didn't seem to end. "Now, if we're going to give the man his money's worth then you gonna have to scream. I call the boy lazy because he will only row a short distance and sit in the bayou. You best scream and put on a show to fool the man."

Queen looked puzzled. *Chouette* took something out of a box and threw it on Queen. Queen jumped, shrieking. A green snake, and this one was alive. *Chouette* threw the snake on the girl again. Queen continued screaming. She screamed every time the snake was thrown at her.

Chouette whispered, "Child, you will not say a word on the way back to Jefferson. You will tell him you hurt and you will avoid the man."

And so Queen followed the advice of the strange woman. Early the next day, Richard Watersong booked passage on a paddle-wheel steamer to New Orleans.

By noon, Richard Watersong and Queen were walking on the riverboat. The steamer was white with red trim and wide galleries on two levels.

Only the upper level of the boat was unobstructed. The grand bottom gallery was stacked with hay. Richard Watersong learned the boat more commonly carried cotton bales, but there was a drought down river in Louisiana. The stacked hay was currently more lucrative cargo.

Richard Watersong jerked his head then pulled Queen away from the edge. He asked her, "Did you see someone watching us?"

Queen shook her head no.

Richard Watersong looked in the distance. "I thought I saw somebody I knew. I'm probably wrong."

Later in the evening, Richard Watersong realized he wasn't wrong. He walked into the main parlor and stepped backwards from fright.

Sheriff Ralph E. Kingfisher stood over the dice table. The sheriff motioned Richard Watersong toward the crowded gaming table.

"Try your luck at the tables, Richard, because your luck has been pretty good so far. I had a time finding you, old boy."

Richard Watersong said, "Maybe we should talk somewhere quiet."

"I'm fixin to get the dice, Richard. You don't want me to miss my throw, do you?"

The veneer of Richard Watersong's demeanor was wearing thin. He was becoming agitated and worse, showing it. "I want you to quit mocking me and tell me why you are here."

The sheriff raised his arms. "Always so formal. You never loosen up do you? Back in Nac, I can be the high sheriff. Here." He raised a tall goblet of red liquid.

Richard Watersong countenance remained stoic. The sheriff rolled his eyes. "Alright, alright, Richard. Let's take us a stroll."

The men stepped up the stairs without comment to the top tier of the boat. They stopped and watched the paddle wheel spin in the murky water.

The sheriff said, "Eleanor had a lot of suspicions. You know how women think. She sees you and Queen a little too close, too often, and she decides you are committing what the law calls an unnatural act. Now mind you, I tried to talk sense to her. Mr. Richard Watersong, you know most of all how women think. You also know it's against the law. I know you're not a law breaker, Richard."

Richard Watersong said, "What do you need to go home."

The sheriff shook his head smiling. "Now 'need' being a powerful thing. All of us have needs. I saw you come on the boat today with Queen. I know you have needs." The sheriff laughed, having amused himself with his soliloquy.

Richard Watersong touched his vest pocket and was reassured by touching a small, modern semi-automatic under his waist coat.

The sheriff seemed to read his mind. He touched the revolver in his holster. "Eleanor gave me one of these Smith and Wesson Number Threes. She told me there was a new Browning automatic missing from the inventory and she just wanted me to be well armed. I told the fool woman my good friend Richard Watersong would never draw down on his old friend, but you know how women are, don't you. I know you know women, don't you, Richard?"

Richard Watersong said, "Have you sent a wire to Eleanor?"

Again, the sheriff mocked him, instilling agitation in Richard Watersong. The sheriff responded, "Now I am hurt. I mean, hurt you would think I would talk to Eleanor before I heard your side. I learned from the young boy who caught Dock Baxter. Ignorant farm boy came up with a good idea. He found a barrier, a waterway, small though it was. Dock Baxter had to cross the Angelina River. So, farm boy set up on it. A good place to lie in wait. Jefferson is unlikely and little used, but still a gateway to the world, north, south, or even New Orleans and overseas. I am going to guess south, to a place where miscegenation is accepted, even if it still is illegal. So, I go by rail to Jefferson on Eleanor's dime. It is the most unlikely of the possibilities, right?"

The sheriff nods in obvious admiration of his deductive skills. "I wait, then I hear a white man with a young black woman checks into a hotel."

Richard Watersong looked trapped, stuck with no way out.

The sheriff continued, "After they checked in the hotel the man is heard trying to find someone who can stop a baby from being born. Then I find out the couple booked passage on this rare cotton hauler here. Amazing what a few of Ellies's dollars will turn up, if you drag them through slop."

Richard Watersong asked, "What do you want to keep this information to yourself?"

The sheriff's smile was visible, even as the light was starting to fade. "Well now see, there is the brass tacks, isn't it? Because even though you are innocent, these allegations merit a trial. Poor Eleanor and the boys, I expect there are even unkind folks who will blame you for your father-in-law's murder. Now I want you to know I will talk them down, but it will be expensive to be your friend. You having been a little careless with what's yours, versus mine, dealing with the bank and all."

The sheriff smiled even broader before continuing. "Your father-in-law caught you. Some harsh thinking, but investors call such a motive. I am in public office, wanting higher office. It will cost me to defend you. I know you don't want your friends to suffer for protecting you. I think maybe a five-thousand-dollar donation to my campaign might cover my losses."

Richard Watersong said, "I don't have five thousand dollars with me. If you let me get to New Orleans, I can pay you. How do I know you haven't already told Eleanor?"

The sheriff continued his mocking of Richard Watersong. "I could probably be persuaded to see New Orleans if I had a little spending money. I mean, you got to trust somebody, sometime, right?"

"Right." Richard Watersong stared out into the cedars and Spanish moss, watching the sun descend in the horizon. He said the word like he meant it. The same tone and matter-of-fact delivery which sold so many crooked business deals, delayed auditors, stymied creditors, and fooled Eleanor. But this time it was a lie in response to a lie. A fraud perpetrated in the midst of a fraud.

For the first time he was confronted by a mirror. A thought occurred to Richard Watersong; how had he ever gotten away with so much for so long? Was he as insincere as the sheriff? It really didn't matter now, did it? What mattered was whether he could pull off the next line with complete conviction. The sheriff must believe him. He looked the man dead in those cold, grey eyes. "I can probably get together five hundred. I will bring it to your cabin tonight. At the next stop, you are going to send Eleanor a telegram. I will write it. I am buying something for my five thousand dollars. My sons will remember me the way I choose. Means a lot to me. Whatever you think of me, I love my children." Richard Watersong turned away. He grimaced. Was, "it means a lot to me," too much?

He soon heard the answer.

The sheriff said, "Five hundred should get me down the river." He turned and then stopped. "Don't think about getting away. I found you once. I can do it again."

Richard Watersong stared into the darkening world before him. The water was black, and lurking below it were surely snakes and alligators. The thought of spending anytime in the mire of the bayou did not appeal to him at all. Worse, there was a possibility Queeny wouldn't survive. There was no manual about how much time it took young women to recover from abortion. He wasn't about to ask the voodoo queen, even if she were here. Well, there were women in Cuba.

The weight of her possible death lifted from his shoulders. He found the thought a pleasant distraction. Queen had become an annoyance in recent days. He began contemplating the relief if she were no longer traveling with him. After all, it wasn't his crimes. No, Queen was the real reason he'd had to leave his wife, his family, and his career.

The riverboat navigated the lake with the aid of a man-made canal called the Government Ditch. The Government Ditch was necessitated when engineers finally cleared the Great Log Jam on the Red River thirty years ago, which had the unintended consequence of rendering much of Caddo Lake all but impassable to steamers.

Queen was ready. She didn't need to know why she was dressed and waiting for him further down the deck. She was barely visible in the lamp light. This might be the last time he would see her. The thought didn't upset him like he thought it would. Rather, it sent him on a hunt through his memories to the first time he saw her. The first time he really saw her as a woman, not a child. There had been maturity in her dark eyes. For the first time, a wonderment. To another man, it might have been the small crush of a young woman coming of age, a crush upon a dapper older man who could have served as a father figure to the girl, but not Richard Watersong. He prided himself on seeing opportunities other men missed. Sometimes he made his own opportunities, like this young girl whom he had cultivated as a farmer anticipating the harvest.

What an opportunity; a young, innocent girl, more beautiful than any doll and completely enamored with him. She appreciated him and saw him as a powerful man. It had all begun at the back of the bank in the vault. The vault was a walk-in room about ten-foot-by ten, encased in steel with a large door. There was not only a wide disparity in age—they were from entirely opposite walks of life.

Two opposing fronts intersected, one sliding past the other into a torrent spiraling around each other like a funnel cloud until they made a tornado, a tornado that consumed everything good, moral, and decent they possessed. Their sinful passion created a tempest capable of wrecking lives and an entire community. Now, he hated it. In his mind he hated it as much as anyone who had suffered. Yet, tonight the storm would claim another victim.

Richard Watersong debated it one final time. There was no alternative. Looking at his hand in the near darkness, he was barely able to make out the knife. He cursed the chain of events which took him here. He couldn't dwell on them, not now. Richard Watersong would rather dwell on the moments, the passions, and the enjoyments. There were more out there, more to be had in Cuba.

The sheriff opened the door. In one sudden movement, Richard Watersong caught his friend's abdomen with the knife. The Sheriff's steel eyes displayed absolute incredulity. Shock paralyzed him for the moment.

The moment resulted in another knife thrust and another. The small blade of the gentlemen's knife made the stabbing hard work. Richard Watersong was deep in the sheriff's abdomen, constantly thrusting up under the ribs and sternum trying to reach some vital organ.

The sheriff was no longer overcome by surprise. He fought. He moved to try to stop Richard Watersong's bloody hands from carving under his ribs as breath began to leave his body. The sheriff struggled for each shallower breath, never getting his lungs full of air. Looking into Richard Watersong's ice-cold blue eyes, the sheriff saw the determination in his killer's face. The more the sheriff tried to catch his breath, the more air he lost. He was suffocating, drowning in a sea of air.

The two men collapsed onto the floor already awash in blood. The red, viscous ooze was all over Richard Watersong's hands, his white shirt drenched in the former lifeblood of his friend. Richard Watersong dropped the knife inside the sheriff chest cavity and reached deep into the man's body. He tore, ripped, and managed to pull, what? He didn't know, some organ inside the sheriff's chest.

Richard Watersong rose breathless, studying his hand like a mechanic becoming familiar with a new tool. He leaned against the door jamb. Looking for witnesses and seeing none, he walked back into the cabin and took the kerosene lamp. He dumped the fuel from the lamp onto the hay which was stacked on the deck. Richard Watersong looked around again. Seeing no one except Queen, he pulled a match from his pocket. For a moment he debated running in the opposite direction. It was Queen's fault he had to do this, but didn't he make her what she was?

The flames swung up in the air in a swoosh, drawing the air away from Richard Watersong. Richard Watersong yelled over and over again, "Fire. Fire." He grabbed Queen and they leaped off the boat into the black water. Neither could see anything. They sank down, further and further down. The two slipped into darkness. Richard Watersong swung his arms and legs in a frantic attempt to reach the surface but something was holding him.

It was Queen. She was panicking. Queeny was thrashing mindlessly. She was pulling him down by the shoulders and kicking away at him all at the same time. He wanted to yell, to hit her, but if he panicked too, they were both doomed. For him to find a way to the surface was the only hope for both of them.

CHAPTER 7: Richard Watersong's House

Ray Elliott opened his eyes. He was in a small room lying flat on his back. The bed was barely largely enough to fit him. The walls were of batten board construction. When the green lumber had dried, knots had fallen out, leaving holes. The holes had been filled with catalog and newspaper pages. Most of one entire wall was covered in catalog pages. Ray Elliott saw all manner of items listed in the Sears and Roebuck catalog, from harnesses to dresses.

There was only one window. The window seemed wrong. Ray Elliott realized there was no glass, no pane. The sunlight must have awoken him. It poured warmth over him.

He had been dying. Ray Elliott satisfied himself that he was alive. The realization only served to heighten his anxiety about his surroundings. Where was he? How did he get here? He racked his mind and found nothing by way of explanation. A little girl in a sack dress opened the door. She shrieked and ran. Ray Elliott could hear her yelling, "He's awake."

Ray Elliott struggled to get up. It was useless because his head seemed to crash through glass every time he moved. He laid his head back, regretting he ever tried to lift himself. He decided he must be in a medical bed in some kind of jail. It would explain the poor facilities. Then he questioned the conclusion because there was no bar on the window or even a window pane.

Ray Elliott opened his eyes again. Without warning nor noise of any kind, a man walked into the room. He recognized the man, but from where?

"I feared you might sleep all week."

Ray Elliott knew the man, yet his mind betrayed him. Finally, the face clicked from their recent encounter at the bank. He blurted the name out, "Cecil Grant."

The man nodded. Ray Elliott found the acknowledgement to be reassuring, however the feeling was fleeting. He hardly knew Cecil Grant. What was he doing in what must be Cecil Grant's house?

The look of consternation on Ray Elliott was obvious. Cecil Grant said, "You weren't far from the tracks. The railroad detectives would have found you for sure."

"How did I get here?" Ray Elliot heard the weakness in his own voice and it took him aback.

Cecil Grant answered, "I been loading and unloading box cars for the I&GN. There is a lot of us, mostly negro. We work like dogs for nothing. Every time somebody complains, the detectives make an example of them, so we all hate detectives. All any of us knew was the porters said the detectives were looking for you. We got us a kind of system; word moves quicker than new-fangled telephones."

Ray Elliott nodded. "So, you found me first."

"You alive, ain't you?"

Ray Elliott nodded again. "Don't you want to know why they were chasing me?"

Cecil Grant flashed a broad smile. "We know. You been out almost three days. You woke up for a little while last night, but I couldn't tell if you understood me."

Ray Elliott nodded again as if he understood. Then he stopped because he didn't understand. "I don't understand now, either."

Cecil Grant's smile disappeared. "Brace yourself, the news is all bad."

Ray Elliott grinned. Nothing could be much worse than having to hide and being a wanted man.

Cecil Grant continued, "Your uncle is the famous lawman, William Preston Henry."

"Yes." Ray Elliott was puzzled. A thought was occurring to him. William Preston Henry didn't make it to the State Penitentiary in Rusk? Like he had feared, William Preston Henry and Dock Baxter had gotten caught? It couldn't have happened. The man was a legend. Legends always get their man. There is not a novel in an outhouse in Texas where the hero loses his prisoner, at least not for long. No one could catch William Preston Henry

Cecil Grant said, "He's dead."

"Who is dead?"

"William Preston Henry."

Ray Elliott shook his head. He was disoriented. This wasn't real. He wasn't here. William Preston Henry doesn't die. Ray Elliott drew the man out of his cave. A man doesn't survive bloody charges in famous civil war battles, a thousand scrapes with Comanches, and shoot-outs with outlaws to die because Ray Elliott asked him to do a favor. There was only one response and Ray Elliott uttered it. "You're lying."

Cecil Grant's dark eyes looked like dark slate, unyielding and determined. "Mister, I would not lie. I got nothing but my name and my family. Richard Watersong owns this house. You know it. I got nothing, but I don't lie.

William Preston Henry is dead."

"How did he die?"

"Newspaper says Dock Baxter murdered him, too. Says he was afraid William Preston Henry was going to turn him over to the railroad detectives. They were holed up at the main depot down in Palestine—"

Ray Elliott interjected, "Makes no sense. Why risk a train station? He was going to ride to the state prison in Rusk."

Cecil Grant answered. "I don't know. Maybe he decided he had a better chance on a train. Palestine is a huge station, and it is a short trip to Rusk. Trains are moving all the time. It's the other part of it which doesn't make sense to me."

"What part doesn't make sense?"

Cecil Grant looked back to Ray Elliott. "I can't believe Dock Baxter killed William Preston Henry. They say he did it because he was afraid Will Henry would turn him over. I knew of Will Henry. He was a friend to black folks and old Will Henry was tougher than a timber rattler. I can't imagine he would have turned over Baxter to save his own skin. No, those railroad detectives are liars. They killed William Preston Henry and blamed Dock Baxter."

"Where are they holding Dock Baxter?"

Cecil Grant looked puzzled.

Ray Elliott asked, "Did they lynch him already?"

Cecil Grant shrugged. "Newspaper claims he got away. Nobody knows how."

The news was startling. It raised more questions than answers. Ray Elliott was lost deep in thought and Cecil Grant slipped out of the room as quiet as he entered.

Ray Elliott pulled the blanket over his shoulders. The

warm sunlight was giving way to a gentle breeze. There must be some shudder on the outside of the window. No one could have a window without a pane unless there was a way to shudder it. The air had a crisp, almost fall-like smell.

After Ray Elliott had studied on the matter long enough,he pronounced in his mind the judgment. This was the worst possible series of events which could have happened. Everyone believed Dock Baxter had allegedly killed one of the wealthiest men in this part of the world and that he'd added one of the most famous lawmen and war heroes to his tally. Both men being war heroes meant people would never stop looking for Dock Baxter, which in turn meant they would never stop looking for the man who saved Dock Baxter from being lynched.

Ray Elliott believed he was responsible for William Preston Henry's murder whether it was at the hands of Dock Baxter or railroad detectives. It still seemed unreal. The William Preston Henry who had lived in Ray Elliott's imagination was ten foot tall and immortal. The real man was small, living in a cave, ground under the boot heel of ill fortune, yet he still possessed an unyielding fortitude, a way of carrying himself which Ray Elliott admired. Now he was dead. It was all Ray Elliott's fault.

All because of a stupid promise to a murderer which never should have been made. Ray Elliott acknowledged to himself the commitment from the other part of the promise, to kill Dock Baxter himself. Then a thought crossed his mind. What if Dock Baxter were innocent of both murders? Both Richard Watersong and the railroad detectives seemed like plausible candidates.

In Ray Elliott's mind, innocent or guilty didn't matter

anymore. He couldn't allow any more innocent people to die trying to protect Dock Baxter. William Preston Henry's only crime had been trying to help his ignorant nephew. Still, if he killed Dock Baxter, how was it not murder? He closed his eyes, wanting to think no more.

Ray Elliott soon discovered Cecil Grant's wife Martha was responsible for much of his care. She was a small woman with kind eyes. At first, she spoke little but over the course of the next three days, Martha revealed that the daughter he had seen was only one of four children. Ray Elliott discovered children were a conversation starter for a proud mother.

There was the oldest, ten-year-old Rodney, whom his mother described as mischievous, but not really bad. Then an eight-year-old also named Martha, who went by Junior in the family. Martha the Junior was painfully bashful. There were two more daughters, ages five and three. The five-year-old, Rachel, had been stricken with polio. Taking her to doctors was the primary setback which had made Cecil Grant have to work near nonstop to make ends meet. The story hit home with Ray Elliott, who had a little sister in poor health. The image of Liza Jane rose into his mind.

Cecil Grant came in after dark. He sat with Ray Elliott.

Ray Elliott asked, "Are they still looking for me?"

Cecil Grant nodded. "Not only the railroad people but everyone. There is a five-hundred-dollar reward for your capture."

"You could do a lot with five hundred dollars. Maybe get Rachel some proper care." Ray Elliott pulled himself into a sitting position.

Cecil Grant ignored the comment. "You look so much better."

"Feel better too. Time I got out from under your roof."

Cecil Grant said, "Not my roof. Mr. Richard Watersong's roof, like everything else in this place."

Ray Elliott said, "Where is Dock Baxter?"

"Long gone."

"Where?"

Cecil Grant looked away. "Your best chance is to get to Dallas and take another railroad to Mexico. I know a man who will lend us horses and we can ride all night. I put you on the train and come back as easy as you please."

"No." Ray Elliott caught himself. He hadn't intended to raise his voice.

"There is no finding Dock Baxter. All the law and the railroads are looking."

Ray Elliott said, "But you know more. Your friends at work know what the railroad detectives know and Dock Baxter's family won't talk to law, but I bet they will talk at church and in their own community. You could find out for me."

Cecil Grant answered, "I was joshing about the telephone system. Because we all black doesn't mean we all talk."

Ray Elliott said, "I am the one who let Dock Baxter get away, and I am responsible for William Preston Henry's murder. I am not going to go hide in Mexico. I can't live till I fix this."

Cecil Grant said, "There's no fixing it, only living, and there is no living for you here."

"I got a little money. I need you to set me in the right direction and give me a horse. Then I am on my way. It isn't safe for me to stay here. We both know if they find me here then all of you will get hurt." Ray Elliott displayed the cash given to him by William Preston Henry.

Cecil Grant ended the conversation. “Rest one more day. I will find out what I can.”

PART II

Journeying from the Truth to Lies

CHAPTER 8: QUEEN'S SECRET

Richard Watersong and Queen stayed in New Orleans longer than expected. The delay was a welcome opportunity to collect themselves after their harrowing escape from the burning riverboat. In fact, every passenger got away, except for one. The couple used their new names to check into the Hotel Monteleone, where Richard Watersong delighted in providing Queen a taste of so many new pleasures: champagne, *beignets*, rich foods, and amazing hats, dresses, and shoes.

They were married at a plantation outside Natchitoches, Louisiana. Richard Watersong told her the owner was an old friend, but somehow, she knew he was a new friend made with money, much like the preacher who married them was ordained with money.

Richard Watersong even got a photographer to take a picture. Queen so hoped one day she might send the picture home to her sisters. It was an overcast, forbidding winter day, but to her it was beautiful, and everything she had dreamed of all her life. Her remembrance was broken by her new name.

"Mrs. Montague? Mrs. Montague, shall I have the chef prepare another dish?"

Queen felt Richard Watersong touch her arm. Startled, she looked up from the champagne into Captain Clinton's dark eyes. The new name still did not register with her.

Captain Clinton said, "If the jambalaya does not agree with you, then I am sure I can have the chef prepare something else for you."

Richard Watersong remained in the Richard Montague character, promoting his cover story. "Forgive my wife. She is a picky eater normally, and she has been out of her element since Baltimore."

"Mr. Montague, we will reach Havana tomorrow and she must become accustomed to the cuisine. It is much spicier than New Orleans. I feared she had lost her appetite because of our political discussion. After how Roosevelt is threatening to let hooligan unions take over the coal business, I am grateful we are all moving to oil."

"Oil is the future. I wish I had a few acres on Spindletop." Richard Watersong looked longingly across the small dining room.

"If we can keep the government out of the oil business. State rules killed business in the Corsicana field. Government has no business telling people how to produce or sell anything."

Queen said, "I must turn in. I am still getting used to rich food," She looked past Richard Watersong's eyes. Did he suspect she was still pregnant? The coldness in his deep blue eyes revealed nothing.

The next morning, Queen woke to the arrival in Havana. She was eager to step off the boat onto dry land. The city was older than New Orleans, but war, pestilence, and pirates had left it in need of repair. Queen and Richard Watersong followed Captain Clinton to a restaurant near the port for lunch.

Captain Clinton insisted, "You must try the *Seleccion de Mastros*. To call it a rum is to call *beignets*, bread."

"I look forward to it. I admit I have not followed Cuban politics closely, to the peril of my business ventures. I am concerned about the number of U.S. troops, proving even well after the war, Cuba is still unstable."

Captain Clinton raised his hand, asserting himself. "Cuba could not be more stable. Some are starting to call it a second occupation. It sends a message—there will be a third occupation or as many as it takes, because there is too much American money to let Cuba fail. I really believe Cuba will become a state sometime after Oklahoma and Arizona."

"I am pleased hear it." Richard Watersong's head turned as if it were on a swivel.

Queen looked up to see a raven-haired beauty in a tight dress with a rose in her hair. The woman was too obvious, clearly a prostitute, though evidently Richard Watersong did not enjoy the same clarity as his wife.

Clinton interrupted the stare by saying, "She is a *jinetera*. They dance with men or more at the bars without charging up front, and then their relatives, often a brother, will seek money for her being in the family way. I find it best to avoid them, Mister Montague. I prefer an honest prostitute."

Queen frowned, looking at the ground. She breathed deep and finally caught a breath of salty sea air. She was mortified. This was the point in her life about which she had dreamed, married and starting a family. She never dreamed her husband would not want her child, and soon it could be no longer be hidden. Thrown into this delicate balance was the embarrassment of a husband lusting after other women.

Captain Clinton must have known their marriage was a sham, or he would not have spoken so plainly in front of her. She realized Richard Watersong was a faithless, terrible man. Still, she owed him. He had protected her, given up everything for her. She owed him her life. Her head seemed to swirl without moving. It seemed as if everyone was mocking her. As if everyone in the crowded port were watching her. She tried to calm herself, but it was far too late as her stomach unleashed and she threw up all over the table.

Later in the hotel room, Richard Watersong could not be placated. He slapped Queen across the room onto the bed. She screamed in terror at a man who had never shown her anything but kindness, at least by his own hand.

She longed to tell him she was still with child. Wouldn't the knowledge make him stop? Of course, it wouldn't make him stop. After all, he had paid the voodoo queen to kill her baby. Only the woman's fraud had saved the unborn child. Queen looked at Richard Watersong, puzzled, realizing the absurdity of the notion he would be protective of their baby. He backhanded her across the face. Her head slammed into the wall. Her whole world went black, all black.

Six months later Queen screamed in sheer terror. No mother to protect her, nor was her father present, who had adored her in her youth. Worst of all, Richard Watersong wasn't even there. She was advised by the Cuban midwife's broken English. Her husband was on a business deal. Queen knew the business deal involved a *jinetera* or a horse race or a fishing trip.

The pregnancy had been sheer terror for Queen. She stood up to Richard Watersong, calling him on the attempted voodoo abortion and challenging him to do his own dirty work. She considered him a weak man at his core, capable of creating an illusion of power in his own mind by hitting her. Killing the sheriff had been a weight on him, a true millstone around his neck. Often, he woke in a cold sweat at night. He treated his anxiety with alcohol. She had grown to despise the man, a malady she likewise chose to treat with liquor.

She remembered her conversations with Eleanor. The words seemed pointless to their brief, uncomfortable conversations so Queen had disregarded them at the time. Now, they rang in her head repetitively. Like some sort of sinful epiphany, she was now aware Eleanor must have known about the affair. In Havana, without the distracting fear of being caught by friends or family or Eleanor, the woman's voice flooded Queen's mind.

Eleanor had been comparing a pecan pie given to the bank by a business client for Christmas to her own extensive holiday baking. At the time, the look she gave Queen seemed odd. Now in memory, it was as prophetic as her words. "I used to think Richard loved pecan pie. I know now he doesn't because, if you love all deserts then you can't truly love any specific one."

Then it occurred to Queen, Eleanor had suffered the same and with the suffering came wisdom. Queen thought it was jealousy, but in hindsight it was so much more than jealousy. It was a tired acquiesce to what both women had learned was the nature of this man, and by him was how both women came to judge all men.

Richard Watersong arrived long after the birth of his son with rum on his breath. He demanded the child be named Richard Watersong Jr. The name was the same as his first son with Eleanor.

Queen balked. "There wouldn't be a baby if you had

your way."

Richard Watersong lifted the infant son from Queen's arms. "Mine now, and he need never know your secret."

CHAPTER 9: *Caribina De Aces*

The sun was rising, casting a red light through the mangrove forest on the *Las Salinas Flats*. The water in the little bay on the flats was serene, an almost transparent shade of light blue. Richard Watersong caught the movement of a bonefish. The long silvery fish was light but it cast a dark, shadow-like appearance in the shallow water.

He swung his fly rod, first forward, then back in a subtle ballet on the flat bottom skiff. The lure landed near the shadow, and Richard Watersong saw the bonefish angle to the fly. The strike pulled him forward. Then he set the hook. Bonefishing was all the excitement he had read about and more.

He was the only one on the little bay surrounded by the mangrove swamp. The smallish trees revealed a morass of root balls exposed above the waterline, giving the appearance of a primeval scene as old as life itself. The day was already hot, the heavy air providing no breeze whatsoever. The scene would have made a portrait, but Richard Watersong's mind was awash with business plans for his new bank. There was the hotel he was building. Then it occurred to him to combine the hotel with a fishing concession here on the shoals for deep sea boats to a navy of skiffs.

There was money to be made and he could market to all the American soldiers who appeared to be in Cuba forever. They would spread the word about the amazing fishing in Cuba upon their return to all parts of the United States.

Richard Watersong would discuss the idea at the club this afternoon. He had hoped Queen would be accepted in Cuban society. In some ways, the country was open to his marriage, despite labeling his son as a *mulatto.* Yet in more ways, the country was as segregated as anywhere in the South. The club would never accept Queen. She had to understand he needed to do business. Then he caught himself. What did it matter that they spent more time apart than together these days? There were always more women. It made no sense to be drawn back to Queen.

In the late afternoon, Richard Watersong arrived at the club dressed in a seersucker suit, white with blue stripes and white shoes.

"Mr. Montague, you must join us. I am enjoying what you Americans would call a lucky streak."

Richard Watersong was familiar with the traditional Cuban dice game, *Cubilete.* He had not mastered the complicated game. It was like poker with dice to the casual observer. The Cuban Customs officer, Rodolfo Castaneda, was already well known to Richard Watersong.

Richard Watersong waded through the cigar smoke to reach the table. He never forgot or forgave a debt. "Good, then you can afford to pay me back the loan, or at least make a payment."

Rodolfo spoke under his breath and turned slightly from the table of players closely following the game, "Do not embarrass me, Gringo. You are in Cuba. We have no loan. You made a wise gift. Do not test my patience."

The dice were passed to the next shooter and Richard Watersong spoke in a hushed tone, "You asked me to cover your losses in New York because you had no broker. It did not make sense to me, because obviously you had some broker to get yourself into a spot on the call, but I did it for you, and now you refuse to pay me? I will not be cheated."

"You are probably a big man where you come from. You are not there. This is Cuba. You will pay to do business here. You did me a favor. Do not ruin the friendship you paid for." The dice were passed to Rodolfo. He threw twice and each time the crowd was louder, but the third time the group of players exploded, exclaiming in unison, "*Caribina de Aces.*"

Rodolfo Castaneda was a reminder. Despite U.S. troops and business interest, Cuba was a foreign country —a foreign country with a long tradition of corruption. Facts which were both useful and worrisome to Richard Watersong.

Rodolfo Castaneda held his winnings and stared at Richard Watersong. "*Amigo*, Cuba is a paradise and I am the luckiest man in paradise."

Richard Watersong balled his fist until the tips of his fingers were white. This man obviously had the money. However, he had no intention of paying what he called a gringo. Richard Watersong attempted to console himself with rum. Rum failed, for the turnings of his mind never stopped, never slowed, always searching for the angle to achieve the maximum leverage. This was more than merely a matter of money in Richard Watersong's mind.

After leaving the club he found Sofia, the young maid and nurse he had hired for Queen and the infant, Richard. Richard Watersong asked Sofia about locating some men. He needed the kind of men one could trust. Her poor English and his weak Spanish made the conversation a challenge. Wickedness has a certain universal vocabulary, and no language barrier has ever defeated evil. It certainly had not limited his interaction with the attractive Sofia.

The next night, a meeting was arranged with two men in a bar. Joaquin seemed to be the leader of the two. Joaquin introduced himself and Fortunato. Both men downed the rum Richard Watersong had ordered.

The bar was dark and located close to the wharf. There was a dingy, dank smell to the humid air combined with the musty bar and an odor of strong alcohol. Richard Watersong became accustomed soon enough.

Richard Watersong said, “Sofia tells me I can trust you. How do you know Sofia?”

“How do you think we know Sofia?” Joaquin looked incredulously to Fortunato, who was smirking, but then frowned, as if remembering Fortunato did not know English.

Richard Watersong looked all around the dark bar. He could barely see the two men next to him. Joaquin was the shorter and smaller of the two with a wiry build. Richard Watersong spoke, “Someone owes me money and refuses to pay because he is in the government. He does not believe I can collect. I can’t be cheated. I am starting a bank. If word gets out about how I can be walked upon, then no one will ever pay me.”

Joaquin said, “Such problems get expensive Mr. Montague. Maybe more expensive than the debt, eh?”

Richard Watersong struck the table with a force which rocked it. “The message is worth more than the debt.”

“Wise business, thinking of the future. Fortunato and I, we are looking to the future. Our work is limited and we need a full-time job. A job which will give us a, what is the word, not cause any concern, a certain respectability. Sofia says you have many businesses and many ambitions. We could help each other. She says you will run many things in Cuba one day."

Richard Watersong smiled at the flattery. "Sofia is a bright girl. I knew almost immediately she understood how the world worked. *Que paso mi hermanito*, did I get it right?"

"*Amigo* is probably easier for you."

Richard Watersong added, "I could find a place for a couple of men capable of getting things done. The debtor is an important man in the government. He is a customs officer. I am not sure of his full name, but he is known as Rodolfo Castaneda to the Americans and Europeans at the club. He claims some direct line from Spain, proud man."

Joaquin spoke to Fortunato in Spanish, because Fortunato was obviously taken aback by the name. "He is a big man, so he will be missed. Cost extra."

Richard Watersong shook his head. "No, I want him to live. I just want him to remember, and tell others you don't cheat Richard Montague. I will send money through Sofia, gold coin, and there will be three times as much when I see Rodolfo pay me my money in front of everyone at the club."

Fortunato picked up on the word "gold," revealing he knew more English than it had appeared. He nodded his head as Joaquin announced their acceptance, "*Si.*"

The following day brought another long ride. This time Richard Watersong arrived much later in the day. He had arranged to change horses twice, first at a farm and then a stable. Only when he was entirely satisfied he was not followed did he turn to the *Las Salinas Flats.*

He poled the skiff across the shallows. Richard Watersong planned the trip so he would have just enough light to reach his goal and return in the dark. The skiff was blue and its flat bottom barely cleared the shallows.

Richard Watersong was dressed in white, making him and the boat impossible to see at any distance against the back drop of pale blue water, white sandy shoals, and light sky. That is, if there were anyone searching the horizon, because the flats were secluded. It was an industrious person who tried to make a meal from a bonefish. There were much better fish to eat, like tarpon, and far easier places to catch tarpon.

He had poled several hours when he arrived at one of the many stands of mangroves looking to the uninitiated like a hundred or a thousand other forest of mangroves in Cuba. He poled toward the mangroves until he saw something which led him to jump from the fishing skiff into the shallow water.

It was a heavy steel chest pushed up under the root balls of one of the mangroves, and lifting the lid revealed a treasure of gold coins. He began the arduous process of returning to shore in the growing darkness with only his lanterns to guide him as he poled across the flats.

Richard Watersong almost always ended his workdays at the club. The hard work of poling the skiff was a couple of days behind him with the muscle aches still plaguing a man not accustomed to manual labor. Then he beheld the sight he had so coveted.

Rodolfo Castaneda was walking toward him. Richard Watersong took another sip of his *mojito*. The mint and sugar overcame the rum and lime to make a minty tang. Richard Watersong savored the flavor while he slowly leaned back in his chair. He sat on the huge patio of the club overlooking the carefully manicured beach.

The formerly proud Rodolfo Castaneda was presented as crestfallen. He extended a bank draft in a bandaged hand, revealing his thumb and only a stub of his ring finger. His eyes were red with a terror, sweeter, and more intoxicating to Richard Watersong Montague than his fine cocktail.

Richard Watersong placed his *mojito* on the table, then he looked around for an audience before he spoke. He projected his voice as if he were on stage. "*Amigo*, Cuba is a paradise and I am the luckiest man in paradise."

CHAPTER 10: MUSKOGEE, OKLAHOMA, U.S.A.

Cecil Grant discovered a fair amount about Dock Baxter. Still, the I.G.N.R.R. detectives had only one real lead. The lead was so far away and so difficult they were not hopeful of taking Dock Baxter into custody in the near future. Dock Baxter had a sister in the Oklahoma Territory. She was married to an Indian, and they were both known for smuggling whiskey. Not the kind of people who were easy to find.

The task was a tall one. Ray Elliott would have to make his way to Oklahoma as a wanted man. Then he, a white man, had to find enough of a way into Indian and black society to locate Dock Baxter, further complicated by the fact Baxter's sister was already well connected in the criminal world. It was an impossible task. Yet, Ray Elliott was driven by an all-consuming sense of guilt.

But for the promise, William Preston Henry would be alive today. How many others? What if Dock Baxter were a murderer? It was certainly the conclusion best supported by the evidence. How many more might he kill on the outlaw path and whose responsibility was every one of those deaths? The answer was Ray Elliott. He alone was responsible. No one else would die on his watch trying to save Dock Baxter. He had chided himself so many times while recovering from his injuries over the last week.

A week on his back gave him plenty of time to go

through it in his mind. He wasn't the best choice to catch Dock Baxter. He wasn't even a good choice. Given the opportunity to review his foibles, he had found himself lacking in every category. Still, it was his responsibility. Such conclusion was the only one of which he could be certain. Had Dock Baxter really murdered anyone? Had Dock Baxter played him for a fool? Did Dock Baxter have to die regardless of guilt? Though his body stood on Cecil Grant's porch finishing a final cup of coffee in the dark, his mind was bobbing in a sea of doubt.

Cecil Grant said, "If it weren't for Martha and the kids, you know I would ride with you."

"You done enough. I won't let you get hurt the way I got William Preston Henry killed. I owe you my life." Ray Elliott sipped the last of the warm brew. Cecil or Martha, one could sure make good coffee.

There was only a kerosene lamp inside the house to throw light onto the porch. "I can at least get you to the Red River."

Ray Elliott's response was emphatic. "No, you done more than enough. The rest of these things don't make sense to me, but running across you saved my life."

Cecil Grant said, "I would have done it for anybody."

"I expect you would. But it doesn't change what I owe you. If I can ever help you." His voice cracked, and he nodded to Cecil Grant, trying to convey by the movement what was escaping his words, like when he had said goodbye to Martha and the kids earlier in the evening.

Cecil Grant relieved the emotional tension in an instant. "From what you told me; a promise got you into this mess. I wouldn't make no more."

They shared a laugh. Ray Elliott let himself continue

much longer than Cecil Grant. It had been so long since he'd laughed. It was less than a week, yet it seemed a world away since he had enjoyed a light moment.

Ray Elliott managed to ride at night. He subsisted on salt pork, sardines, cheese, and crackers for the better part of a week. He finally reached the Oklahoma border and felt safe enough to take a train. In the early morning, he booked passage to Muskogee, Oklahoma.

He sat next to the window and soon fell asleep. After, Ray Elliott awoke consumed with thoughts of justice. Should he kill Dock Baxter on sight? He was likely guilty and even if he wasn't, hadn't he killed William Preston Henry whether he shot him or not? The man had been warned.

On the other hand, justice was the exclusive province of a jury. Wasn't justice why we had juries? Arguably there were no exceptions. Why have a trial for a guilty person? What possible difference could it make?

Ray Elliott was lost in thought as the world passed by the window. The doubts pushed deep into his mind. He debated what William Preston Henry would do. He vacillated between the gruff old man of reality and the great hero he had invented by the same name.

The Missouri, Kansas and Texas Railroad, MKT, was better known as the Katy. It had taken him from Durant and the start of the low plains into what Oklahomans called the Green Country. The Green Country had plenty of rainfall, forest, and lay at the foothills of the Ozark Mountains. Muskogee sat in the Arkansas River Valley near the confluence of the Verdigris Grand and Arkansas Rivers.

The Katy Depot in Muskogee might as well have been

the Taj Mahal to an East Texas farm boy. It was a huge brick structure which included a hotel and restaurant. After Ray Elliott exited the passenger car, he patted his pocket. He smiled, thinking of William Preston Henry.

The man claimed he couldn't afford a leaf of tobacco, and yet the miser produced a wad of cash for his nephew to spend in his new life on the run in Laredo or Mexico. Where did William Preston Henry get all the money? How long had he saved it? Was is from honest work or some questionable activity? As a child he had imagined the famed lawman, though in life the more he discovered about William Preston Henry, the less he thought he knew the man.

Ray Elliott let the waiter suggest his meal. He was disappointed when it arrived. His experience with steak had been chewy, so chewy it took him too long to eat it. This steak was better than an inch thick, and he was given a little narrow-bladed knife. He looked around, tempted to draw his bowie.

To his surprise, the steak cut easily and was coated in butter, joined by roasted sweet potatoes, and fresh cooked greens. Ray Elliott basked in his first good meal since he left Cecil Grant's family.

The waiter asked, "How was the porterhouse, sir?

"Fine meal." Ray Elliott wasn't sure what part a 'porterhouse' played. His mind was on the task before him. "You did great picking out this spread. You know this country pretty well?"

"Yes, sir."

Ray Elliott asked, "I am looking for a Maddy Dehi. Her husband may be Cherokee or Creek, I am not sure. He goes by John Dehi."

The waiter smiled. “You trying to buy their allotment?”

Ray Elliott did not know what an allotment was. It seemed to be a better story than he intended to kill Maddy Dehi’s brother, so he nodded.

“There are some Dehis about five mile west on the Arkansas River because they call it Dehi crossing. Not really a crossing, more a bend in the river where thieves ambush folks. There are easier pickings, young man.” The worry in the waiter’s voice seemed genuine and gave Ray Elliott pause.

The waiter added, “I am not sure Dehi is a name at all. I think it is some kind of Indian word for outlaw.”

Ray Elliott found the lack of interest shown by a person in the middle of Indian Territory to be odd.

The waiter must have read the look. “I been out here three years, and it is still all gibberish to me.”

Ray Elliott asked where he could be outfitted with a horse. The price was steep and Ray Elliott suspected the waiter and the stable owner were in cahoots. Again, the stable owner asked him about allotments. Ray Elliott felt he had stumbled upon such a believable rouse. Of course, he was speculating in allotments, not on a man hunt.

The ruse made Ray Elliott feel better. Hunting a man to his death was not nearly as exciting as it appeared in the dime novels. In real life, it was an awesome thing to hold a man’s life in his hands. For a moment he considered the idea he was really trying to purchase allotments. Whatever allotments meant, it had to be better than seeking justice.

What was he doing here? Was he seeking justice, or vengeance, or something else altogether? Would he capture Dock Baxter, execute him? Or would such an execution be murder? Ray Elliott was content he was seeking whatever William Preston Henry would seek, without determining whether it was the Will Henry of his imagination or the reality of the man he had known.

He rented a dun gelding. The horse ran like a scalded dog without spur or even squeezing his knees. The dun would barely qualify as green broke.

The Arkansas River was large by Texas standards. Riding the skittish horse was a taxing endeavor. Ray Elliott had to be on his guard every moment. He decided to walk the dun and give both of them a break. There was a sand bar with a drift wood stump lodged on it along the riverbank. It called to him like a siren to sit, take out his canteen, and cut a wedge of the inviting cheese wrapped in his cantle bag.

He had not a thought of what he would find around the great bend in the river or how he would find Dock Baxter. Then, how would he get him back to Nacogdoches? As quick as the thought came to him, he chided himself because he wasn't intending to take the man back to Texas. He had to formulate a plan before he took another step.

To the west, the sky was menacing. The dark clouds sailed across the rolling terrain, casting shadows in their wake like great waves. Ray Elliott was unaccustomed to the broad open country. He began debating how much time he had before dark and how he did not want to get caught in the open by a rainstorm –

"Hands up."

Ray Elliott turned to find three barrels pointed toward his head. Two were rifles about ten feet away with a pistol held by the speaker in between them. Ray Elliott complied. He chided himself for being taken unawares. He had been sitting there like he was the Sultan of Siam in outlaw country.

The man with the pistol was the obvious leader. His skin tone made him look more black than Indian. He wore his hair in long braids. He donned a blue shirt and dark trousers. He called out behind him. “Red, bring the horses. We got him.” His mouth arched, flashing a big, near toothless smile.

Ray Elliott said, “I don’t want any trouble.”

One of the minions with the rifles chimed in, “Then don’t start any.” He laughed with great amusement at his own joke. His fellow ruffians only shared a look between them.

The leader asked, “Why are you here?”

“I’m looking for a Maddy Dehi. I want to buy her and her husband’s allotment.”

The men laughed now, joined by a fourth holding their horses. Their leader holstered his pistol and drew his knife in one sudden movement. The laughing ended as sudden as it’d started. The big bowie moved through the air. “Buy my allotment. Allotment? I will carve an allotment out of your hide.”

Ray Elliott realized the cover story was a huge mistake. “Wait, you must be John Dehi. I misunderstood. I thought an allotment was some kind of gift from the government you might trade.”

If Dehi was one of the names the man used, he displayed no recognition for it today. “Gift,” he spat. “If I take your blanket and rub small pox on it and give it back to you, is it now a gift?”

Ray Elliott couldn't tell Dock Baxter's brother-in-law he had come to kill Baxter, and he couldn't continue the lie. He blurted out the only words which came to mind. "I'm sorry."

"You have to pay the allotment fine."

Ray Elliott asked, "How much?"

The crowd of outlaws erupted in laughter. This time in unison. Ray Elliott looked down at his feet, then something drew his attention up. He barely made out the fast-moving shape of a rifle buttstock before it connected with his jaw. His head swung back like a pendulum.

The outlaws were kicking him, beating him with their rifles. Ray Elliott could only cover up by folding into a ball. He tried to fold himself ever smaller to avoid injury. It was an impossible task. No doubt his ribs were broken, and he became grateful even to inhale a breath.

Every time the beating slowed, Ray Elliott took advantage of the opportunity to slide along the sandbar further from the river and where he assumed his attackers were. He knew they had gone through his pockets and were dividing up their loot. He managed to get some short distance away.

It took this beating to convince Ray Elliott he had not completely healed from falling off the train back in Texas. He languished, unable to breathe without pain, to open eyes swelling and covered in blood, and no way to move which didn't hurt. His fat, split lips were incapable of keeping the gritty sand out of his mouth. It was all too much, and he cried out in an exasperated voice with all of his strength. "Kill me, kill me, please kill me."

No one answered, and only then did Ray Elliott realize the ruffians were gone. They took his money, horse, guns, and what provisions he had. He felt the first drop on his cheek. Soon the bottom fell out, and he knew it wasn't tears. Thunder boomed and sheets of hard rain began pelting Ray Elliott. There was no escape from the torrent.

Thoughts raced through his mind. He was still close to the river as it rose. Would he drown? He comforted himself with the thought he would more likely die of the beating than survive until the water rose high enough to drown him. Why was it funny to him? Everything was a joke and a bad dream, yet it was deadly serious.

He wanted to pray, yet in the same moment he thought prayer was absurd. Should he pray to live so he can kill another man, who may or may not be innocent? He argued the matter with himself and finally managed to commence bargaining with his Creator for the mercy of death.

The sun woke him, stinging and hot. There was no way to know how long he had been out. He swung in and out of consciousness many times.

Ray Elliott smelled smoke and the strong odor of liquor.

"Can you eat?"

Ray Elliott didn't respond. The pain was so great, he didn't even want to imagine moving.

"I got some bacon on a stick."

Ray Elliott heard movement and rustling around, but he couldn't discern the direction or even what might be occurring.

"No? Maybe later. I'm Deputy U.S. Marshal J.E. Sharp and you are my prisoner."

Ray Elliott managed to speak a weak word. "Prisoner."

"Yep, don't know what you did but no innocent white man gets this far along the Arkansas River. You wanted for something? I will figure out what by the time we get to the courthouse. If not, I will charge you with vagrancy on the general principle of being out here near dead. Going to slow me down something considerable."

CHAPTER 11: George Washington Pool

Ray Elliott woke to the damp, stank, putrid smell of urine like he had for more mornings than he could provide an accurate count. One week became two, perhaps a month since Deputy Marshal J.E. Sharp had discovered him. Marking time only made the passage of it more depressing. There were maybe thirty men living in the filth of a large jail cell. The odor arose from a long trough along the south wall of the building.

Given the allotment ruse failed in such miserable fashion, Ray Elliott was quick to present the truth, all of it, to anyone who would listen. Truth had not set him free or even improved his accommodations. To the contrary, Deputy Marshal J.E. Sharp initially expressed interest in the story. He even wrote down the names of the bankers in Nacogdoches, then laughed heartily, exhaling his whiskey-soaked breath in Ray Elliott's face. Deputy Marshal J.E. Sharp bragged about intending to seek a reward for Ray Elliott's extradition.

On a good day he was permitted, under guard of course, to work in Muskogee. He mucked horse stalls or dug on a water well before returning in the evening. A bad day was laying in filth while walking through his mind, repeatedly counting the many mistakes. The constant failures which led him here had cost others so much. William Preston Henry's had lost his life. Ray Elliott could only imagine the damage his actions caused his own family. At best they would be outcast, social pariahs, shunned by all. At worst the white cappers would pay them a visit in the night and there were no good visits.

He relived every moment a thousand times. It was an unbearable, though self-inflicted torture. He couldn't stop himself.

Ray Elliott walked back into the jail, stooped from hard labor. He took his place in the cell with the other men. Then he collapsed into a tired heap on the nasty, foul smelling floor. Something was not as it was every other day. The small amount of sun left in the day was being blocked. Ray Elliott looked up and around.

Before him stood a mountain of a man. He was dark skinned and wore a Boss of the Plains Stetson hat. There was the slightest graying of his short, close-cropped hair, but the lines around his eyes really revealed his advancing age.

"Heard tell you're from East Texas. Where?"

Ray Elliott answered, "Douglas, near Nacogdoches."

"Ever get up to Anadarko, Glenfawn, the Devereuxs, Monte Verdi, the Angelina River? Maybe Cushing? I only heard about it, but I know it's right there."

Each name registered less with Ray Elliott until there was one he recognized. "I heard of Cushing, but I have never been there."

"Who's the law in your part of the world?"

Ray Elliott looked puzzled.

"Sheriffs, judges, rangers, marshals?"

"I know the sheriff, but I never did know his name." Ray Elliott was embarrassed by his ignorance of a place he had known all his life. The embarrassment mixed with the always present despair hanging in the air to form anger. He snarled and looked up at the big man. "I don't have to talk to you. What does a prisoner need with the names of law folks in Texas?"

The black man pulled his open waistcoat away from his body to reveal a United States Marshal Badge. "Amazes you, because the world judges us by what someone is but rarely who the person is."

Ray Elliot saw the man the next morning, when he was carried into court shackled to a group of inmates. The federal courtroom was large. The ceiling was better than fifteen feet with long narrow banks of windows separated by light green walls falling to dark, stained paneling. There was an enormous judge's bench made of black walnut. A dock for a witness stand and two lecterns as well as a bar, jury box, and large gallery were all stained or made of the same dark wood.

Ray Elliott smelled the odor of the polish used on the woodwork. He inhaled deeply, taking a welcome respite from the odors denoting his new life. He wanted to touch the wood but dared not do so.

Ray Elliott witnessed a very loud, dignified court opening. The bailiff's performance was almost perfect, but then he corrected himself from Northern District to Western District when the elaborate recitation went off the rails. The judge walked upon the bench in his robe. He gave the bailiff a cross look, and the man looked at his feet.

The judge began reading out loud. Ray Elliott could make little from the legalize. Then he heard his name. Later he made out Sheriff of Nacogdoches County and the name Ralph E. Kingfisher. Ralph E. Kingfisher must be the sheriff's name. There were other words like default, reset, and show cause.

Deputy Marshal J.E. Sharp walked toward the judge

and spoke in hushed tones. The judge shook his head. He followed the gesture with a look in the direction of the big black man whom Ray Elliott had seen in the jail.

Ray Elliott thought about raising his hand or asking to address the court, but the judge's demeanor never seemed to indicate he was open to the idea. The judge was small in stature and balding, yet he was in absolute control of every event in the room. Nothing went on without a look, a nod, a command, or a hand motion. He excused the inmates with a look to one of the bailiffs.

Ray Elliott was admonishing himself for not taking advantage of his chance to talk to the judge when again he was cast in shadow by a large black form.

"Folks say you rode with Will Henry, true?"

Ray Elliott said, "Promise me I can get back to Texas and I will tell you all about it."

"Texas is nothing but a short rope and a long drop for you now."

Ray Elliott was taken aback by the even, smooth tone. The man was neither making a joke nor reciting a threat.

"Tell me how you came to stop a lynching and cost ole Will Henry his life."

Ray Elliott looked around him. "It's a long story."

"You got nothing excepting time." The big man walked Ray Elliott out of the cell into the sunlight and the two sat across from each other on the steps of the courthouse. The big man motioned to a bailiff at the top of the steps with a rifle. It wasn't necessary. Ray Elliott was weakened by his ordeal and this man was an imposing figure, armed or otherwise.

Ray Elliot basked in the warmth of the sunlight on his face. The nights were getting colder. He struggled to determine where to start the story. "I don't even know your name, mister."

"Folks call me G.W. Pool, short for George Washington Pool."

Ray Elliott nodded and then began his tale from the beginning. He didn't leave an event out, having languished in prison over the angst of each decision which he had made with such decisiveness in the moment. He readily admitted his chief fault; only after he acted had he been capable of weighing alternatives.

G.W. Pool asked a lot of questions, mostly about Will Henry. There were frequent breaks and G.W. Pool provided Ray Elliott his first meaningful meal in a long time. He ate heartily and appeared only to feign embarrassment at his poor manners in an effort to continue shoveling the delicious beef stew.

By afternoon the tale was told. Ray Elliott offered his analysis of each character, including chiding his own conduct. He expressed harsh criticism of William Preston Henry. The weeks in prison reminded Ray Elliott the real Will Henry did not live up to the legend in his mind, something short of the hero who should have saved the day. In hindsight, it had been absurd to entrust protection of a negro to a former slave owner and confederate soldier.

This last point evidently proved too much for G.W. Pool. It appeared the man's ire was invoked in defense of Will Henry. "You're not judging Will Henry by the person he was."

Ray Elliott looked up at the mountain of a man, studying him for a moment.

G.W. Pool shrugged his shoulders. "Will Henry got up and left his cave knowing it meant his death. He took you and Dock Baxter, guided both you and Dock Baxter through the world for so long as he had breath in his body. He gave his money and eventually his life for both you and Dock Baxter because of who he was – Mr. Will Henry."

Ray Elliott sat back, taking the picture of William Preston Henry in the new light. The emotion of the moment combined with the despair of confinement and almost overwhelmed him. He pushed against the cold, gritty cement of the steps, regaining his composure.

G.W. Pool continued, "Will Henry wasn't married to a black girl. It wasn't that kind of love. You heard about the great fire what burned down Henderson before the war?"

Ray Elliott nodded. "Yankee abolitionist and his slave woman. They hung both of them."

"The woman you're telling was Will Henry's negro wife was the slave woman's daughter. Will Henry came home from the war and watched the girl abused, beaten, even by her own who had to raise her. No one knew who her father was, so folks began to tell she was born of an unholy union with ole Lucifer himself. She got moved from relative to relative. Will Henry let her stay at the jail a few nights, only to give her a break. He was a sheriff over in Panola County back then. Folks turned on him, including his wife. She told him, 'God didn't call her to raise the Devil's spawn.'"

Ray Elliott asked, "What happened to the slave woman's daughter?"

"All you need to know is what happened to her broke Will Henry's heart and pushed him into a cave until he walked back out for you." G.W. Pool rose, nodding to the bailiff at the top of the stairs and walked away.

The next day Ray Elliott became convinced he had

insulted the only person who had expressed any interest in really listening to what he had tried to tell everyone. He also confessed his judgment of William Preston Henry was false. G.W. Pool was right. William Preston Henry had given his life for Ray Elliott's misguided pursuit of justice. The conviction of his sin finally led him to prayer.

It was after a prayer he opened his eyes to see the great shadow again. This time G.W. Pool said nothing as he walked Ray Elliott out of the jail and into the courtroom.

They and the judge perched on his high bench were the only people in attendance.

Regardless of the small population of the great room, the judge spoke in his booming voice. "Raise your right hand. Other right, Mr. Elliott. Repeat after me. I, Ray Elliott, shall faithfully uphold the U.S. Constitution and the laws of the United States as a Deputy U.S. Marshal in the Western District of the Oklahoma Territory, so help me God."

After Ray Elliott completed the oath, he lowered, then raised his hand again.

The judge looked over the bench and down his spectacles at the young man. "You want to know what happened?"

Ray Elliott nodded.

"Deputy Marshal Sharp sent word to the sheriff of Nacogdoches, Texas about your capture, hoping to claim reward. After the telegrapher told me, Deputy Marshal Sharp chose to bring the matter to my attention. It seems the Nacogdoches sheriff had been unwilling to state in an affidavit the allegation that you and a fugitive, a fugitive whom he considered his racial inferior, were able to escape his custody. He had sworn out allegations of murder against Dock Baxter for both the banker and William Preston Henry. Such was submitted to the proper authority. However, there are no charges against you."

The judge leaned back, motioning toward G.W. Pool. "G. W. is the best marshal in the territory and has been longer than you have been alive. I knew he hailed from East Texas originally, so I asked him to meet with you and to hunt Dock Baxter. It is not my place to decide if the man is guilty. There has been a proper demand for his apprehension to face charges in Texas."

The judge continued in a softer tone. "I originally believed having you assist G.W. was useful because you can identify the fugitive. I thought better of it when I heard the death of a Texas lawman may be the result of the position in which you placed him, but G.W. insisted. He knew you would go back to Texas otherwise and face certain death, lawful or otherwise from the Nacogdoches sheriff. So, you are now a part of the oldest tradition in law enforcement Mr. Elliott. You have been voluntold."

The tone rose, and the judge leaned forward to the edge of the bench to finish his speech, pointing at G.W. Pool. "This man is like a brother to me. I once saw him bring his own son before the Court. It was the greatest commitment to justice I had or will ever witness. Should harm befall him, I will hold you accountable Mr. Elliott."

CHAPTER 12: UNDERSTANDING WHAT VS. WHO

Ray Elliott soon discovered G.W. Pool was not a conversationalist. They rode northwest out of Muskogee roughly parallel to the Arkansas River. Ray Elliot asked about the different areas he had heard the Creek tribe or Cherokee Indian tribe had settled. G.W. Pool ignored the questions.

Ray Elliott asked where they were heading and why. This time G.W. Pool said enough for Ray Elliott to surmise a few facts. Evidently G.W. Pool had done a considerable amount of investigation before the judge ever swore his new deputy into office. G.W. Pool likely knew exactly where Dock Baxter was hiding.

The chestnut gelding was not a strong horse. Under his breath, Ray Elliott complained about the animal. Then he complained about G.W. Pool. After all, he'd had to sign a note. If it was borrowed money anyway, why couldn't he have had a taller, more muscular mount? Likewise, his pistol was an old Richard's Conversion. He wondered if, when the pistol was still a percussion navy model, it had seen combat at Shiloh or Vicksburg. The big military-style flap down holster did not serve to intimidate outlaws.

Furthermore, he had no badge. He was advised by other deputies before leaving Muskogee he would have to buy his own badge from one of the local widows should he live long enough to need one. Perhaps the gallows humor and making fun of the new deputy came with the job. The same men told stories about G.W. Pool. They said the man was living proof of the old adage; the man could stand on a railroad tracks and make a locomotive take dirt road.

But for the slightest grey on the edges of his hair, one had to study G.W. Pool carefully to discover his considerable age. He had a powerful build and moved like a much younger man. He wore a light blue cotton shirt with a dusty brown waistcoat. His horse was magnificent and sported a fine custom saddle with a rifle scabbard mounted vertically at the front of the saddle.

Elliott had seen white horses. They were all light grays, dapple grays or flea-bitten, yet this one was ghostly white. G.W. Pool admonished Ray Elliott. “Best step back from Sarah. There is no better horse but she don’t take to gawkers. Liable to bite you, boy.”

Muskogee sat in the Arkansas River Valley near the confluence of the Verdigris, Grand, and Arkansas Rivers. Traveling west on the Arkansas River soon revealed a country becoming less green. It was more rolling prairie, especially the further north the two men traveled. Ray Elliott asked on a constant basis, ‘How far, how long, where are we going?’

G.W. Pool ignored the incessant whining. Even to Ray Elliott, his own requests sounded like the babblings of a spoiled child seeking attention. The weather was getting cooler and their general, northwestwardly track had them riding into a cold breeze, prompting Ray Elliott to comment. Such was another failed attempt at conversation.

By the end of the third day, Ray Elliott abandoned all hope of discussion. At first, he had been concerned G.W.

Pool had ridden around the area on the Arkansas River where Ray Elliott had encountered Dehi. As time passed, he speculated G.W. Pool knew exactly where Dehi's home base was located. It wasn't readily accessible. Hideouts generally weren't easily located.

They made camp over a little dry wash. Ray Elliott questioned the decision until G.W. Pool showed him a little spring a short way down the wash. Ray Elliott went to gather firewood but G.W. Pool told him they were running a cold camp. Ray Elliott complained bitterly about the cold, figuring G.W. Pool would ignore him again. G.W. Pool walked back to his bed roll and pulled out a duck coat. He threw the coat to Ray Elliott, who smiled in gratitude.

The two men ate left over bacon from lunch complimented by hot water bread.

"I expect we are right on the Creek Freedman's camp."

Ray Elliott couldn't believe his ears. He looked at G.W. Pool then looked around at the emptiness. Why talk now? Maybe the man needed to think and was finally ready to engage in conversation. Ray Elliott leaned forward and in a slow tone asked, "What are Creek Freedmen?"

G.W. Pool looked at Ray Elliott as if they had been engaged in deep discussion for days. "Creek Indians now, but they started off slaves who labored for Creeks. After the war they were freed, but wanted to stay with the Creek, so the name Creek Freedmen. I am showing my age because I should probably just call them Creeks."

Ray Elliott asked, "Indians owned slaves?"

G.W. Pool answered, "Surprises you, because you judge like the world. Man chasing a dollar was like as not to own slaves. Most of the civilized tribes had some slave owners; some even fought for the South."

Ray Elliott took a second piece of hot water bread and wrapped a stringy piece of bacon around it. "It don't seem civilized to own people."

The big man's dark eyes looked down. Ray Elliott feared he had made another mistake, like his poor understanding of allotments, which sounded like a good thing, yet was in point of fact only another way to take Indian land. He wasn't sure whether he should apologize or not. He added by way of apology. "I don't know civilized Indians nor slavery. I mean, you done a lot more living through things than I have."

G.W. Pool ended the awkward silence. "There was nothing civilized about slavery." He had lifted his head, then he looked away into the darkness. He added, "I am hoping this Dock Baxter and his sister judge by the what and not the who. I will leave in the morning. You will wait here for me."

Ray Elliott wanted to ask any number of questions. How long should he wait? What did, "Judging by the what and not by the who," mean? How close were they? He remained silent. Ray Elliott realized he valued this man and did not want to push him any further, not anymore. Maybe the old man was going to walk right up to the door and ask Dock Baxter to surrender. He certainly seemed to have the brass for it.

When Ray Elliott awoke, he was still surprised by the fresh air filling his lungs. It tasted sweet; there was a fall crispness to it. G.W. Pool had replaced his already modest clothes with a threadbare wardrobe akin to homemade overalls. His shoes were poor, simple leather shoes. He completed the look with his small bedroll quilt for a coat and a straw hat of obvious homemade construction.

Ray Elliott watched him walk out of sight to the north of the small encampment. He had little idea what the man intended. He had nothing to do but speculate.

G.W. Pool could see the house in the clearing. The house was part log cabin and partly mud walls with a grass roof, though all parts were poorly constructed. There was a field without barns or out buildings and the corral needed repair. The door was a crude collection of thin boards nailed together. Such as the door was, it was fortunately facing the south while the back of the structure stopped the north wind from continuing to whistle through the hills.

G.W. Pool stepped about twenty yards from the door and yelled toward the house, "You, in the house. I am just passing through and want to work for a little food. Is there anybody in there?"

A shotgun barrel extended from an opening between the boards making up the door. A woman's voice yelled back, "I got my man and both my boys with guns on you mister, so you better reach for the sky and show me your pockets."

G.W. Pool complied with the request. "Can I just have some water before I start out again?"

The voice said, "You are trespassing already, so maybe we will just go get the law."

G.W. Pool pleaded. "Please, no ma'am. I got a little trouble with the law and I will be on my way. Just don't tell them I came through."

The voice both commanded and asked, "You stop right there. Why does the law want you?"

G.W. Pool had already removed his straw hat. Now he folded it in his hand in an anxious motion. "Not sure. I was making bricks in Dallas and the boss's daughter brought him lunch. I didn't have no lunch, so I watched what they had. The boss said I was looking at his daughter and he was going to get the police. I left right then and hopped a train. I been walking or riding boxcars ever since."

The harsh tone of the woman's voice softened. "I figure you are a liar, but there is a wood pile over there to your right with an axe. You split all of it into little stove wood stakes like the ones next to the axe and I will feed you. Only out there in the yard, though."

The sun revealed it was nearly noon by the time G.W. Pool had completed the task. He figured the woman had by far got the best end of this deal. All the more reason she would believe he was a starving outlaw.

A young man emerged with a wooden plate full of beans and some sort of meat. G.W. Pool had a modest lifestyle. He was not unaccustomed to missing a meal, making his portrayal of a starving man all the more convincing. G.W. Pool could not be certain, still the young man did match Dock Baxter's description.

Later, a woman who G.W. Pool figured to be in her early thirties came to get the plate. She was wearing a dirty grey dress with a cigar hanging from her mouth.

She said, "I figure you are alright, being old and broke down like you are. I tell you what mister, you fix the corral this afternoon and I will feed you and let you sleep on the porch."

G.W. Pool, even in his seventies, proved hard work was not a stranger to him. He finished, exhausted, unarmed. If his plan failed, there was no help. He stopped to study the sky. It was menacing, and it occurred to him his situation was equally grim. The tenderfoot he left in camp would likely discover his body in an empty homestead. G.W. Pool soon thought of something else. He was not one to ponder long on danger.

He'd finished another plate of beans and stew when the sky erupted. The woman waived him into the house, out of the freezing rain.

The house was dark except for a pair of candles and the large fireplace. The air was stale and stout with body odor. G.W. Pool had to put his hand near his nose to keep from being sick before he would finally develop some tolerance.

A young man was lying on a little bed in the front room while the woman was pointing G.W. Pool to a chair. G.W. Pool had learned certain questions marked him as a law officer, so he made small talk about the weather. He asked about the country to the west.

The man and woman passed a stoneware jug between them, offering none to G.W. Pool. He was grateful for the poor manners. He needed to stay sharp and was pleased these two were dulling their wits. Over time she spoke more freely explaining her husband was away on business. G.W. Pool suspected the man was running liquor to Indians in violation of federal law.

He laid back on a set of burlap sacks keeping him off the dirt floor. It was comfortable enough. He had trouble staying awake. He was certain the young man was Dock Baxter. Only an outlaw would let an old man work alone like a dog while he laid up all day. Little would be lost if this young fellow met a rope.

G.W. Pool rose quiet and slipped into the bedroom where the woman was asleep and he removed her old shotgun. He put it under the burlap bags which made up his poor bed. Then he took the rope belt from the young man's pants and tied Dock Baxter's hands to the wooden cross member of the bed. The young man stirred, still groggy from the liquor.

G.W. Pool stepped outside and felt the night chill. He determined sleep would be best, so he retrieved the burlap bags and moved them onto the porch.

He was rousted by a shrill scream, "Dock, old man got my gun and got you tied up!" She continued screaming indecipherable curse words.

G.W. Pool pointed the shotgun at the frantic woman who had not managed to make much progress waking her brother. It now occurred to G.W. Pool she could have simply cut his throat instead of shrieking for help. No plan was perfect and most folks panicked in tough situations.

G.W. Pool forgave himself, realizing many years ago there was a certain amount of luck in all success. He pushed out of his mind the thought he was getting old, his thinking muddled.

G.W. Pool began yelling over the irate woman's screams. "Calm down! You knew your brother was an outlaw. Even if he had a reason to shoot the banker down in Texas, there's never a reason to shoot a lawman. Careful I don't take you back with me. You best be grateful I didn't catch your husband running corn whiskey or you would be visiting him in the Federal Penitentiary."

Ray Elliott knew his trust was well placed when he saw G.W. Pool leading Dock Baxter through an early season light snow from the woods beyond the hillside.

Ray Elliott saddled both horses and then he saddled the pack horse which was no longer being used as a pack horse. G.W. Pool tied Dock Baxter's hands to the saddle horn.

Ray Elliott tied down some items formerly on the pack horse onto G.W. Pool's white horse because it was by far the best mount. Dock Baxter's eyes met Ray Elliott's, prompting a good cursing by Dock Baxter.

Ray Elliott asked the question which had been burning on his heart for weeks. "How did William Preston Henry die?" He didn't see the butt of the pistol swing by his head until it landed on Dock Baxter's head.

G.W. Pool said, "We are in the land of his sister's people. We tarry. We die. He can lie to you later if you still want to hear it—"

The loud report of a rifle ended the one-sided discussion. After a moment of silence, when the two men continued to prepare to break camp, there was a series of shots in rapid succession.

G.W. Pool stepped into the stirrup and swung into the saddle. "They coming." Ray Elliott slid his spurs back, and the chestnut jumped forward as best the little horse could.

CHAPTER 13: THE RACE

In his mind, Ray Elliott questioned the wisdom of G.W. Pool's tactics. His chestnut gelding was game, but a poor match for almost anything the Dehi might be riding. The pack horse which carried Dock Baxter was worse. The pack horse was an ancient, flea-bitten gelding, which is sort of white with rust-colored freckles. The only fast horse was Sarah, G.W. Pool's big white mare.

Worst of all, they were not headed back to Muskogee where help might be obtained, nor were they headed south, nor northeast toward Arkansas. They were headed northwest, which took them ever deeper into Indian territory and ultimately Kansas. Ray Elliott tried to console himself by contending G.W. Pool was choosing the most unlikely route to outfox Dehi because no one in his right mind would travel in this direction. Therein was the problem; even with this route as a rouse, no one in their right mind would travel this direction.

G.W. Pool set the pace. He cantered for a period, walked the horses, and then made the men dismount and walk. It was an obvious effort to save the weaker horses. Despite the sensible strategy, the horses were weakening by midday.

Ray Elliott reasoned that if the pursuers knew the condition of their mounts, then for certain the criminals chasing them would gallop them down. But they couldn't know, could they? Surely G.W. Pool had to have a plan. Dock Baxter was obviously scared to ask anything after

G.W. Pool earlier proved how well he could quiet a man.

For Ray Elliott, the only meaningful conversation he and G.W. Pool had passed concerned black people who stayed with their Indian slave masters so they could become Indians. Ray Elliott figured G.W. Pool might as well have told him about the man in the moon. Like everything else in this place, it made no sense.

Ray Elliott surveyed the landscape. It was a vast sea of grass. The slight elevation changes appeared as huge, gentle waves rolling across a green and beige ocean. There was no end, no beginning, and nowhere to hide or take cover. This was too much; G.W. Pool was leading him to his death.

Ray Elliott asked, "Is the plan to outrun the Devil right into Hell?"

G.W. Pool stopped. "Suppose you know better?"

Ray Elliott sneered. "Well I wouldn't run from Indians by running deeper into Indian country."

"You still judge a man by what he is, not who he is?"

Ray Elliott exploded, raising both hands in a torrent of movement. "That's stupid, like everything else. I can't understand how you lasted to be an old man."

G.W. Pool asked, "Why haven't they overtaken us?"

Ray Elliott answered, "Saving horses."

"Not Dehi. They probably carried extra mounts anyway. They are watching, riding deliberate. This is Osage country." For the first time since Ray Elliott had known him, G.W. Pool smiled.

Ray Elliott smiled too. "So, Osages hate Creeks?"

G.W. Pool shook his head. "No, but like all decent folk, they are not much on liquor smuggling criminals. Maybe one more branch crossing and Dehi will back off, brother-in-law or not."

Dock Baxter's head fell. G.W. Pool's smile got broader. G.W. Pool asked, "Don't suit you?"

Dock Baxter looked at G.W. Pool in a sheepish manner. "You think you white, don't you? You know they will lynch me first rattle out of the box."

G.W. Pool argued but only to a limited extent. "I can't say you won't swing, but odds are the federal marshals and rangers can keep you through a trial. There has to be a trial."

The assertion pulled Ray Elliott into the conversation. "Don't have to be a trial if he is guilty."

G.W. Pool said, "Been believing for forty years in law and jury. Best tools we got to patch the world Adam and Eve broke, outside of Jesus."

G.W. Pool saw them first. He grabbed the reins from the ancient pack horse Dock Baxter was still riding. Lifting his foot in the stirrup he yelled, "Get mounted."

Ray Elliott moved even though he didn't see anything. He heard the shot before he saw the rider and in the same moment heard the zip of a bullet pass by his head. He swung his spurs back hard into the chestnut and the little horse jumped forward into a gallop. Soon he was ahead of G.W. Pool, who was hindered by Dock Baxter and the pack horse.

Ray Elliott stopped looking back. He realized it was to no avail. There was nothing he could do to stop the Dehi gang from gaining on him. The race continued and he could tell the chestnut was giving out. Why should the horse die too? He debated stopping and making a stand while the horse continued. Should he jump off or turn and stop? Then he saw it.

At first it was just a low spot with darker vegetation, then he realized it was a spring-fed creek. He looked back at G.W. Pool and saw the man was still holding the reins to Dock Baxter's horse. If they could get to the water, they could make a stand.

The darker vegetation seemed to rise up to meet them. It was men, a wall of frightful giant Indians with painted red faces. There was no way to turn. He would have to crash into them. Ray Elliott closed his eyes. The wall opened and closed again almost as quick. The line exploded with rifle fire and Ray Elliott opened his eyes. To his surprise he was alive and still mounted. He stopped and turned to see the Dehi gang running back the way they had chased him.

Fear had held Ray Elliott, occupied all of him and as sudden as it began the emotion was replaced by elation. Soon gratitude was substituted for elation. The old man knew the best way out and he had guided Ray Elliott through a maelstrom.

Ray Elliott turned to find the big white mare half way up the opposite bank. Ray Elliott smiled, while the big mountain of a man only leaned forward, then swung backward. Ray Elliott saw the blood, now dark, against the dark shirt, yet unmistakable. G.W. Pool fell from the saddle.

CHAPTER 14: A Seed for Justice Falling on a Rock

Ray Elliott sat outside one of the domeshaped houses. It was covered in animal hides added to a kind of prairie thatch. His benefactors were the Osage. G.W. Pool had been right. So many Indians Ray Elliott met had been virtually indistinguishable from anyone else, except for these Osage Indians. The Osage looked exactly like the pictures in Ray Elliott's school textbook.

A woman in a knee-length deer skin dress was good enough to bring him some potatoes and squash. After a time, she brought some dried meat. He thanked the young lady and complimented the meal. He assumed she did not understand him, so he was startled when she responded. "You are welcome. Are you a lawman, too?"

The question took Ray Elliott aback. He didn't feel like a lawman or a man or anything, only a complete failure. He looked over at Dock Baxter, tied to a saddle and laying on the prairie grass. All this because he tried to protect Dock Baxter from a lynch mob. The man was most likely a low killer, anyway. In the process, he had gotten one good man killed and likely another dead too.

How many more had to die in this vain effort to secure a trial for a man who was destined to be lynched, anyway? Even if Dock Baxter were innocent, the answer had to be none. Why hadn't he accepted that this was the way the world worked? To contest injustice had only compounded it. His thoughts were interrupted by an awareness that the woman was still looking at him.

Ray Elliott said, "Yes ma'am, I'm a lawman. Thank you again for your hospitality."

Despite his angst over the situation of his own making, the woman was attractive and her smile contagious. Even in the midst of such a low point, he looked out over the prairie and breathed in the smell of fresh grass combined with the aroma of his first real meal in some time. Dried beef and pemmican didn't count as far as he was concerned. He felt the warmth of the sun on his face and thanked God he was alive.

Ray Elliott looked back at the wigwam. He prayed for G.W. Pool's recovery. He stared at the entrance the rest of the day. Near dark, a tall man in a dress shirt and trousers stepped out of the entrance. He introduced himself. "You must be Ray Elliott. I am Dr. Liam."

Before thinking, Ray Elliott blurted out his first thought. "You look like a real doctor." In the instant, he realized it was stupid and insulting. "I'm sorry."

Dr. Liam smiled. "I was educated in Pennsylvania, which is unfortunate because there is nothing modern medicine can do for Marshal Pool. I am sure there are some remedies of the people, but I don't know what they are."

"Is he going to die?"

Dr. Liam looked down. "Well, I did learn not to be so blunt, even in the white man's school. There is always hope, always prayer. There is nothing more I can do."

Ray Elliott likewise looked at his boots and then gazed upward and extended his hand. "Thanks for everything you've done, Dr. Liam."

Dr. Liam shook his hand. "All the people know the black rider on the white horse. He's the only white man who always keeps his word." Dr. Liam had amused himself with his little joke about the black-white man. The jovial moment passed all too quick.

Ray Elliott asked, "Will it tire him out too much for me to see him?"

Dr. Liam spoke his response like the words were too heavy to utter. "It doesn't really matter anymore. Go see him." Dr. Liam placed his arm on Ray Elliott's shoulder.

The wickiup looked so primitive from the outside, yet inside shone an oil lamp and several straight-back chairs with a basket weave pattern. G.W. Pool looked better than Ray Elliott expected. He was leaning up against the down pillow with a heavy cloth where the bullet perforated his bowels. Ray Elliott looked away. What a horrible way to die. He forced himself to look back at G.W. Pool.

"Not as bad as you think. More like life is pouring out of me more than bad pain."

Ray Elliott said, "Dock Baxter cost you your life and he will pay with his."

"Don't need any more blood on my hands. Take him back to the judge. The Osage can help you get to a federal court in Kansas. You take a train into Arkansas, then back to Muskogee. You're a lawman. Lawman works for justice. He doesn't make it on his own. Trials make justice."

Ray Elliott sneered before catching himself. "He can't get a fair trial, anyway."

G.W. Pool raised his hand to stop Ray Elliott. "Making up your mind quick is a good quality in a lawman, but not when you decide wrong. The world is broke, so you want to quit. Let me tell you what only the judge knows. I was born a slave right there in Rusk County, Texas. My slave name was Ezra." He used all his might to turn enough to show the mass of scar tissue pulling up from his back into an irregular stack of wrinkled flesh.

He laid back and continued. "I was married and happy with my family living down near the Angelina River. The war was over, and we were finally free. Wicked men killed my wife and daughter. I buried them there on the bank of the Angelina. Where I want to rest, next to them. After their murder, I was filled with hate. I killed me one of those demons. Still no relief. My heart only craved death more. I ended up staring down a loaded gun only a hair's breadth from going to Hell."

"What happened?"

"Fellow stepped between me and Hell. A white man was willing to give his life for me because it was right. Because he was the law. I made up my mind right then he wasn't what he was, a white man. No, he was who he was, a Christian. Isn't most of the Bible about who Jesus is? The way I figure it, what a person might be, don't make any difference to the Almighty. God is asking who we are. Are we his people or not?"

G.W. Pool had to stop and take a labored breath before he regained part of his composure. "Later I found out the man died trying to save someone else, so I took his name. I knew he wouldn't mind. George Washington Pool. God don't need but a mustard seed."

Ray Elliott asked, "So you think I should let Dock Baxter go?"

"No. I can't tell you what to do. I can only tell you what not to do. Don't kill him. It's not your place. You won't be the law anymore. You put yourself in place of the law, in place of trial and jury, and you're not the law, not justice."

Ray Elliott looked away. "Maybe it is justice. By my count, he's got three good men dead."

G.W. Pool exhaled. "I won't miss this old world. Man's not ready to fix what he broke. He's too busy tearing apart what's left of the garden." G.W. Pool's words were slower and slurred.

Ray Elliott implored him to rest and not speak. "We will talk more tomorrow." Tomorrow brought no more words from George Washington Pool. Ray Elliott closed the man's eyes and fought back tears. He took the man's pearl-handled Schofield and walked into the sunlight.

He kicked a still sleeping Dock Baxter, who remained tied to the saddle horn. Dock Baxter saw the gun moving down into line with his head. "What are you doing?"

Ray Elliott answered him. "Keeping a promise."

In an instant, the hammer fell on everything Dock Baxter ever was and everything Ray Elliott could have been. No one else was going to die keeping Dock Baxter alive.

Ray Elliott concluded perhaps he and G.W. Pool were both right. A jury verdict was justice. Still, sometimes the price of justice was too high, too costly. The decision, the conclusion, and the killing were never far from his thoughts. For years, every time he closed his eyes, he saw Dock Baxter. His soul was divided against itself, and his only defense was necessity. He told himself the phrase he would repeat so often, 'It had to be done.'

CHAPTER 15: THE WAY BACK

Ray Elliott was exhausted. He leaned against the base of an enormous white oak tree along the banks of the Angelina River. His hand rested on the cool river bank, covered in a carpet of rotten acorns and gritty mud. He looked up through a canopy of orange, round-ended, many lobed leaves. The massive oak must have been more than 150 feet tall. Surely this tree saw the man he had known as G.W. Pool at his happiest. The great oak must have witnessed the woman and child he had loved all those many years ago.

The federal judge in Muskogee was named Porter, and he didn't carry through on his threat. He shared stories about his friend, G.W. Pool. Judge Porter celebrated the man he called a brother and prayed for Ray Elliott's safe travels.

G.W. Pool had found fulfillment while happiness had escaped him in Oklahoma. He had married, but the woman was faithless and left him to raise their son. The son likewise married a faithless woman whom the son later killed. Judge Porter said the other marshals refused to serve the murder warrant, so great was their admiration and affection for G.W. Pool. So G.W. Pool brought his own son to trial where the son was convicted and is serving a twenty-year prison sentence for manslaughter. The son would be paroled soon at the request of Judge Porter. While G.W. Pool lived, he had forbidden the judge from special treatment or even a kind word to the parole authorities for his son.

Under the great oak tree, Ray Elliott sat exhausted as the winter light was fading. He walked back over to the fresh grave and rolled the heavy blanket wrapped body into it. There was no way to know where the man he knew as G.W. Pool had buried his family. This spot would have to do. He began to shovel dirt over the body.

Ray Elliott shivered while riding into Nacogdoches. For his entire nineteen years, no one had noticed him. He was Roy Elliott's boy, one of those Elliott kids, and he never drew attention. Anonymity became normal, so he had shied away from any kind of limelight. Today was different. He was different.

Gone was the uniform of a farmer. Judge Porter had helped outfit him in the clothes of a lawman. He wore G.W. Pool's Schofield in an elaborate tooled holster and he rode the great white mare, Sarah. Behind him trailed the little chestnut gelding and the pack horse with Dock Baxter's body wrapped in heavy blankets.

Judge Porter had telegraphed ahead to local officials advising them Ray Elliott had rendered great service to the law. Still, no one knew exactly when Ray Elliott would arrive, so the outpouring was a surprise. People emptied into the street. Horse and mule teams on the streets pulled aside so the drivers could watch Ray Elliott pass.

He wanted to ride to his home in Douglas. He had resisted the urge to send a telegram. He had best explain himself in person. People wouldn't understand what he had done. Still, he had to be able to convince his mother and father. He missed his siblings, most of whom he never believed he would ever long to see except for his favorite.

Little Liza Jane was what set all of this in motion for

him. It was the need to raise money for her illness, which caused his parents to send him to town with eggs and chickens. He imagined a healthy little girl jumping and hurling her arms around his neck. The daydreamed warmth of her embrace pushed away the shivering cold.

Ray Elliott's mind shifted to thoughts of the sheriff. The sheriff, whose name he now knew, was Ralph E. Kingfisher. If Kingfisher was his name. Kingfisher had been the name of a gunfighter. It wouldn't surprise Ray Elliott if the sheriff had stolen the name to increase his standing. The man was all about putting on airs.

Ray Elliott had tied his horse and stepped toward the sheriff's office when the door opened. A young man about his own age walked out with a star on his chest. He knew of the person. His name was Mason, and his father was a blacksmith in Garrison.

Ray Elliott asked, "Where is the sheriff?"

Mason Pritchard answered in a bold voice. "You're looking at him."

Ray Elliott was puzzled, yet extended his hand and began to introduce himself. "I'm—"

"I know who you are. I been expecting to arrest you." Mason Pritchard displayed a set of handcuffs in his right hand.

Ray Elliott reasoned you don't display handcuffs in your gun hand if you are truly intent on arresting someone. "You're not arresting anyone. Sheriff Kingfisher wasn't going to swear that I bested him so there is no warrant. Now get me Sheriff Kingfisher before I tell him to leash his pup."

The quip surprised Ray Elliott. It sounded a lot more like something William Preston Henry would say, not Ray

Elliott. Nothing seemed like him anyway. He had gotten William Preston Henry killed, buried another good man. In the meantime, he had tried, convicted, and executed Dock Baxter for what? He wasn't sure anymore. He figured he had seen enough death for a lifetime.

Mason Pritchard said, "Sheriff's been gone a long time with no word."

"Looking for Dock Baxter?"

Mason Pritchard shrugged. "Kind of looking for Richard Watersong looking for Dock Baxter."

Ray Elliott motioned to the pack horse. "There is Dock Baxter. I will swing by tomorrow to collect my pack horse. I want to get back to my people before dark."

A small crowd had gathered. A smirking Mason Pritchard said in a manner intended for the crowd. "Mister, you ain't got no people."

Ray Elliott looked past the deputy at the crowd. He saw no reason to continue with the smart aleck boy. Evidently, the young man had picked up on how to show off for a crowd from Sheriff Kingfisher. Ray Elliott mounted the great white horse and began a trot with the little chestnut following.

The days were growing shorter, and he had misjudged the time. Dark overtook him not far from his home. There was enough moonlight to navigate, and besides, he could find his way home in pitch dark.

He wondered what the deputy meant. He was fairly sure his parents would not be happy with him, but once he explained it, they could understand. Like Judge Porter reassured him, they had raised him to do right, so certainly they had an appreciation for it, the judge had concluded.

Where was it? Did he miss the house? How could he miss the house? There was the field, the wood line, and the old barn. The old barn had some other structure added onto it. It was sheets like some kind of tent.

A voice yelled, “Step off your horse or I’ll shoot.”

Ray Elliott recognized the voice. “It’s me, dad, it’s Ray.”

“Aww Ray.” His mother repeated the wail while his father lit a lamp.

In the light he could see the sheets making a tent were open, facing him. His brother and his sisters stood motionless in their night clothes.

His father did not wait for the question. “Burned us out.”

Ray Elliott asked, “White cappers?”

“Don’t know. Deputy Pritchard says it was Dock Baxter’s family getting even for you catching him. I don’t believe such. Now you seen it. Turn your fine horse around and ride. This family paid enough for your foolishness.”

Ray Elliott’s mother cried out in a high shrill.

Ray Elliott’s response was immediate, as if somehow the news was communicated to him without words. He looked, and franticly swung back to his father. Someone was missing. “Liza Jane?”

“She couldn’t handle the smoke. By the time we woke, she was overcome with it. You told us what we were to you when you run off with a murderer. You more kin to him than your own family. What folks say about you is true—”

His father ended with a litany of racist remarks. Ray Elliott knew it was grief cursing him, not his father, but still, it stung no less. His own anger and frustration were rising as a result of losing his sister. He was being filled with rage at who: his father, white cappers, Dock Baxter, the sheriff? No, the only person he knew was responsible was him. He slumped in the saddle and rode away.

Ray Elliott slept under the stars; except he didn't sleep. He was tormented by his failings. It crossed his mind to pray, but prayer only filled his mind with all the prayers his father led the family in for Liza Jane's recovery, sometimes praying that she would live through the night. Besides, God couldn't hear his prayers. He had given all he loved to save the life of a murderer whom he later shot in the head himself. What would he do? Where would he go? Where do killers go when they are not killing? The sun broke over him with his eyes still open.

Ray Elliott rode to the sheriff's office to collect his horse. Perhaps Judge Porter would take him as a deputy marshal, or, as the sheriff had suggested, the rangers' frontier battalion. However, he now realized Sheriff Kingfisher had only been coming up with an idea to get rid of him.

Mason Pritchard met him at the door again. "I took your nag down to Old Auggie."

"Who burned us out?"

Mason Pritchard looked around and then blurted out his answer. "Some of Dock Baxter's people, but I can't get them to talk. I asked several darkies. They ain't telling. I can tell you who I talked to if you want to know."

Ray Elliott didn't figure Mason Pritchard did any questioning of anyone. "I'm more interested in who the white folks are that you didn't want to talk to."

Mason Pritchard acted like he did not hear Ray Elliott. "Eleanor Watersong wants to see you. You know where she lives."

Ray Elliott asked, “Why does she want to see me?”

“You being such a big high and mighty outlaw hunter and all, I reckon she wants to cat around with you while her husband is gone.” Mason Pritchard laughed hard enough the star on his chest was bouncing. “How do I know what a rich woman wants with you?”

“She still live in the big blue house?”

“Well, you know where it is.” Mason Pritchard pointed. “You know right there on the rich folks’ street. Sort of got a lot of gables and wings around it like a storybook castle.”

Ray Elliott rode away, debating whether to go to Eleanor Watersong’s mansion or not. The grand lady certainly did not want to ‘cat around’ with him. She probably wanted to ask him if he had seen her husband or Sheriff Kingfisher on Dock Baxter’s trail. Of course, the deputy could have asked him for her. What did Eleanor Watersong want with him?

CHAPTER 16: Ellie's Request

'Wings' on a house and this kid thought he was a hick. Ray Elliott pulled the collar of his duck jacket up over his neck to where it almost met his hat. It wasn't hard to find the biggest, richest home in town, and it didn't hurt matters that it was the only blue house of all the Victorian-style mansions.

An older housekeeper opened the door and showed Ray Elliott to a small parlor off of the foyer. The little room was full of expensive furniture, book shelves, and was adorned with several oil paintings. A painting depicted a landscape of bluebonnets and Indian paintbrushes. Another showed Lukas Halten in his war uniform. There were two little tables covered in what Ray Elliott surmised were white, crocheted little covers. He stood with his back to the fireplace.

Eleanor Watersong entered the room and made her introductions. Ray Elliott grinned, chuckling to himself. Eleanor Watersong was always made up to the nines, but today it was clear she had spent even more time. She looked like she had walked off the canvas of a magnificent portrait. In his mind, Ray Elliott laughed at Mason Pritchard's little joke. What in the world could Eleanor Watersong want with him, and why would she try to impress him?

She was so nice. Would she give him the time of day if she didn't need something? Yes, she might. Eleanor Watersong had a gentle, sincere quality. He resisted the urge to blurt out, 'Why did you want to see me?' His curiosity began to wane as he savored his surroundings.

Everything in the house was beautiful and fragile. Her perfume reminded him of the crisp, clean aroma floating off a fresh cut hayfield. Her hazel eyes matched the light green pendant she wore. Still, neither the lavish home nor the beautiful lady overcame his grief or even eased it. Perhaps the prison in Oklahoma had given him a new appreciation for a pleasurable moment, despite his depression. He wanted to savor the moment before the conversation moved past pleasantries.

Eleanor said, "I am sorry to hear about your home and sister."

Ray Elliott appeared startled. "I forgot how news travels here."

The housekeeper entered with a pot of tea and a plate of what looked to Ray Elliott like flathead biscuits. She tried to pour Ray Elliott a cup of tea. He declined. He couldn't fathom any possibility of not breaking the cup. He did eat one of the biscuits and take another.

Eleanor seemed to read his mind. "Yolonda, please fix Mr. Elliott a plate of the roast and potatoes we had last night. I suspect being on the road, you have not had a cooked meal in some time."

He tried to protest, yet it was entirely pro forma. He had laid awake all night, too upset to sleep or even think about eating, but now hunger was overwhelming him.

Ray Elliott found the kitchen more to his liking. He had a big glass of water and a full plate of the roast and potatoes at a little table in the kitchen. Eleanor seated herself in the straight-back chair across from him. She insisted he call her Ellie and made polite conversation about the weather until he completed his feast.

Ray Elliott asked, "Ellie, did you ask me here to find out if I saw your husband or Sheriff Kingfisher in Oklahoma?"

"I fear Sheriff Kingfisher may be dead, and Richard was, at least for some period, in New Orleans."

Ray Elliott looked at her for a moment. The easy-going veneer had been dropped, and she was deadly serious.

Eleanor continued. "I know my husband was in New Orleans because he assembled the money he stole from my father's bank. He was clever enough to have it under false names in stocks and various business ventures which he liquidated from New Orleans."

"Where is he now?"

"Panama, Brazil, Cuba, China for all I know. He is somewhere on a beach spending my father's hard-earned money with his mistress."

Ray Elliott looked down. "I didn't know you knew about her."

"Queeny was like family to me, so I was the last to know. I should not have been surprised though. Richard always had a wandering eye. My father begged me not to marry him. I knew better." The sadness in Eleanor's face echoed the sarcasm.

"I'm sorry."

"No one held a gun to my head and by the time I knew, it was hopeless. I had two sons who needed a father, and he was a good father until he walked out." She drew a deep breath. "The bookkeepers caught it first at the Henderson Bank. I am fairly certain my father was going to confront him or had recently confronted him at the time of his murder. So, you see why I needed to meet with you."

Ray Elliott looked back into her eyes. It was easy to be mesmerized by the lyrical quality of her voice. His own tone was short and harsh. even when he tried to be softer, more elegant. “I don’t know anything about stealing money.”

Eleanor leaned closer to Ray Elliott. “Do you know whether Dock Baxter really killed my father?”

“There was a time when I thought your husband murdered Lukas Halten. I am convinced I was wrong and Dock Baxter did it, but I couldn’t prove it and don’t see how I could ever prove it now.”

Eleanor’s countenance fell. Whatever answer she prepared or had hoped to receive, whether good or bad, carried the certainty of a final answer. The truth was still unknown. “I hired Sheriff Kingfisher to find Richard and make him return whatever funds could be located. He had a theory about Richard. He speculated Richard and Queen went by way of Jefferson down the Red River to New Orleans. I am worried he was right and Richard killed him for it.”

Ray Elliott said, “I feel for you. I really do. Still don’t understand what I have to do with all of this.”

Eleanor began to weep. “I need you to find out what happened to Sheriff Kingfisher. If my children’s father is a murderer, then I don’t want the boys growing up with it in their face every day. We will leave and go as far away as possible. If not, then I will try to hold the banking business together until my sons are grown.”

Ray Elliott looked at her. He was amazed. If she could determine all of this, including many things he had not been able to deduce, then why didn’t she go?

She answered the question as if she heard his

thoughts. “I have to try to keep the banks afloat. I can’t go.” Her weeping turned to sobbing.

Ray Elliott suspected the enormity of the situation was hitting her. After all, what she described was that marrying over her father’s objection had not only brought her misery; it may have brought her father’s death. On the other hand, even as independent and resourceful as she seemed, she was capable of turning on tears to get her way. Were these tears sincere? After a moment, he realized it didn’t matter. He wasn’t going to say no to her whether the tears were fake or not.

“What do you want me to do?” He extended his hand across the table.

Eleanor took a minute to compose herself. “I want you to find Sheriff Kingfisher.”

Ray Elliott asked, “The deputy can’t find his sheriff?”

“You met Mason Pritchard. I need answers and Sheriff Kingfisher is a good place to start.” She extended her hand over Ray Elliott’s own. Her hand was warm, and it reminded Ray Elliott of all the affection he anticipated from the reunion with his family. He had no family now. In a strange way, she was all that was connecting him to the world. The thought embarrassed him and he pulled his hand back.

Eleanor pulled back too. “I’m sorry. I forget myself. I apologize.”

Ray Elliott wanted to tell her it wasn’t the reason he pulled away. He wasn’t sure why he pulled away. He had lost so much, so soon. Taking more only served to expose him to more hurt when it was lost. Hurting was useless and unmanly. He wasn’t going to hurt anymore.

“I had better get on the road. I can probably still get a

train out if I move quick. Excuse me, ma'am."

She corrected the ma'am comment. "Ellie, please."

Ray Elliott stepped out the door while Eleanor continued to hold it open until Yolonda chided her.

"Eleanor Alderose Halten Watersong, you get in this house." Yolonda's tone was terse.

She had her hands on her hips, facing Eleanor like she had done many times in Eleanor's youth. "You are fooling the boy. Playing with him to get him to do what you want done. You were raised better. Your father would be ashamed."

Eleanor closed the door. "Don't get upset. I am desperate. Even if I went after them, men don't tell women, not like they talk to other men. I wasn't going to let it go far, and he didn't want me, anyway."

Yolonda's demeanor remained dire. "It didn't work because the boy is not trash. You remember who Eleanor Alderose Halten was before the Watersong got added to your name. Don't make me call you down again."

The stare from Yolonda would have burned through stone. Eleanor looked away.

Yolonda had the last word. "You ain't too big for me to beat, Ellie."

CHAPTER 17: Finding the Future

Eleanor chose the hotel in Jefferson. As a result, Ray Elliott was treated to a new technology. The hotel had a telephone and he phoned Eleanor upon his arrival. His first telephone call was uneventful, except she shared with him her exasperation with her sons who failed to clean their rooms. Ray Elliott had difficulty fathoming each child having their own room.

Local law enforcement failed to turn up anything about Sheriff Kingfisher. It appeared Eleanor had also made the reservations for the sheriff. The circumstance prompted the desk clerk at the hotel to inquire as to Ray Elliott's purpose.

Ray Elliott said, "His name is Ralph Kingfisher: snappy dresser, probably helped himself to the best meals and liquor while he was here. He had a pair of boots with 'sheriff' embroidered across the tops and a fancy diamond tie tack."

The clerk studied Ray Elliott. Soon, Ray Elliott realized he was missing the necessary inducement—cash.

"Yes, dead."

"Dead?" Ray Elliott studied the clerk. "You can't just say dead. What happened to him?"

The clerk stood mute until more bills were produced by Ray Elliott. "The *Caddo Queen*, last of the paddle wheelers, burnt up and sank over on the Louisiana side. I don't know for sure it was your sheriff, but word on the street was he was a snappy dresser and he left for the

Caddo Queen. So, I assumed he was your sheriff."

Ray Elliott asked, "Well how do I find out?"

The clerk's palm extended again. Ray Elliott grudgingly dropped six bits to grease the open hand.

"Go over to Caddo and talk to the Parish Judge and the Police Jury." The clerk looked at Ray Elliott like the idea should have occurred to him.

"What is a Police Jury?"

Ray Elliott's primer in Louisiana governance was as expensive as it was cursory. Jefferson was wedded to Shreveport, Louisiana more than the town was connected to most places in Texas. The Police Jury was essentially the governing body of the county or parish. Ultimately, Ray Elliott discovered the Police Jury required a report on major disasters, like the *Caddo Queen*'s burning and running aground.

Catholic Parishes were well established when the United States purchased Louisiana. There was no use in attempting to establish any other form of local government. The president of the parish's Police Jury was an amiable fellow and despite his professed love of all things Texas, he was more conversant in French than English. However, he was able to guide Ray Elliott to an English translation of the report.

Ray Elliott spent two days researching the steamer accident and arson to gain some context for the report. The report recited that each crewmember was interviewed from the captain to lowest porter. There was no indication of a mechanical failure. In fact, there was sufficient time to navigate to the shoreline, so the fire resulted in only one death.

The official finding was inconclusive. However, all

knew arson caused the end of the *Caddo Queen* as well as the death of the unknown man. The body was unrecognizable. Ralph Kingfisher was listed on the passenger manifest. The fact eliminated any doubt in Ray Elliott's mind. Still, he would have preferred a picture of an identifiable body before it was interned.

Ray Elliott found a Richard and Queen Montague on the passenger manifest. Richard Watersong was a college graduate. In school, he had participated in many drama presentations. Ray Elliott knew enough to know Montague and Capulet were names used in *Romeo and Juliet.* It was exactly the kind of play on words Richard Watersong would find humorous or ironic or something.

Once Ray Elliott explained his strong suspicion that Ralph Kingfisher was the deceased individual, he was provided a box. There was a handful of items which didn't burn like a badly damaged watch and something which established certainty. Included was a tie pin with I&GN etched in faux diamond.

Ray Elliott returned to the hotel in Jefferson. He shared a brief discussion with the clerk about the many rumors concerning the *Caddo Queen.* Out of desperation, Ray Elliott asked a question. "Did you ever hear of a man named Richard Montague or a Queen Montague, a black and white couple?"

The clerk said, "We get a few Richards but almost no Queens and very few mixed couples."

Ray Elliott said, "Miscegenation?"

The clerk answered, "It is the twentieth century; the modern term is mixed."

Ray Elliott smiled. "Mixed is better."

The clerk smiled, too. "I have an answer and then I

have an expensive answer."

Ray Elliott threw the remainder of the cash from his pocket onto the counter. "I'm sure expensive is better."

The clerk looked around and then spoke in a hushed tone. "The man had a problem. The woman was with child and he wanted her without child."

"Without child?" Such a thing had never occurred to Ray Elliott.

The clerk continued. "There are ways, expensive ways."

Ray Elliott grimaced. "I suspect it is very expensive. Where did you suggest Richard take the young woman?"

The clerk raised his hands to feign ignorance then answered. "There is a black lady in the lake. Why?"

Ray Elliott moved closer to the clerk. "I want to meet with her and I am willing to pay for her time."

The clerk leaned back. "I will get word to her, and if she agrees then her man will come to your room and take you there."

Ray Elliott started to walk away, then turned and asked the question he had to ask. "Did Queen even know she was going to have her baby taken?"

The clerk gave him an incredulous look which answered the question. Ray Elliott went back to his hotel room and waited.

It was still dark in the early morning hours when there was a knock on his door. The young man said little, even when pressed by Ray Elliott. About all the information he provided was that they were going to see Marie Laveau. The name meant nothing to Ray Elliott.

His guide rode a mule and Ray Elliott kept Sarah at a slow walk. His thoughts were of Eleanor. What would he tell her? Yes, all her fears were true. Her husband was having an affair with Queen and more; Queen was pregnant with almost certainly a half sibling to her own sons. After the news shocked her, then he would have to add the child was not going to be born because of Richard Watersong's actions probably overcoming Queen's objections.

Would he give her Sheriff Kingfisher's tie pin? It was reasonable to assume Richard Watersong killed the man. If he were capable of one murder, wasn't he capable of the murder of her own beloved father, Lukas Halten? She didn't listen to her father when he tried to save her from the heartache of marrying a philanderer. Her refusal to accept his advice cost her the life of her father. How could one survive such guilt and grief? It would crush Eleanor.

He kept empathizing with Eleanor. She had to have debated confronting Richard Watersong with her suspicions. If she had done so, would it have saved any of the misery? Even Queen was a victim of Richard Watersong who could have been saved. He could have been saved from the loss of his family; maybe even Liza Jane would have had more time.

Ray Elliott concluded Eleanor was innocent. Richard Watersong chose to set in motion a hurricane of destruction when he succumbed to his lust. Still, Eleanor would not see it. She would blame herself.

The image of the grand lady weeping flashed before his eyes. He remembered how he couldn't be sure she wasn't using the tears to get her way. Despite the possible insincerity, Ray Elliott remembered the overwhelming compulsion to do anything to stem those tears. She couldn't really cry on his watch. He wouldn't stand for it.

The mule stopped. The man lit a candle lantern and motioned toward a canoe. Faint rays of orange were just breaking the dark horizon. The poor illumination from the lantern only permitted Ray Elliott to make out the form of a shack and on the porch, a black lady with wild hair, matted into serpent-like shapes. He introduced himself.

"I know who you are. You want to know about the girl."

Ray Elliott asked, "Is she all right?"

"No."

"What did you do to her?"

"The man did enough. I tried to protect her."

"Where is she?"

The raspy voice from the darkness answered, "I don't know."

Ray Elliott argued. "You say you tried to protect her. You were the one putting her in danger."

The response was terse. "I don't help girls who don't want help."

Ray Elliott was perplexed. It never occurred to him a person he thought a witch had standards. In desperation he asked, "What can you tell me?"

The sun was breaking through the curtain of darkness hanging over the vast bayou wilderness making up Caddo Lake. The orange light did little to cut through the night.

The woman said, "I've heard of you. We asked around. You think I'm evil. You're the one who caused the deaths of the famous lawmen Will Henry and G.W. Pool. You killed Dock Baxter in cold blood."

Ray Elliott said, "You're nothing but a fraud."

"I'm the fraud, lawman?" The first red rays were breaking through the night. The woman motioned toward them and then laughed in a guttural clatter.

Ray Elliott's face was flush. He threw the last of the money Eleanor had provided onto the porch. "Spare me your fortune reading, witch."

As he stepped away, she raised her voice. "The sun doesn't fear breaking the darkness. It brings truth everywhere it shines. If the light hides its truth, then we are all lost to the night."

CHAPTER 18:
THE PLACE FOR TRUTH

Ray Elliott arrived back in Nacogdoches. He changed clothes and rode to Eleanor Watersong's home. She wasn't home. Yolonda was dressed in her finest attire. He realized it was Sunday morning.

Yolonda said, "She is at church, where I am going now. Where you ought to be. There is a sacred harp singing this afternoon at the church. She will be there."

Ray Elliott had figured Eleanor would want to meet alone. "Does she want me to go there? I don't want it to look bad, like I am hurting her reputation."

Yolonda laughed. "I would not have told you if it would hurt her. You both going to a singing don't make you a couple." Perhaps her next comment was a joke, but Ray Elliott took it as an admonishment. "Lessen you already thinking you are a couple."

Ray Elliott turned bright red. "No, ma'am."

Yolonda said, "Eleanor is dealing with a lot of guilt for what she let Richard do to her father's banks and the shame she let him bring on her sons. She has a big heart. Let her find a way to crawl out from under some and I expect she can find a place in her heart for you."

Ray Elliott was mortified. He looked at his feet. "I am not going to sing. I will come by when they eat."

He walked back to his horse. Yolonda yelled, "Once you seen her really cry, she can't fool you again."

Ray Elliott went back to the wagon yard behind Auggie's stable. He had spent Eleanor's expense money and he wasn't going to take anything else for trying to help her. At some point he would hit Auggie up for some part time work. The short-term plan only highlighted the fact he had no long-term plan.

Nonetheless Eleanor was foremost on his mind. What would he tell her? The truth was, all her suspicions were likely true. No matter how bad it hurt her he had to tell her the truth.

He didn't want to walk to the church. His decision had nothing to do with the cold weather or the wind whipping through him. Each step was heavy. It made more sense to walk away. Ride away now and let her forever wonder. The not knowing was better than the truth.

He heard the singing long before he saw the tent. The tent was open on two sides while the other two held back the wind. His mother had been a singer. He wished she was here now, not suffering without a home.

Did she hate him? A mother can't hate her son. He had heard stories about young criminals executed for their crimes and their mothers cried and were inconsolable at the hangings. What had he done to merit being shunned?

Ray Elliott wasn't a singer and it made no sense to him to spend good money on an organ and a warm church to stand outside in the cold. The singers formed a hollow square. When he was younger, Ray Elliott tried to make out the words. None of it had made sense. He'd tried singing on the wagon ride home when his mother had finally shared with him there were no words, only sounds.

A new leader stepped into the hollow square and called a number. Ray Elliott stopped and listened to the dark melodic tones. As the song continued, he closed his eyes. In his memories, he could hear his mother along with the rest of the large square. He didn't want to open his eyes because as long as they were closed, he could imagine she was seated in the treble section. Their home was still standing. He had not shamed his mother and father. He was never robbed and jailed in Oklahoma. Little Liza Jane and the rest of his siblings were standing on the porch waiting for him to return from cultivating his failed tomatoes.

Ray Elliott didn't notice the music had ended until long after it was over. He opened his eyes and there was Eleanor standing before him. Her bright red hair and attractive features stood out in contrast to the dark smock-like dress she was wearing. He realized she was wearing black, as if Richard Watersong were dead. Eleanor and her sons would be so much better off were Richard Watersong dead. In death, even scoundrels were treated with honor. The wife of an adulterous leech could claim no such status.

She asked, "Is Sheriff Kingfisher dead?"

"Yes."

Ray Elliott opened his mouth to continue and Eleanor gave him a look he instantly understood. "Mr. Elliott, I and my children rarely have a day like today. Please wait until after dinner to discuss the particulars."

"Yes ma'am. I will be at Auggie's livery."

"No sir, I insist you join us for dinner. Someone will make a couple of fires so it is not too cool in the tent. What happened to calling me Ellie?"

"In public?"

She smiled. "Hardly scandalous, Mr. Elliott."

He added, "Call me Ray."

In short order, a number of long oak planks were laid over sawhorses, forming a long table covered by white cloth. No time passed and the tablecloth was covered with dishes. There was beef roast, chicken and dumplings, pork ribs, purple hull peas, and sweet potatoes as well as bread covered with butter, and all manner of preserves and jellies, from figs to pears and marmalades.

Eleanor found him at the small table set up for tea "I expect you need a set of sideboards on your plate. I see you got a lot of the roast."

Ray Elliott asked, "Did you make the roast?"

Her smiled moved lower. "No, I made the chicken and dumplings."

"I was going to go back and get chicken and dumplings."

"Yes, you will, and the peach cobbler."

He nodded. "My favorite."

There were several of the long makeshift tables. The two of them sat across from each other at one of the long communal tables. It struck Ray Elliott as somehow wrong, but why escaped him. They were in a church activity setting. Her boys were at the children's table. Even with Eleanor married, it really broke no rules to sit across from the lady.

Conversation ranged from the weather to the singing. Ray Elliott was consumed the entire time with how he was going to tell Eleanor all he had to share with her.

Despite the recent tragic events, her smile seemed genuine, as if she had lost herself for a short time. He knew now what was missing when he saw his parents.

No matter the poverty, the tomato blight, sick children, and a note to pay, when his father looked at his mother she would light up. Then his father's face would soften. From the expressions, Ray Elliott and his sibling knew it was all going to be alright. It was what was missing when he saw his parents near the ashes of their home, lamenting the loss of Liza Jane. Nothing would ever be alright again.

He didn't relish crushing Eleanor. It wasn't only when she cried, her hazel eyes hinted toward green and looked so soft. She was like a butterfly, too precious to touch, too lovely not to try.

Fortunately for Ray Elliott, the cobbler was inviting. The lightly browned crust highlighted the orange color of the syrupy peaches. He would have eaten the large helping on his plate anyway, even if it weren't suggested by Eleanor.

After a long dinner, he suggested they talk inside the sanctuary of the church. It was secluded and an acceptable place to be alone with her. Eleanor told him to wait on her because she wanted to check on the boys.

The sanctuary wasn't empty. A young man presented himself as Brother Talbert.

The young man addressed Ray Elliott. "Do you have a special prayer request?"

"Are you the pastor?

The young man wasn't much older than Ray Elliott. "You might say what passes for it." He announced himself as a graduate of a seminary whose name Ray Elliott did not know, but it occurred to him, he really didn't know any seminaries, anyway. "Brother D.L. is the pastor. I am learning from him. I assure you the Lord hears all prayers, even ministers in training's and lawmen's."

Ray Elliott stepped back. "I'm no lawman."

Brother Talbert said, "Folks are saying our sheriff has run off and you are going to replace him."

"What about Pritchard?"

The young man frowned and shook his head.

The refusal to comment was in line with Ray Elliott's impression of the deputy. He had little better impression on this preacher or the county's leaders.

Ray Elliott said, "Folks were ready to run me out on a rail when I left town a few months back and now easy as you please, they want to make me sheriff. Makes even less sense than singing outside in the cold while you got a new organ laying fallow in an empty church."

"You're the one who caught Dock Baxter when the sheriff couldn't. Then you went and caught him again. Pretty good lawman work if you ask me. The only thing better would have been if you had already scalded the skin off the murderer."

The phrase stuck out to Ray Elliott, "scalded the skin off." Why did the preacher say it? Where had he heard it before? "Preacher, I have to tell someone something they don't want to hear. It will change their life forever and I don't know how to do it. I am not sure I have the courage to do it."

"Is it the truth?"

"Yes."

Brother Talbert turned and pointed to the large porcelain baptismal elevated above the alter and under a large cross. "Brother, we can't turn away from truth in the face of the Lord."

It hit him like a shovel across the back of his skull. Ray Elliott's knees folded like he'd really suffered a blow. In his mind, he heard the threat again from the night he spirited Dock Baxter out of town. "We'll have to get us a bigger rendering pot; we got two of them to scald the skin off of now." He couldn't be sure it was the hothead who yelled out.

The voice was similar, and how many people talked about scalding the skin off someone? There were other threats, like necktie party for hanging, shooting, killing whatever else, but scald was unusual. Ray Elliott had helped his father butcher hogs. After the hogs were dead, they scalded hogs to get the hair off the skin. Even then it wasn't proper to describe such as 'scalding the skin off.' Talking about scalding anything was odd.

Ray Elliott gripped his hand into a fist and then conscious of it un-balled the hand. He had to keep in control of himself. He couldn't be one hundred percent sure this was the hothead. A strange thought occurred to him. Why should he want to hit this man? It was himself who'd executed Dock Baxter.

Ray Elliott looked up at a large porcelain baptismal above the alter and under a cross. "Preacher, I expect everything in here is designed to inspire a man to live up to the truth and come clean. Why if a fellow was living a lie right here at the altar, I imagine he would flat burn up where he stood."

Brother Talbert nodded. "I reckon so Mr. Elliott. You must have come for a quiet moment and here I have been doing all this talking. Excuse me, I will get back to the tent."

Ray Elliott continued debating in his mind whether Brother Talbert was the outspoken hothead trying to help incite a lynching. If so, he had taken hypocrisy to a new level. Preaching God's love by day and lynching God's children by night. He shook his head. Surely not.

Eleanor had arrived. He began to speak and she placed

her finger to his lips. "I know I was dying to know. I still am, though not tonight. It makes no sense. You won't understand. There aren't many good days."

Eleanor's eyes began to water in the corner. She looked away. She pulled her finger from his lips and ran her thumb across the edge of her right eye. Ray Elliott could tell she was fighting back tears, desperately trying to block the spigot. "The boys have had a hard time and they were happy today. I want to take them home with a smiling mother, at least tonight. Come by the bank."

She looked around at the great baptismal and altar. "The bank is probably a more appropriate place to hear the truth, anyway."

CHAPTER 19: Will the Truth Set You Free?

Auggie buried his head in the wagon of hay. He pulled away, still drawing the crisp sweet odor deep into his lungs. Ray Elliott looked at Auggie like there was something wrong with the man. The old man licked his lips. Auggie said, "Get you a snoot of it, boy. Better than snuff."

Ray Elliott responded, "Not going to get this wagon unloaded any sooner."

Both men began forking the hay into a short loft. The work was hard and hot, even in the winter. They had started before dawn: mucking stalls, haying horses, drawing water. Putting up hay was only the most recent on an endless list. Like a farm, a stable was forever a work in progress.

Ray Elliott sat his fork down and tried to draw a breath without a lung full of hay. It was unusual for him to tire this early. He had never been afraid of hard work.

Auggie said, "We got to have a wage. Can't have you work like a Hebrew slave without straw and not get paid."

"Apply whatever you think is fair to my room and board. If you think there is anything else, give it to my folks. Lord knows I have caused them enough trouble between the house burning and Liza Jane."

"You didn't kill Liza Jane. She was always going to die."

Ray Elliott looked at his feet. "I am sure I sped it up

some."

Auggie took his old black hat off and swung it at Ray Elliott. "You might have had some fault in the fire. You did what you believed was right."

The look on Ray Elliott's face showed Auggie he was not achieving the desired response. Auggie added, "How do you harvest taters?"

Auggie asked again. Ray Elliott answered, "You hitch up a middle buster and make a furrow."

Auggie nodded. "You bust it right down the middle. You don't try to dig little holes, guessing where the taters are growing. Bust it right down the middle. Way a lawman lives. Stop all this guilt about Liza Jane. She was dying her whole life. All three of the doctors they took her to told your folks the same."

"My folks lied to me? We prayed she would get better near every day."

"Your folks tried to spare you kids some misery and make the time you had count. As for praying, it's another good tool for a lawman."

Ray Elliott looked Auggie in the eye. "How do you know what a good tool for a lawman is, much less me being a lawman?"

"Leave it at I have known a lot of them. Man got to have his secrets, Ray." Auggie turned away.

Ray Elliott nodded. "You keep yours then Auggie."

"I got myself hankering some tater soup, maybe a tall sarsaparilla."

The idea made for a splendid lunch and renewed Ray Elliott for an afternoon of work training horses. He had asked Auggie to call it a day a little early so he could go to the bank. He tried to clean up a little and make himself presentable. After all, he could at least wash his face and change shirts.

He decided to walk to the bank. Ray Elliott was lost in thought until he realized he had stopped in the street. It was the first time he had walked to the bank since the fateful day, which changed his life forever. He wasn't lifting his feet.

Ray Elliott was filled with trepidation about going back to where it all started. His mind was swimming with recriminations about all the things he could have done to avoid the harm he had both caused and suffered. Auggie's words came to him, "Bust it right down the middle." He had done everything he believed was right at the time. This time he released himself from the endless second guessing.

Ray Elliott's attention was drawn back to the moment. Some children were screaming in the street near the bank. They were forming a crowd around something. It wasn't a crowd; it was a group of boys kicking and hitting something.

Ray Elliott went running into the juvenile fray. The children stopped. Ray Elliott found the target of the boys' attack. A boy dressed in a sailor's suit was getting pummeled. The attackers scattered while Ray Elliott helped the boy lift himself out of the mud-filled street.

"What are they hitting you for?"

The boy was quiet. He looked up at Ray Elliott through tear-filled eyes. The tear-filled eyes gave his lineage away. Soon Ray Elliott realized he didn't need to ask. There was the same greenish blue coloring to the boy's eyes as Eleanor's. A closer inspection revealed he shared even more with his mother. To Ray Elliott's mind, there was nothing about the boy which denoted Richard Watersong.

The boy said between sobs. "They called my dad a dirty word."

"What?"

"My mother won't let me say it."

Ray Elliott thought a minute. "When I was a kid, we could call it by what it started or ended with."

The sobbing and heavy breathing had slowed to a stop. "It ends with lover."

Ray Elliott said, "Kids are cruel. Mostly when they are jealous or afraid. I expect they are jealous of you because your family owns the bank, all it is."

"I saw you with my mother at the singing. You are not going to tell her, are you? She says I am supposed to walk away."

"I'm Ray Elliott." He extended his hand to the little man.

"Richard Watersong Jr. Friends call me Richie."

"I want to be your friend, Richie."

The boy smiled. "Please don't tell my mom."

Ray Elliott said, "Moms don't understand; no one can walk away. You keep covering the ground you stand on Richie. Go home and see if Yolonda can clean you up before your mom gets there."

The boy looked a little puzzled. Ray Elliott realized he may have shown himself too familiar with Richie's family. The boy's face revealed he considered Ray Elliott a kindred spirit. Such seemed to occupy the child to the point he wouldn't dwell on any concern which Ray Elliott's familiarity with his family had raised.

The bank had the same unmistakable musty smell. It was as if the whole bank was fermenting. He wondered if money molded or curdled. Ray Elliott had never seen enough long enough to know. He amused himself with the thought.

Ray Elliott walked to the cage of iron and oak holding the bankers. He announced, "I am here to see Eleanor Watersong."

A young man in a dark suit and tie wearing a starched collar pointed him to a bench. Ray Elliott took a seat and he waited. He studied the entire bank from his vantage point. He was seated at the side, perpendicular to the door and almost next to the long counter topped by iron bars.

He read the sign over the entrance many times while he waited, *A heart at peace gives life to the body, but envy rots the bones, Proverbs 14:30.* After he had waited a good while, he laughed to himself. What was a heart at peace? Did the money ferment so much these rich folks got drunk from it? Because those who didn't have the money had the envy. Like his dad had told him, he was old enough to know how the world worked.

He could see the envy, the rot overtaking the faces of folks coming in to pay on their notes. Money bought doctors for children, food for families, and building supplies for homes. On the other hand, interest compounded to the point cotton, tomatoes, and other crops grown in the acidic and often gravel-filled soils became a master no slave could appease.

Eleanor walked out from back behind the cage. She wore a long grey skirt and a white ruffled blouse. She apologized, "I am sorry to keep you waiting. Come on back to my office."

Ray Elliott followed her, noting to himself she didn't call it Richard's office. Maybe she had always had an office in the bank or maybe it was a sign Richard was dead to her.

A huge oak desk separated them. Eleanor asked, "I hear you saved my son today."

"I figured word would get to you without me telling you. I made a promise to your son and I would like to keep it."

Eleanor asked, "You promised to lie for him?"

Ray Elliott leaned toward her and her stern demeanor melted. "I promised not to tell on him. He got a bad set of cards. You have to let him play them out for himself or he will never have any sand." In her green and yellowish eyes, he could see she did not necessarily agree with him, but still chose to let his comment pass.

Eleanor said, "He likes you."

Ray Elliott pondered how she could know.

"He tells Yolonda everything. She shares your view of parenting and I don't betray her confidence because she shares with me what my son will not tell me."

Ray Elliott added, "He had a tough row to hoe. Kids are jealous of him anyway because he's rich—"

Eleanor interjected, "Rich is relative. I spent most of the day writing letters, making telephone calls, begging big banks in Shreveport, Houston, even Chicago to help us."

"You mean even the bank borrows the money."

Eleanor quipped, "Did you think we grew it because we were rich?" She paused and looked down at the desk for a minute. "I am sorry. It has been a long day. I have to tell the boys we are going to move into my father's house in Henderson. We can't keep both households."

Ray Elliott tried to console her. "Might be a blessing to

make new friends and get away, even if it is only a little ways down the road."

"Don't make me ask."

Ray Elliott accepted the cue. He had spent a fair amount of time from Shreveport to Jefferson to Nacogdoches debating what he would tell her. He surprised himself when he blurted out, "Your husband is dead."

The tension in Eleanor's face subsided. She exhaled. There were no tears. She studied Ray Elliott.

"There was a fire on the steamer *Caddo Queen*. Sheriff Kingfisher's body was recovered." Ray Elliott placed the tie pin on her desk. "Your husband's body was not recovered. Nevertheless, I am satisfied he died in the fire and subsequent sinking. The lake is deep on the Louisiana side and I would not expect to find his body."

She continued looking at him.

Ray Elliott fought to look her in the eye, "As for Queen, I don't know. I can only conclude Richard and the sheriff thought they had a lead on Dock Baxter."

She looked at him with an open mouth gaze. Ray Elliott was concerned. Had he added too much? The idea the men were chasing Dock Baxter might have given the lie away. He consoled himself with the fact she likely knew he was lying. It was what she wanted to hear. It was how her sons needed to remember their father.

After all, why rob Richie of the treasured memories he did hold? The lie would buoy him in the future fights over his father's honor. Ellie wouldn't have to carry the shame of divorce from an adulterer who abandoned her. She could be a sympathetic widow whose husband died a hero, chasing a murderer. So much good from one lie.

Eleanor nodded. "You must have Christmas with us. You are without family through no fault of your own and you have done me, my boys, and Yolonda a great service." The tears erupted down her face.

Ray Elliott reached across the desk and took her hand to comfort her.

CHAPTER 20: FREEDOM JAIL

Christmas was like a magnificent dream, especially when compared to past holidays. Ray Elliott's own family had never celebrated Christmas on the scale of Eleanor's family. The Christmas tree was foreign to Ray Elliott. His nervousness at the invitation soon ended as he warmed to the festive atmosphere the tree promoted.

Likewise, the baked goods were a welcome treat. Yolonda and Eleanor had decorated cookies to the point they were far too pretty to eat.

The boys were playing with new toys. Richie's demeanor was so much better. Granted, the last time Ray Elliott had seen him he had been beaten down by a gang of tuffs. Yet still, there was a spring in his step, a brightness in his eye which made him look like a kid again.

Richie had a toy battleship he pulled with a string until the string broke. Ray Elliott knotted the string back together. Richie reached out and hugged him like Ray Elliott had revived a loved one. Ray Elliott recoiled, and still the boy leaped further into his arms.

It was the first time Ray Elliott had been hugged since his little sister Liza Jane. She had a way of grabbing him around the neck. He missed her. Here was another family, a family which accepted him and loved him. Still, it wasn't his family. It was Richard Watersong's family.

The idea was never far from his mind. As if Eleanor realized it, she did everything she could to make him at home. Even Yolonda asked Ray Elliott to carve the turkey.

When he completed the unfamiliar task. Yolonda pronounced it, and him, acceptable, "You'll do."

After the kids retired to their bedrooms, Eleanor presented Ray Elliott with a gift. It was a pocket watch. The gold case was smooth and cool to his touch. He opened the timepiece and there was a picture of Eleanor inside the case across from the watch face. Ray Elliott tried to refuse the gift. It was too nice and didn't compare to the poor present he could afford.

Eleanor told him every time he looked at the watch, it would remind him it was their time. Time had been such a hinderance in Ray Elliott's mind. What was proper, appropriate for what was now a widow? It was forever their time. This moment, this home could be his.

Ray Elliott's gift was far too humble. He was embarrassed to pull from his vest pocket a glass tiger. When he saw the figurine in the general store, it reminded him of Ellie. The object was strong, beautiful, and powerful while still so fragile.

Eleanor held it to her heart and began to weep. She leaned toward him, and almost to Ray Elliott's surprise, he kissed her. Then she kissed him with a longer, fuller kiss.

He walked to Auggie's barn in the dark, filled with excitement about the future. He had never had such a fine meal in such a magnificent home with such a lady. If you had told him months ago life held an opportunity like this one, he would have scoffed. Yet here he stood on the precipice of dreams. It made for a sleepless night.

A group of leading citizens found him at Auggie's livery in the morning. To no one's surprise, Deputy Pritchard had tired of a lawman's life. No one knew for sure what happened. Likely he stepped on to a train and out of

Nacogdoches forever.

Ray Elliott had been nominated by a number of citizens who had attended a Commissioner's Court meeting, including Auggie. There was no real way to say no. The job paid $80 a month, with a room and meals at the jail.

Life at the jail did not start well. It wasn't too far from the railroad tracks, and the whistle of the trains sounded without schedule or warning. He literally lived in a cell, albeit a little nicer with a new bed and mattress, both of which were finer than anything he had ever had.

The winter days moved quick. He patrolled more at night and spent the afternoons with Eleanor. It was during a late lunch at the bank when she made a request.

"My lawyer needs you to make an affidavit."

Ray Elliott asked, "What's an affidavit?"

"A statement sworn under oath." Eleanor continued with her meal.

"I don't understand. What kind of affidavit?"

Eleanor seemed perturbed. "I have to prove my husband is dead. Just business. This way, I have the authority to handle everything for the banks with these ignorant laws treating me like I am a child to be raised by the man I married."

Ray Elliott nodded, yet he didn't understand.

Eleanor looked cross. "You will sign the affidavit, won't you?"

"Of course." Ray Elliott's response was tempered by the thought that lying was one thing, lying in writing another, then a sworn affidavit. He followed her a short distance to an attorney's office where he read a pack of lies, more or less in line with the falsehoods he had told

Eleanor.

The lawyer's office was small. The floor-to-ceiling oak paneling stifled him. Air was short. He couldn't breathe effectively. He took the pen. The secretary raised her hand. An oath was administered. He signed.

Then Ray Elliott excused himself. He needed to go to the privy. Before he could reach the outhouse, his stomach erupted. He dropped to his knees and continued to vomit. The ground was cold, the dirt dry. Dust coated him as he continued to heave.

What was wrong with him? This wasn't him. The dust-filled air strangled him. He fought to catch his breath and stand. Walking back to the jail was arduous.

The air seemed a little sweeter, easier to breathe at the jail. He sat in a large chair behind a roll-top desk and peered out the window at the tracks. He listened to the lonesome whistle of the train. His mind left his miseries and took him to pondering where the train was traveling. What freight or passengers were being moved down the rails? His mind drifted to places spanning the globe.

Places where the sun kissed fertile valleys of ripe crops. Places where tracks carried the produce over the snowcapped mountains. Places where palm trees reached above warm beaches. Places where no one knew he was a liar.

Ray Elliott reached the pull on the right-hand drawer and pulled out a bottle of Old Crow his predecessor had left behind. He lifted the cork and punched his ticket to anywhere excepting here.

So, the days were spent with Eleanor. Her very breath was life to him. More than life, she was an intoxicant constantly pulling his soul to her—the very definition of attraction.

The nights were spent at the jail where the air was free and he was only a train whistle away from anywhere on Earth. Days moved into weeks and the odd torture between the pleasure and pain both destinations provided consumed his soul.

Ray Elliott got up to begin his final patrol of the night. The final patrol was where he checked all the doors all the way up to North Street. He was walking down an alley when he saw a man consorting with a prostitute. It was his job to move them forward through the darkness to a darker place on the outskirts of town, not to necessarily arrest either, because there was no way to stop a crime as old as a mankind.

Ray Elliott stepped closer to roust the liaison. He pulled the man's shoulder and stepped back in absolute horror.

It was his father. "Daddy, what are you doing?" All at once, the realization that his question was ignorant overcame Ray Elliott. They both knew what he was doing.

His father swayed toward him, rotting from the inside out with liquor. "Well isn't it my dear boy, Ray. Ray, my boy, made a big lawman. Sporting the high and mighty Halten's woman."

"Daddy, go home. Go home."

"Right boy, because I got a quilt hanging over a brush arbor for a home. I got three hungry mouths to feed and a woman blaming me for everything gone wrong since the Garden of Eden. Tell your big lies about Richard Watersong. Everybody knows he took Queen to South America. Better to bed the rich banker woman. She's a tart like your mo–"

The Schofield landed true. Ray Elliott's father collapsed in a heap and the woman ran away.

In the morning Ray Elliott's father hid his face in shame and ran out of the jail when Ray Elliot opened the door. There would be no reunions, not today anyway. He wanted desperately to ask about his siblings and chide his father for disgracing his mother. Somehow the man didn't really seem like his father, anyway.

He was like the real William Preston Henry, a cheap shadow of the man he was supposed to be. A man shouldn't see his father weak. In hindsight, Ray Elliott knew the weaknesses had always been there. He had chosen not to accept them in his youth.

It confirmed his belief he had chosen well when he lied about Richard Watersong. Little Richie should never have to see or even know his father was no better than Ray Elliott's own. Still, the lie would forever stain his soul and he knew it.

About mid-morning, Brother Talbert walked into the sheriff's office and jail. Ray Elliott offered the man a cup of coffee.

"How can I help you, Preacher?"

"It is more about how I can help you. There is some poor talk you need to hear."

"Pastor, I promise you, I hear more talk than is fit to repeat."

Brother Talbert continued, "Seems the darkies have received a letter from Queen. Supposedly she is in Guatemala with Richard Watersong. Your own sworn testimony shows it is a lie."

Ray Elliott said, "I expect there's no harm in believing lies."

Brother Talbert said, “There is, oh there is. You most of all should see the harm to the Halten family and the natural order.”

“I don’t understand.”

Brother Talbert stepped to the side and back. “If the Halten’s are liars, then why pay back their money? If you are a liar, then why follow the law? You can see how the natural order breaks down.”

Ray Elliott said, “That’s what this is really about, isn’t it? You want me to go roust a few folks for you to make sure they remember where they belong, right?”

Brother Talbert responded, “Why are you getting upset? I thought you of all people would understand. We have to manage the truth to maintain order.”

Ray Elliott stared stone-faced at the pastor for a long moment. There was little doubt the pastor knew he had lied. It was necessary, which made him a liar no matter how he sliced it. However, he couldn’t convince himself lying was ever right, and to hear a preacher promote it was too much. “So, we can turn away from truth in the face of the Lord if it isn’t the truth we need to hear.”

“We are not understanding each other.” Brother Talbert turned and walked away.

That afternoon Eleanor asked Ray Elliott about Brother Talbert. Her tone started terse and moved from there. “Well, everyone says you were rude to him.”

Ray Elliott asked, “Who is everyone?”

The tiff erupted, becoming their first argument. Ray Elliott suspected Eleanor encouraged Brother Talbert’s visit. It was a terrible thought. In his mind, Ray Elliott questioned how well he knew the woman. He knew she placed a great deal of emphasis on her standing in the community. Such was why he had protected her from the truth. Now he was learning how much appearances mattered to Eleanor. There was no doubt in his mind she knew the truth.

CHAPTER 21: WHERE YOU ARE

The argument made him sick to his stomach. He felt like the walls in Eleanor's small office were collapsing on him. He stormed out of the bank, which in and of itself would aggravate Eleanor because it made their disagreement public.

On the way back to the jail, every step released stress from Ray Elliott. The weight was coming off his shoulders.

Spring was being heralded by the white flowers of the spindly dogwood trees blooming. He was taught the Cross at Calvary was made of dogwood and ever after the tree was reduced to spindly branches incapable of providing the implement of crucifixion ever again. He stopped long enough to touch the soft pedals. He remembered he was also taught every time he lied it was as if Christ was crucified all over again. The silly things they tell children.

There was a welcome surprise at the jail. Old Auggie had pulled a chair up next to his desk. Ray Elliott asked, "You need me for any lawman work?"

"Can't an old friend visit?"

"Proud to have a friend today."

Auggie asked, "Woman troubles?"

"How do you know?"

"Not really much goes on in this town. Richard Watersong made the New Orleans Picayune, several big articles. It will be a long time before folks stop talking." Auggie pulled out a bag of chewing tobacco.

"Well."

Auggie stopped dragging the tobacco out of the leaf pouch. "Well what?"

Ray Elliott raised his tone. "Well, what are they saying?"

"Nothing has really not been said. Watersong is in Guatemala, Honduras, latest is Cuba. He's living like a king or working as a cowboy for grub. Queen had his child or lost his child. Anything you want to hear has been said." Auggie finished placing the tobacco in his mouth and used his boot toe to drag a spittoon over to him.

Ray Elliott asked, "What about me?"

Auggie spat and ringed the spittoon. "I don't put store in talk. You know that."

Ray Elliott insisted, "What do they say?"

"Really why I came. I wanted you to hear it from me. I can't get to spitting it out. There's no good way to put it."

"Say it."

Auggie slapped his knee and sat straight up in the chair. "Brother Talbert is saying you and Eleanor have been carrying on for some time. She sent you off to kill Richard Watersong after her old bo, Sheriff Kingfisher, failed at the task."

Ray Elliott kicked the desk. "Nobody could believe it."

"Folks like a good story. Whether it's true don't much figure in."

Ray Elliott slapped at his holstered gun. "He pretends to be a preacher. Talbert is trash. He needs killing."

Auggie raised his hand. "He's not worth it. Talbert will always be with us, and if he weren't a preacher, he would be mayor or judge or something else. He will get his in the end. Don't you hasten it."

Ray Elliott turned more sullen than mad. "It's my fault.

I lied—"

Auggie interrupted, "Man shouldn't tell all his secrets."

There was an uncomfortable silence. The look in Auggie's dark eyes told Ray Elliott the man knew what was real and what was lies. The old man stared out the window at the railroad tracks. "I'm not telling you any of my secrets. But you asked me how I knew what it was to be a lawman. I've had a lot of living on both sides of the law. Got to be who you are. If you can't be who you are, where you are, then brother, start traveling."

Ellie came to Ray Elliott in the night at the jail. She appeared in front of the jail door and he opened it. He wasn't sure if she had awakened him by knocking. He thought a knock must be why he went to the door, yet he couldn't remember hearing anything. His only memory was the familiar perfume and the way her warmth cut the cold night even from a step away.

She said nothing. He had nothing to say. This was what he wanted, what they both wanted. She stepped inside in an instant, and her light green eyes drew all his attention. A woman far beyond anything he could ever covet and here she was. He shut the door, and she took a step toward him.

She continued to say nothing, yet the actions were loud. This was a commitment. What held him back was it wasn't simply a commitment to Ellie. It was a commitment to a series of lies he would never outrun, never escape. The jail had been his only respite from a world where his own falsehoods were constantly constricting him.

All he had to do was not run out the back door. He smiled for a moment, amusing himself. It's a jail; there was no back door. The moment he smiled, Ellie leaned her lips to his. His mind told him to run. His heart told him it was the wrong time. Ray Elliott heeded neither.

There was no way to separate himself from her, and he made no effort to do so. He awoke believing it was a dream until he looked over and saw Ellie in the darkness near him.

He watched her sleep and tried not to ponder the future. She turned and moved toward him. "Yolonda told me this was a bad idea. She says you need space. She says, 'I am crowding you.'"

Ray Elliott didn't respond. There was a long silence, so she repeated herself.

"I'm not crowding you, am I, Ray?"

"Of course not." Ray Elliott rolled out of bed, and began getting dressed.

"When should we have the ceremony?"

"Ceremony?"

Eleanor spoke with a smoothness which made Ray Elliott believe the comment was rehearsed. "Only a judge. You don't think I would come here like this if we weren't going to be married? An appropriate amount of time has passed."

There was silence again.

Eleanor insisted, "We both knew it was where we were headed. Besides, you will have an election in a couple of months, and we can't have a bachelor sheriff."

Ray Elliott exhaled. "Of course."

After Ellie left, Ray Elliott paced. He looked around at the overflow cell, which had been made into an apartment. The remainder of the jail was behind a large steel door. There was no place to sit or stand where he was at ease.

The locomotive whistle cut through the morning. Ray

Elliott found himself walking toward the tracks. He could breathe without his lungs being compressed and feeling short. He remembered how good it felt to stand strong, for things to be closer to right.

Each step moved Ray Elliott backwards in time to who he was. Yet there was a future of freedom for the taking down the railroad tracks. The smoke, the grease, and the fire beckoned his sense of smell, leading him further toward the rails. The steam drove the train further into the future with every revolution of a great locomotive.

He was running, and it was exhilarating. The metal rail was cool to the touch. Elation overcame him as he swung onto the railcar, and so ended the beginning.

PART III

Thirty Years of Harvesting the Seeds Sown

CHAPTER 22: CUBA 1929

"A 1929 Duesenberg J model. Few were built because of the stock market crash. No one can afford one." Richard Watersong was standing on the docks in Havana, watching the enormous crate being moved from the ship.

There was only the wisp of grey along the edges of Richard Watersong's dark hair and an impeccable tan to reveal the passage of near thirty years in Cuba.

Richard Jr. asked, "Are you sure you got the straight eight-cylinder racing motor?"

"There is not a road in Cuba I would want to ride 100 miles per hour." The answer deflated his son. Richard Watersong thought to himself how much his son was still a boy despite his twenty-eight years.

Richard Jr.'s mulatto status in Cuban society had closed some doors. But whether it was Cuba or private school and college in New York, the boy had never known real hardship.

Joining the father and son was Richard Watersong's two longtime employees, Joaquin and Fortunato. The pair had provided the muscle necessary for so many endeavors. Their effort and a wicked fortune had smiled on Richard Watersong.

Richard Watersong had built a bank for capital, then he used the capital to develop a fleet of fishing boats prior to the United States prohibiting alcohol near the eve of the Roaring Twenties. The unique position provided him with the opportunity to smuggle Cuban rum into the Florida

Keys and later, all of the United States.

The enormous profits from illegal liquor were used to build a powerful business conglomerate of shipping and banking. Richard Watersong soon built an empire and amused himself with the best of everything.

Finally, the crate swung onto the dock. Richard Watersong awaited the falling of the crate walls. Bright chrome gleamed in the Cuban sunlight followed by a deep rich lacquered candy apple red. The Duesy had a tan convertible top with enormous whitewall tires.

Joaquin was moved to give thanks saying, "I am glad the Americanos like rum so much they had to outlaw it."

Richard Jr. asked. "Take us for a ride?"

"You have to ask the owner." Richard Watersong threw the keys to his son. A gigantic smiled flashed onto Richard Jr.'s face.

Richard Watersong put his arm across his son's back. "You made a good deal negotiating with some tough New Yorkers. Anyone can run rum to Florida; the key is a distribution system from New York, Chicago, and all of America."

The automobile coach was a masterpiece of leather comfort. The ride was dampened by the enormous weight of the Duesenberg, and only the wind blowing past them reminded the riders of the speed the luxury coach could attain.

Deep, thick saddle leather enveloped plush seats. Even in the open air, the aroma of the leather was strong and intoxicating.

After the excessive speed, Richard Jr. slowed the Duesy to a crawl where he could be heard. "Can I show it to Mom?"

Fortunato and Joaquin looked at each other, yet neither spoke. Then the two shared a gaze of apprehension aimed at Richard Watersong. Richard Watersong ignored them. "Sure."

They drove past the gate of the palatial mansion with grounds manicured to perfection, accented by a large fountain in the center of a circular driveway. The Duesy came to rest in the circular drive. A young servant ran to get the lady of the house.

Queen stumbled slightly, coming down the short wide stairs to the driveway from the main entrance. "*Mi hijo*, son, I missed you so much."

The tiny woman was only nearing fifty, but she looked much older. "Come in this house. Your brother and sister have missed you." Queen gave Richard Watersong a bitter, cold stare.

"Dad gave me this. Isn't it amazing?" Richard Jr. hugged his mother tightly before releasing her and running to his siblings at the door, where two small children stood in awe of the amazing red and chrome automobile.

Richard Watersong used the opportunity to approach Queen, whispering, "Couldn't stay sober, could you?"

Queen's tone was curt. "You gave up your right to criticize me when you walked out on your children."

"Junior is my son. Those poor retards are the product of your drunkenness and old age."

Queen swung at Richard Watersong, missing by a narrow margin. She lost her balance and began to fall. He grabbed her. He spoke in a low tone. "Keep it together for our son or we will see how you fare without my money."

Queen responded to the threat in kind. "One day, and

I hope it is soon, you will get what you deserve."

"Not today. I know you hate me, even though I kept my word. It's why I don't sleep where you can find me, Queeny. I even bought my own island." Richard Watersong donned a smirk as Queen turned back toward the house.

He yelled out to Richard Jr. "I need to get back. I am going to the Keys tonight. I'll leave your Duesy at the office near the wharf."

Richard Jr. walked back to his father. "Don't go. You have a big organization. There are plenty of people to take a shipment."

"Big shipment. Remember son, trust no one. Weakness begets weakness."

Richard Watersong threw his son a gold piece. His son caught it in air and asked, "Another birthday present?"

Richard Watersong announced, "A lesson. Early minted American Saint-Gaudens. Only U.S. money which does not include 'In God We Trust'. Teddy Roosevelt thought the phrase diminished God. Truth is, it diminishes us."

Richard Watersong boarded the boat, followed by Joaquin and Fortunato. The vessel made up part of his fleet of smugglers. It was far faster than any fishing boat. He took pride in seeing his fleet of disguised smugglers hiding in plain sight.

Richard Watersong prided himself on knowing how and where to fish. He saw boats only in a utilitarian light. It was a long white boat trimmed in blue with what appeared to be a cab, and then an entrance below deck forward of the structure. The boat looked like so many other fishing boats made in the 1920s. In actuality, the vessel was considerably faster, while it was still no match for a coast guard frigate.

Richard Watersong never intended to land on the Florida Keys. He would rendezvous with the American boat at a pre-determined point south of the Florida Keys. There was an appropriate signal of lanterns necessary for the liaison.

The rendezvous boat was a sailing yacht. Not a wise decision. It would draw too much attention. Richard Watersong shrugged. Soon it would be someone else's concern.

"My money?" Richard Watersong pointed to a small leather satchel in the hand of a very dapper-dressed, middle-aged man.

"The boss wanted to make sure you were a happy man, Mr. Montague, so he is paying you with gold coins."

Richard Watersong took the leather case. "Your boss is a wise man. You can tell him he knows his business partner well."

Richard Watersong slept all the way back to Cuba. Joaquin and Fortunato were not as fortunate. They had to look to the boat and only took turns sleeping during the night. The men were in no mood to start a new task when they arrived back in Cuba. Still, Richard Watersong was the boss.

To appease his tired employees, Richard Watersong treated them to breakfast. There were traditional buttered and toasted *tostada* followed by *tostados* with fried egg and ham on them, *café con leche,* and then expresso. The aroma of the breakfast combined with the fresh coffee to revive the tired men.

Richard Jr. joined the feast and was greeted by his

father. Richard Watersong laid out the task. "You know I have bought a private island and had a little home built on it. Well, I need to move a few things, some of it fragile. I don't trust the rest of these Neanderthals to keep from breaking my stuff. Plus, not many people know the location of the island, just my son, and of course, thirty years has made the three of us all brothers."

Joaquin and Fortunato struggled with the crates, including several large heavy crates which had to be lashed to the deck. Richard Jr. and his father were of little use. They did manage to lash extra fuel cans to the deck.

Richard Watersong apologized. "I didn't realize they were so heavy. You don't appreciate all the junk you have until you move."

Joaquin looked at Fortunato before answering, "Must be something expensive to be this heavy."

Richard Watersong said, "Afraid not. I get attached to junk."

The island appeared in the distance, commonly called a key. It was sand covering a coral reef. This one was small with green grass off the beach, but no trees. The only structure was the house.

The house was impressive. A sturdy beach house, built upon stilts. The house was white, trimmed in dark brown with a big open porch elevated on tall piers wrapping all the way around the structure.

Joaquin looked upon the entire small island and the house. "It is perfect for you, *El Jefe*. A place where you can be happy surrounded by your money and count it over and over."

Richard Watersong did not know how to respond. He had not thought about it in those terms. "A little get away."

Joaquin continued, "It is sad, no Fortunato, very sad. El Jefe has no one he can trust to share his money. He won't even tell his own son and 'brothers' they are carrying it."

Richard Watersong stood staring at Joaquin. So enraged, he was speechless. No one spoke to Richard Watersong in such a way.

Joaquin added, "He has made Queen a drunk. Fortunato, he cannot even love the children God gave him."

Richard Watersong turned to Joaquin, exasperated. "Out of line, Joaquin."

Fortunato nodded to Joaquin, urging him on. "His son is a disappointment because he is a *mulatto.*"

Fortunato was now laughing loudly.

Richard Watersong stepped toward Joaquin yelling, "We are going back right now. You're done."

"No, we are not, *El Jeffe.*" Joaquin now turned to face Richard Watersong for the first time since the conversation began, revealing a small revolver aimed at Richard Watersong's belly.

Joaquin nodded to Fortunato. "Make sure we are right."

Fortunato took a small bar and hammer, opening one of the crates as the gold coins spilled onto the deck.

Richard Watersong looked to Richard Jr., who was absolutely panicked. Richard Watersong hated he had put his son in this situation. It wasn't so much he truly trusted the men; he hadn't, though he hadn't seen this one coming. He struggled to fight back his fear, sure he could extricate himself from any situation with time. He took pride in his ingenuity. His ability to weigh and choose the most expedient solution had been honed by decades of criminal ventures.

At this moment, however, he faced the cold realization no solution to the equation spared his life. He set aside his rage and approached the current problem with cold pragmatism. He placed no value on sentimentality, emotion, or life.

He had spent his nefarious career mapping the equation. Now it was his own life and Richard Jr.'s hanging in the balance, yet the math remained the same.

He needed a minute, just a minute to think, so he complimented his adversary, "Joaquin, you completely fooled me. You arranged to have our business associate pay me in gold coins so you could follow me to my stash. Then you got lucky."

Joaquin looked at the pistol in his hand before returning his gaze to Richard Watersong. "You are right, *El Jeffe*. We only planned to follow you. You make it easy. The treasure is already packed on a ship. We are in a desolate place where no one will notice when we kill you. I am a man capable of many more things than you ever understood, *El Jeffe*."

A crying Richard Jr. begged for his life. His father admonished him. "Don't give them the satisfaction. They have to kill us anyway. It's expedient." Richard Watersong smiled. "My money has to support the tribe Fortunato has fathered and Joaquin's prostitutes in Havana. Who gets the lion's share?"

Joaquin shook the pistol back and forth. "No, no, *El Jeffe*. You cannot divide us or talk yourself out of this end."

Richard Watersong studied the boat. There was only one boat, and it was far too far to swim back to Cuba. "I would not dream of it. As they say, the student has become the master. This very day, I told my son, trust no one. I broke my own rule." Richard Watersong raised his arms even higher. "I have always been a practical man. Let's have a drink. Thirty years and all."

Fortunato shook his head but Joaquin nodded to indulge the request. "Fortunato will get some rum."

Richard Watersong said, "Good, I have some cigars to follow it."

Joaquin said, "You will not delay me forever. Nothing personal, *El Jeffe*."

Richard Watersong nodded.

Fortunato opened a big cask of clear liquor.

Richard Watersong was looking over his island and his house, surrounded by a fortune in gold coins packed into the crates. Maybe this was as good a way to die as any. He puffed the cigar and then removed it as he swung the bottle up and took a long pull.

Joaquin and Fortunato did likewise before setting the jug down on the deck.

Richard Jr. declined the offer. There was nowhere to run, yet he panicked anyway, running as fast as his legs would take him.

His legs didn't take him far. Fortuna produced a gun in addition to Joaquin and both men fired through Richard Jr.'s back.

Richard Watersong moved in a blur lifting and swinging the big bottle. The rum broke onto the fuel canisters lashed to the deck. He threw the cigar. A searing sensation burned through his thigh. Thereafter, he fell forward, falling off the boat and into the shallow water. He was face down. Richard Watersong couldn't breathe for the sand in his mouth.

He swung his head out of the water to see the boat engulfed in flame. Fortunato and Joaquin moved with absolute speed. Fortunato swung first his shirt and later a blanket at the flames. Joaquin cut the ropes lashing down the other fuel tanks before yelling, "Push the tanks over."

Fortunato complied, then he slid into the flames and was covered, engulfed in flames. Soon Joaquin succumbed to smoke and was later consumed in fire, fed by the fuel canisters.

Richard Watersong managed to drag himself from the still burning boat. Using his arms to pull his body along the ground, he moved up the stairs to his house one bloody board at a time. He had been prudent enough to have a radio in the home. The prudence saved his life.

Richard Watersong Jr. was buried on a rainy day in Havana. The cemetery was enormous. There were rows and rows of Spanish style vaults standing above the ground. The altitude was relatively low and no one wanted their loved one to wash out of a grave. Richard Jr.'s vault was more elaborate than any other in the grand graveyard.

Queen was inconsolable. The mourners dispersed, a necessity owing to a thunderstorm. After the service, Queen refused to leave. She threw herself over her son's grave.

Richard Watersong kneeled over his wife and held his rain coat over her. She looked up at him then clocked him with as hard a right hand as she could muster. He only turned his head, then moved it back.

She screamed, "You finally killed him, didn't you?"

"Queen, I tried to protect him. He panicked. I loved him with all my heart." The sideways blowing rain blasted both of them.

Queen sobbed. "You took him from me. I hate you." Her hot tears were washed into the cool wetness of the crushing wind.

Even the rough cement of the grave was soaked slick with water and mud. Richard Watersong collapsed in a heap with Queen. "I never told him."

CHAPTER 23: PERCHANCE TO DREAM

Cecil Grant sat in the kitchen behind the swinging door of the dining room in the Southwestern Hotel in Henderson, Texas. He wanted to hear the presentation, yet dared not enter the room. His kitchen accommodations were a necessary concession to the Jim Crow era South. He was anxious to hear the man who was either a great huckster or an unappreciated genius. Community gossip was still deciding the issue.

Cecil Grant's neighbor, some distance to the south, was Daisy Bradford. There was a rumor her property held a treasure greater than gold.

It was a meeting of possible investors. There were no Rockefellers, no Carnegies, no accountants, and no bankers. These were mostly farmers willing to exchange the near nothing they had for the prospect of riches.

Through the louvered door, Cecil Grant saw their white suited, boat hatted prophet. For a moment the disappointment from the realization the presenter had exhausted greener pastures showed on his face. He soon recovered and prepared himself to pitch for twenty dollars, five dollars, anything to drill one month, a week, or another day.

"I am Columbus Marion Joiner. Glad to be in a meeting with farmers and not a bunch of the shyster money men like ran this country into the ground and bled me dry. They drove us all in this Great Depression. No sir, give me men and women of the soil.

"Soil is what I come from, a farm on the Alabama Tennessee border. I am not here to fool you. I am not offering you a bird's nest on the ground. No sir, I am here to give you an opportunity, not to make you a Rockefeller, but to buy a new/used Model T for the family, send the child to school, or leave the cotton in the field this October.

"Nobody ever gave me anything. I learned to read by memorizing Genesis and then later I taught myself the law, well enough to get elected to the Tennessee Legislature. I promise you; politics and the flush times have never runt me. My momma taught me to tell the truth and I ain't never gone back on my raisin, nor shamed my momma."

He had taken off his flat-brimmed straw boat hat coming through the door and now it swung with his arms back and forth as he pleaded his case. He walked through the room gathering all eyes as he walked toward the edge of the kitchen and poured himself a glass of tea.

"I am proud to be among farmers because when you get right down to it, a farmer is what I am. My crop is deep. I aim to harvest it. It has taken thousands of years to grow. I am near seventy and it's time. I intend to bring in the sheaves. Timing is everything, as Shakespeare told us.

"There's a special providence in the fall of a sparrow. If it be now, 'tis not to come. If it be not to come, it will be now. If it be not now, yet it will come—the readiness is all.

"Twice, twice, I have stood over pools of oil. At Earlsboro in Oklahoma, I had to abandon a well just above the great Seminole Field. I ran out of money and had to watch others get rich.

"Later, I brought in the Cement Field, and again money was scarce. It gave me another start. Still, I had to sell out.

I was able to buy leases here."

A bearded farmer from the front of the room yelled out to spontaneous laughter, "Did you buy from the Millville Dry Hole Company?"

Columbus Marion Joiner was not perturbed. He laughed with the farmer and started again. "I know about the dusters at Millville and Overton and Pine Hill, but did you know Humble has bought up leases in Rusk County and there is a table of lawyers over there who are likely not here to listen to my Shakespeare?"

The room turned to three well-dressed men in the corner making the speaker's point. Columbus Joiner continued, "I am a lawyer, so I have enough sense to never trust my business to a courthouse. Back to my point; it is all about ripeness. I won't mislead you. We have had two wells; neither could be completed, but they weren't dry holes. They just weren't completed to the depth the geologist told me was oil."

Columbus Marion Joiner softened his tone, as if he were telling a secret. "All changed now. You saw me walk in with Mr. Laseter. I had to go to Houston and pay a pretty penny. He is a partner in the venture too. There are few drillers with his skill. I know you have heard I pay for groceries, salaries for the crew, haircuts, and even rented this room tonight with certificates from leases."

Columbus Marion Joiner pointed to his head to show his keen business sense. "Because I have invested every dollar in this venture, in this time, in this moment, there are no other deals for me. 'Men must endure their going hence even as their coming hither. Ripeness is all.'"

He said the name Shakespeare before continuing. "When I was a young man, about sixty-seven," Joiner shared the laughter with the entire room before continuing, "I took a trip to Galveston. It wasn't so much a vacation as I really wanted to be near the ocean. I have told you about my earlier success and near successes what never panned out. Well, a lifetime of chasing dreams left me as empty as old King Lear or young Prince Hamlet."

Columbus Marion Joiner motioned like he was sitting on the beach. "I was about so low, listening to salt water pound on those rocks. I thought about how those jagged rocks were formed and how quick they would sheer a man open and end it all. I laid down looking up at a full moon. Well, of course you know me well enough already, to know it made me think of Shakespeare, right?

> To be, or not to be, that is the question: / Whether 'tis nobler in mind to suffer / The slings and arrows of outrageous fortune, / Or take up arms against a sea of troubles, / And by opposing end them? / To die—to sleep, / No more; and by a sleep to say we end / The heartache and the thousand natural shocks / That flesh is heir to: 'tis a consummation / Devoutly to be wish'd. To die, to sleep; / To sleep, perchance to dream—ay, there's the rub: / For in that sleep of death what dreams may come / When we have shuffled off this mortal coil...

"I woke up in the night and my life was changed forever. I had been dreaming about walking through the woods, crossing over a little branch. I could see pin oaks, elms, red oaks, and the stand of pines. I can tell you every bend in the stream, every limb on some of those oaks, because I touched them as I crossed the water, and of course I paid close attention of the curve of the ground. I felt the rough bark of the hardwoods and felt the wet dew on the grass. I had already bought some leases in Rusk County from an Oklahoma oilman, McFarland, back when I was in Oklahoma; add to the investment my friendship with a geologist, Dr. Lloyd. He is back in Ft. Worth because we are busy drilling. Some big companies laugh at him, but he has found more fields than you could shake a stick at. I will swear it to you."

Columbus Marion Joiner put his arm around his colleague's shoulder. "Well, I had drawn a map from my dream; unfurl the map Dan. This is Dan Tanner; he has been with me since the start. A lot of my crew has stayed through thick and thin. One of them is a cashier out at First State Bank in Overton, Walter Tucker." A black gentleman unrolled a leather mat to reveal a colorful map of trees, streams and hills.

Cecil Grant pondered why this Dan Tanner was permitted in the room and he wasn't. He debated entering. No one had told him he could not attend. Cecil Grant decided it best not to have trouble if it could be avoided.

Columbus Marion Joiner pointed to a spot on the map. "I shared this map with Dr. Lloyd and he showed me a map he had made of a huge formation, a lake of oil about thirty-five hundred feet below the surface here in Rusk County. They are both out in the same survey and real close to being on top of one another."

He waited for Tuner to unfold the second map, far more colorful and professional in appearance than the first map. "Are you still not understanding why I am drilling where I am drilling? No sir, I rented a room from a cashier at the Overton bank. The man, Walter Tucker, would later moonlight with me. I commenced to walking the leases."

Columbus Marion Joiner walked across the room, mimicking his journey. "I guarantee you, the folks out at the Overton Drug Store still remember when I came in telling them I had found it right there on Daisy Bradford's farm, not seven miles from where I stood. You should have seen widow Bradford's face when I told her that we needed to drill in her garden." The crowd laughed and seemed enthralled with the oratory.

"I can't explain it. Folks, look at all the great fields. If it were just science, then Standard Oil and the big operators would have them all. I promise they would get the government to pass laws to keep us from drilling. There are new finds yearly in Texas, Louisiana, Arkansas, and Oklahoma; all are open to the little guy, because the little guy dreams."

He was animated, near jumping onto the table. "Every field, every new success starts with the little guy. I got a new, used Model T out there and I guarantee you, Mr. Henry Ford did not dream up the first car. The big man loans, leverages, trades, forecloses, passes laws to protect himself, but he must go to the little guy to harness the dreams fueling commerce. We have the fuel right here to ignite a boom, lifting generations. I am going to pass certificates around for you to look at. They are only twenty-five dollars and you will have what amounts to your own four acres in the lease. I have hit fields twice and I am going to do it again. 'Though this be madness, yet there is method in it.'"

Cecil Grant exhaled. This prompted him to realize he had been holding his breath. The night had overtaken them, and compared to the humid, stagnant atmosphere an hour before. there was a crispness to the air. Likewise, a better aroma filled the air around them.

It wasn't stale and there was no unpleasant odor, despite the hot, packed quarters of the dining room. The farmers, both male and female, were well groomed and dressed in their Sunday best. They were never asked to patriciate in Wall Street or the rampant speculation which wrecked the national boom of the Roaring Twenties.

These people had been too busy subsistence farming while raising a little cotton for pocket change in an ever-decreasing harvest. Those bold enough to avoid king cotton might land a job in a sawmill, trading one hard living for another.

Cecil Grant's daydream was crushed by a woman he had known since childhood. "You not to going to get any money, fool."

Cecil Grant looked like a caught child. "You don't know nothing, Kizzy. I got land close to the dream."

Kizzy mocked him. "'The dream?' If white man gonna let you share in his dream, then why you hiding in the kitchen, fool?"

Cecil Grant argued, "You'll see there are some good white folks. I know one who will help me if I need it."

"Well get your good white folks to help me with these dishes like you said you would."

Cecil Grant looked through the slits in the door and saw people swamping Columbus Marion Joiner. All except one of the young men Columbus Marion Joiner had called out for being a lawyer. The young man, clad in a navy-blue three-piece suit, seemed to hover to the side, waiting to catch the farmers after Columbus Marion Joiner's pitch.

CHAPTER 24: Fortune Favors the Bold

Richard Watersong rarely saw his bank in Havana. The club and fishing concession were his world these days. Every time he walked through the massive entrance, he was surrounded by the beautiful cold marble stone making up the interior of the building. He had to stop and beam with pride.

It was a temple of commerce connected to banking interest all over the world. This institution was so much more than the little wood store front in backward East Texas. There was a kind of palatial courtyard inside the Havana bank, as opposed to the cage cutting across the country bank.

Earlier, Richard Watersong had received a phone call from his manager. He was advised a woman was trying to draw out a large sum of money from her account. Ordinarily not an issue meriting the attention of the bank owner, however, this incident necessitated an alert.

Queen gave the manager a piece of her mind. She completed the tirade in English before turning to Spanish. She didn't notice Richard Watersong walk up behind her. Queen was using her broken Spanish to question whether the manager's ancestry was crossed with a burro at some point.

The manger saw Richard Watersong and gave his boss a look of relief. However, the look soon turned to disappointment. Richard Watersong was hesitant to wade into another battle with Queen. Despite thirty years of alcohol and cigarettes, she could still manage to make herself attractive. For a moment she reminded him of the Queen of her youth. The tongue lashing she was giving his employee brought back to his mind the Queen of middle age. He paused.

He overcame good judgment and asked, "Queen, what are you trying to do?"

She answered him with a further tirade of insults directed at the manger. Richard Watersong raised his hands, motioning to stop her. "He is only following my orders. We don't know if someone is being held hostage and you need to pay a ransom or if someone is trying to con you out of money, so when you withdraw over five thousand, I get a phone call to protect you and your children."

"'My children.' If you had left Richard Jr. to me and he had been one of 'my children,' he would be alive today. You killed our son."

Richard Watersong looked at the manager and the man stepped away. "I am not going to do this in public. It is my bank, my money; tell me why you want it."

Queen's aggressive demeanor did not so much soften as display her acquiesce to a bitter taste. She said, "I am going home."

"Good. I will find someone to drive you."

Queen lifted her head. "Home to Texas. My father is dead and my mother will pass soon. Richard Jr. was all I had here, and you took him from me. I want to go home."

Richard Watersong motioned for the manager to return. "What if you get found out? Can you really face Eleanor and the community?"

"Might be merciful."

Richard Watersong nodded, turning to the manager. "Give her the money and help her make any arrangements she needs." He turned back to Queen, made a rolling motion with his hand and pronounced, "Bye."

Richard Watersong walked away. He wasn't about to get into a fight with Queen, nor was he going to permit himself to express anything except relief she was gone. No doubt he would miss her. One day fishing on the bay or when he looked at Richard Jr.'s picture, he would miss her. Today was not the day.

He moved toward the door when a young man in a blue three-piece suit approached him. Richard Watersong kept walking.

"Mr. Watersong or Mr. Montague; my name is Matthew Kenner."

Richard Watersong did not slow down or accept the man's hand. "Good for you. Everyone should know their name."

The young man tried to block the door. "I have a deal for you, sir. I have been waiting in this lobby every day this week trying to get a meeting with you."

"I suggest you make a more efficient use of your time young man."

The young man held his hands up, pleading for a moment. "You foreclosed on two hundred acres from a Cecil Grant in 1901. Not the bank or the Halten family but you in your own name. What if I told you the land was worth a fortune?"

Richard Watersong smiled, intrigued by the bold young man. "I would say you have lunch plans at my club, Mister—"

"Matthew Kenner." The men shook hands.

Over lunch, Matthew Kenner related Columbus Marion Joiner's dream. Richard Watersong was patient with the story. The young man professed a profound admiration for Richard Watersong. After all, Richard Watersong was the successful businessman Matthew Kenner dreamed of becoming.

Matthew Kenner knew all the information old copies of the New Orleans Times Picayune provided. He described the lengthy process of trying to locate Richard Watersong. He checked government records, but never found an obituary. He continued to search the records and discovered, beginning sometime after 1900, there were many entries for a Richard Montague and as more time passed, even some entries for Richard Watersong.

Matthew Kenner said, "I know what you are thinking."

Richard Watersong looked at the young man. "I suspect you have no idea–"

Matthew Kenner interrupted him. "The two hundred acres you got from Cecil Grant are close to Daisy Bradford's farm. Daisy Bradford's farm is where, rumor has it, Columbus Marion Joiner struck oil."

Richard Watersong asked, "Why haven't I seen it in the Dallas newspaper? I realize they are out of date when they get here but shouldn't there be some report."

Matthew Kenner, "No one is sure what he has and the fact he is even showing some pay dirt is a closely held secret. No one knows how big the field is."

Richard Watersong leaned across the table. "Why did he tell you?"

Matthew Kenner grinned from ear to ear. "I mentioned I am a lawyer. My clients make it their business to know everything in the oil business. Columbus Marion

Joiner has attracted their attention. So, we know he has a pay zone as yet untested. I only found out for sure yesterday."

Richard Watersong interjected, "They don't know where you are, do they? What did you tell them; you're on vacation?"

"Mr. Watersong—"

Richard Watersong ignored the interruption. "The client who is probably in contact with your boss has instructed you to lease everything in the area. You ran the titles and did your job. Then you found a substantial interest and discovered I owned it. You want to lease it for yourself and either drill on it or sell a lease to your own client."

Matthew Kenner looked away. "No. If I was dishonest, why tell you about Joiner's plans and the pay zone?"

Richard Watersong shook his head. "You have flattered me since I met you. Don't insult me now. You come to me and want an oil lease on land I have not given a thought to in thirty years. What am I going to assume?"

Matthew Kenner continued to look away.

Richard Watersong said, "It's the next Spindletop Field or a young man wouldn't risk a promising career. Double dealing your own client is frowned upon in the legal profession. You thought about all of it and you knew there was no way to fool me. So, you did something I can tell was counterintuitive. You were honest with me or as honest as you are capable."

Matthew Kenner said, "I can buy you out or manage your interest, either one."

"How will you buy me out? Mortgage my own property to pay me?" There was no answer nor was one expected. "It is a beautiful day in paradise; let's go fishing." Richard Watersong got up and motioned for the young man to join him.

It was a short ride in the Duesenberg to the *Cojimar,* where one of Richard Watersong's boats met them. The fort at *Cojimar* jutted out from the old pier into the bay. A single palm tree grew in front of the square next to four tower ruins. The beiges and oranges of the brick contrasted the soft greens and bright blues of the water, extending into a horizon dominated by loosely-bound clouds piled high like sticky, white cotton.

Matthew Kenner had never enjoyed fishing. The purpose escaped him because the time wasted irritated him. This process seemed particularly useless. The trolling was tedious. He gained some appreciation for the sport once he landed his first deep-sea fish. Battling a Blue Marlin provided thirty minutes of total exhilaration. The crew rigged the rods again, giving Richard Watersong an opportunity for business.

"I have heard about your proposal but not about you. I don't do business with people I don't know. Tell me who you are, who your people are?"

Matthew Kenner's face beamed with excitement. "I was born and raised in Connecticut. I only fished in streams and I didn't like it."

"I would not have guessed New England. You have almost no accent."

Matthew Kenner nodded with pride. "My mother was a widow with three sons. I was good at school and sports and had the opportunity to go to Yale. After law school, a firm in Dallas offered the best salary."

"So, a Connecticut Yankee in Dallas, Texas. How did

Dallas suit you?" Richard Watersong motioned to one of the few crewmen on the boat.

"I carried documents to the firm's biggest clients, traveling the oilfields from Shreveport, Louisiana to El Dorado, Arkansas. I loved it. I saw fortunes rise and fall on the smallest scrap of information. A graduate of the best business schools might go broke while a pimp chasing the oilfield becomes a millionaire. The common denominator was as old as Latin: *Audentes Fortuna iuvat.*"

Richard Watersong translated. "Fortune favors the bold."

Matthew Kenner hands and arms moved in a blur as he spoke. "You will be even wealthier, my mother will never want again, and I will no longer make fortunes for lesser men."

Richard Watersong nodded, and a crewman delivered a steel pipe to the back of Matthew Kenner's head. The young man collapsed on the deck.

The crewman placed Matthew Kenner in a chair with his feet in a feed trough followed by a slurry of concrete. The wind was increasing and the salt air began to bring Matthew Kenner around. He lifted his knees and tried desperately to thrash his feet, but it was too late.

Richard Watersong said, "Expediency, Mr. Kenner. Beauty, simplicity, and necessity are all employed by chance, fate if you will, to create expediency. For far too long I feared expediency. You could even call me squeamish. Then I realized time was irrelevant and our shameful worship of it reduced man to irrelevancy."

Matthew Kenner's head bobbed back and forth as he pulled on the ropes securing his hands behind his back. "Jesus, you are crazy."

Richard Watersong, “Don’t be so conventional. You said yourself ‘fortune favors the bold.’ What could be bolder? You tell no one you are coming here because you are committing a bar rules violation by perpetrating fraud against your client. You’ve presented me an incredible opportunity. Step back and look at this opportunity with objectivity. I realize it may be difficult. Can’t you see your death is beautiful in its expediency?”

Matthew Kenner screamed, “How did I come to this?”

Richard Watersong ignored the question. “Recent events required replacing my staff. You are providing an opportunity to evaluate the new help. Further, your death keeps secret my ownership of the Grant property until I can get on the ground and move the pieces into place. Why settle for a royalty or one well, even several, when there may be colossal wealth?”

Matthew Kenner’s sobbing was punctuated by an occasional wail. Richard Watersong shook his head and motioned for the crew to throw Matthew Kenner over the side of the boat.

Richard Watersong said, “Other side men; it’s closer to Texas.”

CHAPTER 25: UNDER ATTACK

Ray Elliott knocked the policeman down and rolled him across the floor until he beat out the flames. He was under an all-out attack on a scale he had never witnessed. A series of bottle bombs were assailing the courthouse in Sherman, Texas. The two men moved into a more interior room better, shielded from the onslaught.

The policeman said, "Captain." He trailed off, words failing the officer. Ray Elliott nodded, releasing the man from the obligation to comment further.

Ray Elliott pushed a note in the man's shirt pocket. "I need you to get to a telephone and call Colonel McGee in Dallas. The information is in the note."

The policeman said, "I can't leave y'all—"

Ray Elliott yelled, "You're not leaving anybody. You're going to get past the mob and get us some help." Ray Elliott slapped the man's shoulder and then tore off into the bowels of the courthouse.

Even breathing was difficult for the policeman laying in the floor. His clothes were drenched in gasoline from what were known as poor man's grenades. He reached into his pocket and read the note.

Colonel McGee,

The mob will overtake us soon. I have been ordered not to fire on the crowd under any circumstances. I recently convinced the governor to activate your unit. I intend to lock myself and the prisoner in the records vault.

Captain Ray Elliott

Ray Elliott was short of breath. He hadn't run any distance in a number of years, and even getting down the hallway was a chore. He burst into the County Clerk's office. Two sheriff's deputies were there with the prisoner.

Ray Elliott shoved the inmate into the records vault, and the deputies helped him swing the door shut and locked. The vault room was about thirty-by-thirty with a ten-foot ceiling. There were shelves and shelves of bound volumes and a chest high desk holding stacks of documents clipped together and sorted into different groups.

The prisoner asked Ray Elliott. "Are you sure there is enough air in here?" The two men collapsed on different sides of the room, leaning against the bookcases.

The corners of Ray Elliott's mouth moved upward. He laughed, under his breath at first. Then he couldn't help himself.

The prisoner said, "Call me crazy. You white people are the crazy people. Whole country out there trying to get in here and lynch me and you laughing."

Ray Elliott composed himself. "I haven't studied on the air. I been figuring on how long it would take to get through those hinges with an acetylene rig or whether more likely they will dynamite us."

"Why are you helping me?"

Ray Elliott dropped the magazine from his Colt 1911. He began pulling shells from his pockets. Firing over the crowd's heads had not produced the intended effect. His prisoner tired of awaiting a response and looked at the wall.

"Prisoners don't get lynched on my watch, not while I'm the law." After Ray Elliott holstered his pistol, he lifted a weathered Winchester lever-action rifle.

"Not what the deputies said about you." The remark drew a harsh gaze from Ray Elliott, prompting the prisoner to soften it. "I don't know for myself and you have done me a good turn. I don't want to seem like I'm ungrateful. You could have let them have me. You haven't even asked if I'm guilty. My name is George Hughes."

Ray Elliott looked as if he would laugh, yet he only sported a thin smile. "I know your name."

"So, you think they will get an acetylene torch and cut through the door."

Ray Elliott answered, "Hopefully, because otherwise they will blast it off and there is no way to know how much dynamite it would take. Doesn't matter much anyway, because I guarantee you, they will use too much."

George Hughes smiled. "I understand what you found funny."

There were a series of dull thuds against the door and what were probably voices shouting that were barely audible in the vault. George Hughes asked, "Do they have torches?"

"Rest easy. It's too soon. They are likely beating the hinges with sledge hammers. We still got time."

"Time for what?"

Ray Elliott was puzzled, "I don't know." The words surprised him, yet they were undeniably true. No way guardsmen would reach him in time, even if everything went right. He knew in law enforcement, especially in a crisis, there was little which went right. The governor might change his mind on calling out the guard. The soldiers might get beat back by the mob, especially if ordered not to fire. Logistical concerns might delay the national guardsman. There were a thousand reasons they couldn't make it in time while only the thinnest sliver of hope.

Then a thought struck him as even worse. What if the soldiers fired into the crowd? It was an unfit comparison, but still his mind jumped to school book pictures of the Boston Massacre. He looked at George Hughes. Was he worth it? Was a rapist worth killing some hot-headed farmers? Ray Elliott remembered when he would have spent his life farming.

Until the day he crossed paths with Dock Baxter, any other life never occurred to him. He knew what it was to be a farmer; how precarious an existence living on the difference between rainfall and a late frost was. Hardest of all, he remembered, was the work scrabbling through the rocky soil of East Texas.

Most of the farmers were scared and willing to follow anyone pressing for action, showing out for other men or their own wives. Some of them wanted no more than the distraction of a day away from the hopelessness of the Great Depression in one of the hardest hit sections of the poorest region in the nation—the Deep South.

Even the elements favored a mob. Unusually heavy rain prohibited field work. Hence, there was a large concentration of idle people in town. Ray Elliott didn't need thirty years in law enforcement to identify such circumstances as a fertile seedbed for wickedness. Many times impromptu courts of racial intolerance replaced the legitimate criminal justice system.

The foul system of racial laws was an older form of governance, existing in most places prior to the arrival of courthouses and lawyers. The tenants of the practice had been necessary to keep an ancient labor system from collapsing of its own inherent wickedness.

It was a disgraceful and insidious holdover from a time when slavery was considered in the South as indispensable as soil, water, and sunshine to King Cotton. The entire process was marked by an overhanging fear; a horror so foul it dares not be confronted, only forever avoided at all costs–the sheer terror of righteous judgment at the hands of the oppressed. The antithesis of loving your neighbor as yourself.

Ray Elliott was lost in deep thought when he was startled by the memory of waking in the jail cell in Oklahoma so many years ago. A look revealed George Hughes had urinated down the leg of his overalls. Ray Elliott assumed the additional foul stench revealed George Hughes had soiled himself as well.

George Hughes said, "You hear. No more hammers. Means they giving up, right? Or the soldier boys are here, right?"

George Hughes's countenance fell when Ray Elliott pointed out what he believed was far more likely. "The acetylene rig is here. We don't have too much longer now."

CHAPTER 26: LAW AND FORGIVENESS

George Hughes was heaped in a pile of tears in the corner. Ray Elliott didn't fault the man for fear. Death was not the worst of alternatives.

Trapped in the vault was not the way Ray Elliott had planned the day. He had scheduled every minute for himself and George Hughes. Jury selection until noon, followed by opening statements and witnesses. He already knew keeping the prisoner alive was going to be a near-run thing.

He was walking the high wire, yet he had done it so many times. Experience provided the necessary balance. Thirty years of experience had made him a hard man. Like the proverb about iron sharpening iron, he had matched wits with the sharpest of outlaws and modeled the steel constitution of the best captains and sheriffs.

The fault in his plan had been the level of indecisiveness by the political leaders. Ray Elliott never expected bold leadership from local or state officials. People elected leaders who reflected themselves and the same public possessed noble qualities in measured quantities. However, humanity possessed prejudice and lawlessness in great volume.

By mid-morning, Ray Elliott was convinced the situation was untenable. He'd surmised only a show of force would dissuade the growing mob, and even then there might be bloodshed. If he had rangers, militia, even national guardsmen, then the farmers would return home.

Overwhelming force was the best way to ensure the peace. However, the governor acting through the adjutant general of the rangers took the opposite view. Among other reasons, it behooved them to avoid expense.

The governor also feared a larger force would antagonize a delicate situation. He'd assumed the mob would subside once the trial had actually commenced. Wouldn't action eliminate the perceived need for unjust action?

The governor went so far as to prohibit Ray Elliott from firing on the crowd under any circumstances. Somehow, a leader would have anticipated the order would leak out, but the governor failed to do so. The effect was an emboldened mob, in a near instantaneous fashion.

Added to the lighted match was George Hughes' plea after jury selection—guilty. Ray Elliott next appealed to the district judge. There had to be a change of venue, and it had to happen now.

At first the judge seemed receptive. However, he pointed out the trial would be much shorter since there was a guilty plea. The prosecutor would present abbreviated evidence about the crime for the purpose of the jury affixing a punishment. Moving the case could be interpreted as a lack of confidence in the essential goodness of his constituents. The judge would instead take the matter under advisement.

The victim's testimony served as a powder keg thrown upon an open flame. Indecisiveness and an insistence on assuming the goodness of people, rather than anticipating and circumventing the wickedness within men's hearts, made an altercation certain.

The mob would eventually take the door down. His

death was a certainty. Worse, they probably wouldn't stop with lynching George Hughes. A mob this large and strong would likely continue lynching Hughes's family. Hughes's family would soon deteriorate to anyone black. Whole neighborhoods could be put to the torch.

The governor and the district judge were going to need a scapegoat. Ray Elliott realized he was an excellent candidate. If he died, then blaming him would be even more convenient for the politicians.

Still, he didn't curse his leaders. The people elected leaders, so their actions were necessarily right, meaning legitimate as opposed to correct. The same was true of juries. Their verdicts were just because there had to be an end to the endless debate. What was justice?

He need look no further than the vault door to appreciate that mob rule offered no alternative to even a flawed form of representative government. He looked down at the star on his chest and then back to the vault door.

The vault door shielded him, George Hughes, and most important, the legitimacy of the law from murderous demagogues. Like the door, badge toters such as himself were cut down from time to time. Someday the door would be replaced, for vaults and safes were always being built stronger. Ray Elliott took a strange comfort in his end. Somewhere God was calling another young man, probably stronger, to wear his shield. A person capable of both decisive action, and cool reflection prior to action when the situation called for it.

His duty was soon to end. He took out his gold watch and viewed the photograph inside. Thirty years had done nothing to diminish the beauty of the likeness. He debated it again until he satisfied himself; right or wrong, the past was moot now.

For Ray Elliott and those who understood duty, his death would have meaning, even a certain nobility, which lesser people would never understand. He pulled his mind back to the moment. Ray Elliott looked at George Hughes cowering in the corner.

George Hughes was rattling on about something. He was confessing. Though typical of confessions, it included minimizing his conduct by blaming the victim and her husband for cheating him. Ray Elliott ignored the diatribe.

At one point, George Hughes accused Ray Elliott of disliking him. It was a curious comment. It occurred to Ray Elliott he had never pondered on the matter.

George Hughes was a prisoner whom he had a duty to protect. The comment had astonished him from a person he thought incapable of surprising him.

Thirty years of investigating criminal conduct made George Hughes an open book to Ray Elliott. He had almost referred to the man as Dock Baxter to one of the deputies earlier in the day. If only he could go back in time with the wisdom he had gleaned from his career and interrogate Dock Baxter.

Ray Elliott didn't like to dwell on Dock Baxter too long. He had never been sure the man was guilty. He had only assured himself Dock Baxter needed killing before more good people had died.

The answer to the question had become apparent. No, he didn't like George Hughes. Some people needed killing; no one had ever needed raping. It was a vile crime perpetrated by one whose intent was to rob an individual of dignity.

Murder robbed the victim of every day, every breath, every moment remaining in the victim's life. Such a theft did not always include dignity.

Dock Baxter had died with dignity. He had died with the question of his guilt still unresolved. He debated whether his killing of Dock Baxter was a murder. He had avoided the subject of Dock Baxter so many times over the years.

Ray Elliott thought about the promise he'd made Dock Baxter and what was in store for George Hughes once the hinges were cut off the vault door. He would make no promise, no mercy, to a rapist.

George Hughes said, "You don't like me because I'm colored. You'll do your job even though you hate me."

Ray Elliott shook his fist. "I don't like you because you're a rapist. I am going to die with you because you are colored."

George Hughes grinned. "I didn't think of it that way. You got to die because I'm not white."

"Since we are dying together because of you, against my better judgment I got to ask what every lawman knows won't make sense." Ray Elliott slid further down against the wall.

"What you got to ask me?"

"I see stealing, there might be circumstance for it, and killing a man can be necessary, but raping a woman—"

George Hughes said, "They cheated me; more than cheated me, they stole from me. They had the money and wouldn't pay me. Both of them laughed at me. What could I do? Like folks said, nobody is going to believe an animal."

Ray Elliott asked, "Animal?"

"Been called a baboon all my life. I only went there to

get my money from her. Even when I had a gun aimed at her, she was better than me, threatening me. I saw a way they would have to remember me. Every time they were together, every time they thought about each other, they would remember George Hughes. A way to teach them I was a man." George Hughes looked away.

George Hughes had struck out at an unjust society; a society which robbed him of his dignity. He lashed out, trying to oppress his oppressors.

The rationale made a certain sense, although it wholly failed to relieve George Hughes of criminal responsibility. George Hughes chose to cross the line. Whether society moved him toward the line was immaterial. Still, Ray Elliott recognized social injustice was as incongruent with a just government as criminal conduct.

Ray Elliott pronounced, "All you taught them was what you learned: hatred and envy."

George Hughes continued looking away. He was still weeping. Ray Elliott debated if it was from remorse or regret at his fate.

Ray Elliott said, "I appreciate you not lying to me. I have heard enough women's stories to know this lady was raped. Maybe twenty years ago I could get fooled, because I admit there are some cases of buyer's remorse and innocent men, especially black men, get accused. What I can't understand is why you didn't try a not guilty plea?"

"Brother Earl preached to me about choosing lakes of fire and eternal damnation or life in paradise. Not much choice when you study on it. Every word he said was backed up by the Bible. He convinced me to confess what I did and seek God's forgiveness. You think God forgives me?"

Ray Elliott's demeanor moved from surprised to perturbed. "I don't know what God does or doesn't do."

"We going to die here tonight. Don't you think we should pray or something?" George Hughes was sitting up on his knees looking at Ray Elliott, who sat slouched against the wall.

Without warning, a concussive blast rocked the room. George Hughes disappeared in a wall of smoke and debris.

Ray Elliott's head was rocked against the wall. There was no way to move. A bomb of sound and pressure moved everything against the wall, sending a wave through Ray Elliott's body.

He touched his head. He was bleeding from his ears. The shattering force had lifted everything in the room and then dropped it from a distance into the room.

Before Ray Elliott collapsed, he smiled. God must have answered George Hughes's prayer. Out of the corner of his eye, he saw men lifting the body of a dead George Hughes.

They would lynch his corpse. And it might have even saved a number of homes from arson had the mob taken its ire out on Hughes.

CHAPTER 27:
A PLEA FOR HELP

Eventually, the governor declared martial law in Sherman. The shooting of arsonists and looters was authorized. Order was restored. However, the vigilante riot made front page news far beyond Texas.

Ray Elliott sat in a straight-back chair across a desk from a livid man sporting a fine suit and a handlebar mustache. In a way, the general reminded him of Sheriff Kingfisher. The comparison to the adjutant general was only as to style, not substance.

The general threw a stack of letters across the desk. "This one is in Massachusetts. Tells me how he has seen the Texas Rangers in the movies. Those rangers always get their man and stand for truth and justice. He prays his son will never know real rangers get overrun by mobs and let innocent folk get put to the torch by racists. Course he writes it all in Yankee, a bunch of 'wherefores' and 'thereins.'"

Ray Elliott picked some letters from his lap and the floor, placing them on the desk, then started to rise.

"Then you come walking in here and want to quit. Are your feelings hurt? You're not a babe in the woods, Elliott. There are a lot of politics around this mess, which means you get blamed and get a reprimand, taken out of command for a few months: not fired, not demoted. This governor has been good to lawmen in Texas. You want the Fergusons back in the governor's mansion?"

The general didn't wait for an answer. Ray Elliott had

been fired for crossing the Ferguson political machine in a failed attempt to curtail corruption. He sat back down in the chair, convinced he owed both the general and the governor.

The general barked, "Here is what you are going to do. You are going back to Sherman officially as a witness, but in point of fact you will have your company. Find the leaders of the mob. Get them arrested. I will find a way to force the trial to Dallas or Fort Worth. After, and only after we have tried the criminals responsible, will I consider your request for resignation."

It hadn't occurred to Ray Elliott his resignation required permission. Such a circumstance seemed impractical.

Ray Elliott looked into the general's eyes and realized the order was a plea for help. "Yes, sir."

Many were arrested for the lynch mob violence. The venue was moved to Dallas. Months passed from May into the early fall of 1930, and only two were actually convicted and sentenced to short prison sentences.

Ray Elliott was disappointed. The governor pointed out to him how atypical it was to try to convict members of a lynch mob. Specifically, white juries convicting white men of arson and inciting violence against blacks was beyond exceptional.

Ray Elliott was at Camp Mabry waiting to meet with the governor when the adjutant general's clerk chased him down to deliver a telegram.

> NEED YOUR HELP RICHARD WATERSONG HAS COME BACK TO TAKE HIS HOUSE – CECIL GRANT, NEW LONDON, TEXAS.

Ray Elliott, like most rangers, had provided security

for the governor. The two had shared many conservations while traveling. However, he had never actually had a formal audience with him, a meeting at the governor's request. He had also never seen such envy as when he passed a full capitol lobby and outer office of people.

The governor turned from behind a rolltop desk to a table between him and Ray Elliott. "Elliott, what is this quitting foolishness?"

"Retirement, sir. I believe I have earned it."

The governor laughed. "I didn't think rangers had a retirement. If you do, I promise it is not much."

Ray Elliott said, "I made my mind up a while back and today I got a telegram from a man I owe my life to. He was asking for my help. I feel guilty I'm not already on a train."

The governor's face had turned somber as Ray Elliott spoke. "Wouldn't a company of rangers help your friend more than one?"

Ray Elliott retorted, "No, if it is what it sounds like, a badge will only slow down what might need doing."

The governor leaned back in his chair and raised his tone. "Do tell. Who is this man who can command you while the Governor of Texas cannot do so? What kind of predicament is making you turn outlaw?"

Ray Elliott leaned back. "I don't know, sir."

The governor let pass a few curse words before catching himself. "Tell me what you know."

Ray Elliott had heard the patronizing tone applied to others. In prompt fashion, he presented the telegram. He added, "Richard Watersong foreclosed on Cecil Grant's house. He also embezzled a fortune from his father-in-law's bank. Like I said, Cecil Grant saved my life. I owe him a debt of honor. As for Richard Watersong, I had hoped, prayed, and wished he was dead."

Ray Elliott had to stop. The point was powerful. How he had wanted Richard Watersong dead like he had told Eleanor. The lie had already cost him the woman he loved, the life he wanted, and pushed him down a lonely, cold path for the better part of thirty years.

Ray Elliott said, "What I can't wrap my head around is why a millionaire thief would come back from who knows where for some gravelly acreage in Rusk County, Texas."

"Isn't the Daisy Bradford Number Three in Rusk County?"

After a long pause, Ray Elliott decided he must have had a puzzled look on his face because the governor kept motioning for him to respond.

The governor pointed toward the outer office. "All those people are here about Rusk County. Some want martial law to protect an, only possible, mind you, oil field so large they are already calling it the Black Giant. The others insist the best way to develop the resource is to let the free market regulate itself, even if we have vast open pools of oil sitting in East Texas and no way to market it. Meaning, if there is no market, how can there be a free market? What do you think; enough of a fortune to bring a thief out of hiding?"

CHAPTER 28: The Giant Awakens

The governor walked out of the office, and returned accompanied by a well-dressed businessman in a silver suit. The businessman's steely eyes compelled attention, despite the man's modest stature.

The governor introduced the man. "This is James Denzel, a good UT alum originally of Madisonville, Texas and currently an oilman in Shreveport."

"Ray Elliott." Ray shook Denzel's hand.

"I'm going to let Denzel educate you for a little while, and if you still want to go, then I am not sure how I can stop you; but wear your badge. It's the California gold fields and the Wild West all rolled into one. Kilgore added five thousand people overnight, all looking to escape this Great Depression." The governor stepped out.

Ray Elliott said, "Mr. Denzel, I am sorry you are getting drug into this. Apparently quitting requires approval."

Denzel laughed. "I need the governor to see things my way. He needs you to see things his way. So, I am volunteering to help."

Ray Elliott joined in the light banter. "The oil business seems a lot like the police business."

Denzel said, "The governor makes it sound like you don't have any idea how big the Joiner field really is. Where is your friend's farm, anyway?"

"London."

Denzel nodded. "Close to the Daisy Bradford Number Three. The Crim Well was more than eight miles north of the Daisy Bradford and it is much bigger. There is a Lanthrop well still being drilled, nearing what they hope is the Woodbine Sand. It is over twenty miles from the Daisy Bradford Number Three."

Ray Elliott nodded. Denzel started again, indicating he did not find the nod dispositive. "Do you understand we are talking about the largest oilfield in the world?"

Ray Elliott answered, "No."

"The governor is getting pressure from big oil companies. They are complaining about waste and crime in this new field. They want the sole authority to develop the field. They contend they are far more orderly and less wasteful. Putting acreage in the hands of big oil to develop who knows how many years from now when big oil thinks the price is appropriate is not the answer. The independent oilman can develop the resource most efficiently. With reasonable regulation, the independent can protect the formation. Oil will create vast new markets in time. This is an engine Texas and much of our nation can ride out of this depression."

Ray Elliott asked, "Why are you trying to sell me?"

"The governor knew what was in your telegram when it arrived at Camp Mabry. He trusts you because you took the heat over Sherman like a good soldier. He can stand up to Big Oil except if his constituents think East Texas is Sodom and Gomora. Then he has a more formidable problem."

"So, you convince me and I convince him." Ray Elliott grinned, joined by Denzel.

The governor returned. "Elliott, Denzel will fly with you up there in the morning. Don't worry, I have flown with him. Good at the flying part; it's the landing he has trouble with." Denzel and the governor erupted in laughter. Ray Elliott did not appear to see the humor.

The following morning was cold, at least cold for Austin. Ray Elliott wanted to ask if the cold weather affected the plane. It stood to reason the motor might be harder to start or might run more poorly in the cold. After the laughter yesterday, he was reluctant to show fear.

He had put his neck in this noose by agreeing to fly, and it seemed a little late to start crying now.

The bi-plane was silverfish grey. *Stearman* was written on the vertical tail section. There were only two seats, both in open, separate cockpits. Neither offered much in the way of protection against the elements. Denzel directed Ray Elliott into the forward seat and offered him goggles.

Ray Elliott discovered a previously unknown anxiety as the plane lifted. Then he felt the exhilaration from the speed of the climb. It was as if his knees were raised into his chest.

Denzel used the railroad tracks as a guide, following their general northeastern path. After a while, Ray Elliott recognized the Brazos River. The Trinity River was unmistakable and the tall pines and dark hardwood forest denoted his homeland: East Texas.

They were following the International and Great Northern Railroad. The tracks extended all the way to Longview. Ray Elliott saw in his mind's eye the tie pins of the I&GN Railroad detectives and Sheriff Kingfisher. He remembered his inexperience thirty years ago, yet how Sheriff Kingfisher was the one who failed the ultimate test of their profession. A person could be vigilant for decades and in one careless moment hasten their end.

Richard Watersong was a dangerous man. Likely, Richard Watersong was more dangerous with thirty years of his senses honed from always looking over his shoulder. Ray Elliott chided himself for another consequence of the lie. Even if people deduced Sheriff Kingfisher's death was murder, then Dock Baxter would be blamed, not Richard Watersong.

Thirty years after he lied to spare Eleanor and her sons the mortification of becoming pariahs in Southern Society, unintended consequences were still arising. There had been women in the intervening thirty years. The relationships failed because none could compete with the lost dream of a life with Eleanor.

The same desire which drove him to walk out on her and step onto a train thirty years ago was compelling him to turn, even if it meant jumping out of this plane. He pondered the absurdity of the feeling.

Ray Elliott tried to ignore the emotions conflicting within him. He was a harsh judge, especially harsh on himself. His judgment was crushing. He was a liar and a killer, and he would be found out, unmasked. Still, he owed Cecil Grant a debt of honor. Even a man without honor could appreciate the obligation it demanded.

There were tall drilling derricks linked by more noticeable long mule trains carrying everything from equipment to large tanks, vessels used to transport oil. Upon crossing high over the Henderson to Tyler roadway, which was choked with cars and trucks, Ray Elliott saw Denzel pointing at a wellsite. Whether it was the Daisy Bradford Number Three or the Deep Rock Oil Company's Ashby Number One, he didn't know. Denzel had mentioned too many wells for Ray Elliott to keep them all clear in his mind.

There were enormous mule teams; some must have numbered fifty mules. He also saw vast open pits of shimmering black liquid. The pits were long rectangles for the most part, and they looked like great black ponds glimmering in the winter sun. There were many sites being prepared for drilling covered with tractors, boilers, and all manner of heavy equipment.

The plane made a lumbering turn to the east, revealing a countryside alive with people. As they approached what he knew must be London, Texas or more likely New London a short distance away, there were groups of shacks and tents, along with a handful of more permanent structures like company stores being hastily built in camps.

Ray Elliott had difficulty recognizing what had been a small farming community. He was able to identify New London because he saw the tracks of the Henderson and Overton Branch Railroad connecting to the I.G.N.R.R.

Denzel wagged the plane right to left slightly and pointed to his right. Ray Elliott reasoned this must be the Lou Della Crim Number One. Denzel had told him how Lou Dell Crim wouldn't miss church, when first told the well exploded with its twenty thousand barrel-a-day bonanza.

Kilgore was alive with drilling rigs being erected next to buildings. Some buildings had been knocked down to put up derricks. The roads were clogged with traffic, all dreamers intent on escaping the depression with the Black Gold.

They reached the Sabine River. The river reminded Ray Elliott of trips to the Angelina River in his youth to harvest catfish.

There was another railroad in the distance, the Texas and Pacific connecting Longview in East Texas to Dallas on the plains of North Texas. There was definitely less activity now, but there were still a number of cars, horses, and mule trains as they flew to the northeast.

Ray Elliott saw the drilling site come into view and realized this must be the Lanthrop well Denzel had described. The flight gave him an appreciation for the scale Denzel had tried to explain.

Denzel turned the *Stearman* further toward the east, flying over Longview before landing the Stearman on a runway which was little more than a pasture outside of Marshall, Texas. The Stearman came to a stop near a small tin building and Denzel jumped out of the plane. Ray Elliott tried to follow the lead, but his legs were like water and he nearly fell.

Denzel admonished, "Careful, it takes a little time to get your legs back."

"I don't know if I'll ever fly again but it was exhilarating, thank you," said Ray Elliott.

Denzel raised his arms like he was pleading. "No telling how many times I flew over the field. I bought this Stearman to fly from Shreveport to my leases in West Texas. It never occurred to me I was flying over the largest oil field in history right under my wings."

"I do have a question."

"Be glad to answer it, if I can."

Ray Elliott leaned against the building. He was still getting his bearings. "Suppose I own an acre and drill a well on my neighbor's property line; aren't I stealing my neighbor's oil?"

Denzel spoke in a lighter tone and a slower cadence,

but his words were heartfelt. "No more than shooting a deer crossing onto your property. However, you are landing on the debate sweeping all corners of Texas Government: do we limit wells by acreage or limit production by allowable barrels per well? How do we protect the resource for the future and yet reward the independent producer like Joiner who found this field with a worn-out rig, ripping tires off old trucks to throw into a used-up cotton gin boiler, all the time praying for a few more feet of depth?" Denzel was near laughter in admiration. "If you'll join me for lunch, I would like to share my plans."

Ray Elliott caught himself grimacing before he tried to smile. The oil business was interesting and very interesting to those involved. However, he had devoted a considerable amount of time to it in the last day. There were more pressing matters on his mind. "No, thank you. I will catch the train to Overton. I really need to check on Cecil Grant. If Richard Watersong is still the snake I remember, then it may already be too late for my old friend."

CHAPTER 29: CECIL'S PROMISE TO MARTHA

Ray Elliott had a difficult time finding the Grant's farm. Thirty years ago, it had been a modest place, yet it displayed hard work. Ray Elliott appreciated a well-tended farm, having helped maintain one himself.

Since it was winter, it wasn't surprising the fields were unworked. What was surprising was the fields didn't look like they had been planted earlier in the year. They were overgrown with briars, even pine and persimmon trees.

The fences were down. The roof on the small barn had fallen down. The house had fared better. Still, whatever had once been painted had long since given way to grey, denoting the sun-bleached lumber.

Martha's smile had not aged. She rose slowly from a rocking chair on the porch, still a small woman. Ray Elliott had some doubt whether the chair would support a normal-sized person.

He tied the reins of the rented horse around one of the four, large post holding up the tin roofed porch. Martha wrapped her arms around him. "Cecil will be so proud to see you, Mr. Ray."

Ray Elliott said, "Just Ray, Martha, no mister." He was reluctant to hug her at first. Martha had not been prone to such affection, at least not with him. Ray Elliott feared the reception was because the family was in such grave trouble. Cecil Grant would not have sent for him if he could have handled it himself.

Ray Elliott asked, "Where is old Cecil?"

"He is poorly, bad poorly. Most days he can't get up much at all. He will feel better knowing you're here." Martha's near constant smile only waned for a moment.

Ray Elliott looked around. "Are all the kids grown up and gone?"

Martha looked away. "Rodney died in the war in France. Rachel didn't outlive the polio; pneumonia got her. One of my girls moved to Dallas and I don't know if she is alive or dead. Junior married a preacher, and they have been a blessing to us. We got two grandbabies." She motioned for him to follow her into the house.

If anything, the house was sparser and more covered in the sales catalogs for wallpaper than before. Cecil Grant sat up in his bed when Ray Elliott reached the door. The house was dark. Electricity had not reached the Grants. There was a sweet and sour smell which was hard to place.

Ray Elliott stepped back, then forced himself forward. The years were not kind to Cecil Grant. He looked emaciated. His cheeks and features were hollow, giving him a death-like appearance. Now Ray Elliott recognized the odor. He was smelling death.

Ray Elliott was grateful the near darkness helped mask Cecil Grant's face. It was painful to see the once proud, strong man in such a state. Cecil Grant must have realized how much Ray Elliott was startled.

"Doctor thinks it might be cancer. Can't be sure until he opens me up and I am not going to let him do it." Cecil Grant leaned back, breathing heavy.

Ray Elliott looked at Martha. "You got to take care of yourself for Martha's sake."

Cecil Grant paused a moment. "No, not going to leave Martha a bunch of debt." He struggled for breath before continuing. "Why you're here. I would not have sent for you for myself."

"What has Richard Watersong done?" asked Ray Elliott.

Cecil Grant motioned toward a stack of papers on the window sill. It was the only part of the room with any light. Martha reached them first and handed the papers to Ray Elliott, who tried to hold them to the light.

From time to time Ray Elliott had served some civil process lawsuit papers. He had also cleaned up a number of oil boom towns in his three decades of service. On one occasion, he had even occupied a disputed portion of Texas which was ultimately ruled to be Oklahoma by the United States Supreme Court. All of these experiences gave him some understanding of oilfield claims and real estate law.

He recognized the archaic common law pleading of a trespass to try title lawsuit in Texas. Such suits often resulted in violence. Law enforcement become embroiled in these civil disputes. Poor families didn't have wills. If they could afford a lawyer to draft a proper will, then they certainly couldn't afford probate proceedings. Instead of a title proceeding through family members from A to B to C in the county clerk records, more often A bought the property, then D, who was A's great-grandson, sold a portion of the tract to Z, although nothing in the deed records recited the relation or inheritance. Then add to such common circumstances frontier surveying, poor property descriptions, and homemade deeds. Once real estate became valuable enough to merit a lawsuit, lawyers had no difficulty finding an issue.

Here, the complaint was less convoluted. Richard Watersong had foreclosed on Cecil Grant. The English justice system had come down through history with the primary goal of establishing legal title to property. But English common law was not the only influence on Texas.

The Spanish system recognized wives as true partners in a marriage to the point of vesting one half of the property earned or otherwise obtained during the marriage to them. That is to say, even if Richard Watersong owned the land, his wife at the time, Eleanor, owned half of it.

There was an additional legal wrinkle. Frontier states like Texas placed a premium on the cultivation and development of property over the rights of absentee land speculators. Laws authorized citizens who lived on property and made valuable improvements to establish title after a certain number of years. This concept of adverse possession meant Cecil Grant still had a valuable claim.

Martha had excused herself and returned, hoping to take advantage of Cecil Grant's alertness to get him to eat some chicken broth. He refused.

Ray Elliott continued reading the voluminous documents. There was a temporary injunction prohibiting Cecil Grant and his agents from drilling or entering into leases to drill. The injunction was set for a hearing before the district judge tomorrow. He debated how to explain all these matters to Cecil Grant before realizing the man likely understood most of it. After all, the proud Cecil Grant had waited until the proverbial last minute before sending for Ray Elliott.

Cecil Grant asked, "Can you make anything out of it?"

"I can and I suspect you did too." Ray Elliott stepped back toward the darkness of the bed. "You need a lawyer."

Cecil Grant shook his head. "I read in the newspaper about how they ran out on a rail the only lawyer who would help them black folks in Sherman." He coughed. "Right after they burned the colored neighborhood."

Ray Elliott said, "This isn't Sherman."

Cecil Grant motioned to Martha. "Already had lawyer do all I need: get the deed."

Martha handed Ray Elliott a document, and he read it. Cecil and Martha Grant were deeding to him their entire farm. Ray Elliott looked up. "I don't understand."

Cecil Grant coughed and motioned to Martha. She said, "It was my idea. Cecil won't live much longer. You know how important this land is to him. His father had been a slave. He bought the property through the Freedman's Bureau." Cecil nodded almost in tears. Whether it was his imminent death, the story of his father, or the fear of leaving Martha alone, the man was overcome.

Martha placed her hand on Cecil's hand. "Cecil feels like you owe him so he wants you to fight Richard Watersong for me, for him, for our grandbabies."

Ray Elliott took a step back. "I don't understand. Why deed it to me? I do owe you and I will help, all I can, anyway."

Cecil Grant leaned up. "Which is why I trust you and no one else." Cecil Grant struggled for breath. "Nothing much lower than a colored woman under the law. I don't want Martha treated dirty." He tried to speak while his breath was failing him.

Ray Elliott finished the thought. "Bad enough the way Richard Watersong treated you. He would have even less respect for Martha and you can't go to the Almighty with her on your heart."

"Martha is a strong woman. Not her fault. I am the one who brought Richard Watersong into our lives. It's all my fault. I promised her I would fix it. You're going to keep my promise for me." Cecil gasped.

Ray Elliott looked from Martha back to Cecil. "I will fix it. I promise."

Martha accepted Ray Elliott's offer to watch over Cecil Grant. However, she was not to have a rest. In the night, Cecil woke and began talking without making sense. He did not recognize Ray Elliott's voice and his hand was chilled.

Martha reached her husband. He recognized her touch. Cecil Grant expressed his love for Martha. Alternatively, he begged for her forgiveness for having failed her. Ray Elliott stepped out of the room. Martha comforted Cecil as best she could.

There was no loud shriek, no thunderclap from the heavens. Martha walked past Ray Elliott whispering, "He has gone home."

PART IV

A Trial for a Trespass That Wasn't

CHAPTER 30: RUSK COUNTY JUSTICE

Ray Elliott suspected Martha was in a state of shock. Her affect was flat. Perhaps Cecil Grant's death was merciful. It appeared to Ray Elliott that Martha, combined with the guilt of leaving her in dire straits, were the only things which had been tethering Cecil Grant to this world.

Ray Elliott rode a short distance to inform the daughter, known in the family as Junior and her minister husband. Junior followed him back to her childhood home. Cecil Grant had prepared for death. His family knew he was ready to go home. Martha and Cecil Grant had discussed with Junior the promise Cecil Grant intended to extract from Ray Elliott.

Junior said, "I didn't want them to ask you. Oil money is not worth getting people killed over."

"You let me worry about getting killed. You have to take care of your mom. Would you take her to your house to stay for a while? I want to complete the ruse as much as I can." Ray Elliott stepped onto the porch, beating his suit coat with a heavy brush.

Junior followed him. "My husband is distant kin to some of Queen's momma's people. Richard Watersong is more than a con artist. He is a racist, murdering thief."

Ray Elliott looked at her. "You might be right. Not the first one I have had to face down."

"You don't really know. He built a crime empire in Cuba. When Prohibition got passed, he became the supplier for rum smuggled into the U.S." She looked back at him like he still didn't understand.

She raised her voice. "He's like Al Capone, only bigger. Some lawyer interviewed Queen's family trying to find where Richard Watersong was living. He seemed to think he might get a little piece of whatever fortune there might be under our feet. Word in the family is Richard Watersong's men fed him to the sharks in Cuba."

Ray Elliott grinned. "I chased a lot of outlaws on the Mexican border during Prohibition. In their kind of business, the guy with the scariest reputation never gets cheated. They create or enhance rumors. It's only good business."

Junior shook her head. "Can't tell you anymore than I could tell Daddy."

Ray Elliott paused for a moment. He had been so convincing, he had found what seemed like real courage in his bravado. He had been forced to scramble for fear Junior would realize her comments hit home. If she or Martha saw fear, then he would have let Cecil down.

Richard Watersong posed a danger before he took up murder. What had thirty years of crime done to the man?

In Ray Elliott's mind, Richard Watersong had died somehow on the boat to South America or he was enjoying life on a beach. Never did Ray Elliott deduce the obvious. Richard Watersong would use his ill-gotten seed money to build a crime empire. After thirty years of amassing wealth at all cost, Richard Watersong placed even less value on human life. Ray Elliott continued his attempt to reassure Junior as well as himself. "If you mean I am as stubborn as your father then I'll take it as high praise."

Ray Elliott rode to the courthouse in Henderson. Much had changed in thirty years, including the courthouse.

Gone was the stately courthouse in the center square, replaced by a new Art Deco, multi-story building down the hill. The great stone building was modern, boasting a large, open stairwell to the second floor which took up half the front facade. It made the courthouse accessible, giving the appearance it was open to all.

No doubt planners had designed the grand structure to see the county through the future. They could not have anticipated the recent boom. The hallways were cramped with landmen and lease hounds, the people who reviewed the deed records to determine mineral ownership and then tried to obtain signed leases from such owners. They had set up makeshift desks and typewriters in every nook.

Ray Elliott made his way to the County Clerk's Office and filed the deed from Cecil and Martha Grant. He took the file marked 'Duplicate' with him and walked the stairwell to the third floor.

He stepped into the courtroom. Light filled the room from massively tall windows. The ceiling fans stood still. They hovered over a gallery of over two hundred individual theater seats.

Ray Elliott turned to face the bench to his left. Over the bench, an enormous picture of General Smith stood watch, extending from the top of the bench to the ceiling. General James Smith was a veteran of the Red Stick War, the War of 1812, the Texas War of Independence, and the Cherokee War which had precipitated the birth of Rusk County.

On the wall to the right of the courtroom entrance was a smaller portrait of a gentleman, much brighter than the dull likeness of General Smith. The caption under this portrait read, 'Honorable Mathew Duncan Ector, Second

Judicial District, Seventh Judicial District and learned appellate jurist.'

The courtroom was crowded exclusively with white men wearing dark suits, one of whom announced, "All rise. This honorable court is now in session, the Honorable R.T. Brown presiding."

Judge R.T. Brown projected his voice across the courtroom. "Posted next to the door in the hall is the ancillary docket. I will call each case in order and you will present your request for injunctions, sequestrations, and whatever additional temporary relief you are seeking. I am also amenable to setting final trial dates. Number One, Buckelew et.al. vs. Columbus Marion Joiner."

Judge R.T. Brown smiled a wry smile, thumbing through a ten-inch stack of papers. He looked down before turning to his left and said in a stern tone, "I have read the pleading and affidavits, at least about two dozen of them. I would prefer the moving parties, petitioners, realtors and plaintiffs limit their arguments to one or two. Who speaks for the Movants?"

"If I may Your Honor, Myron Blalock of Marshall by agreement of the moving parties. I shall serve as lead counsel solely for the purpose of today's hearing.

"I am assuming, Your Honor, the Court has overruled our request for *ex parte* relief, given Mr. Joiner's counsel is present."

Judge Brown responded, "You may assume only that I took the matter under advisement and found it proper to proceed with all parties represented."

Myron Blalock retorted, "Then for the purpose of preserving the issue, note our objection to the Court's failure to rule, Your Honor." Judge R.T. Brown stared at the attorney. The courtroom was silent; more than silent, it was still. The judge gave no indication there was a limit to his ability to maintain an uncomfortable silence.

Myron Blalock began again. "Your Honor, we come here in equity, wronged by blatant fraud. I will not recite all the allegations in the affidavits. The same numbered stock certificate was sold eleven times. I personally investigated an instance where one fifth of the same lease was sold ten times. There is a gallery of witnesses I will present today, Your Honor, evidencing the most blatant of frauds. We will prevail in these suits. Secondly, Your Honor, our clients have no adequate remedy at law. We cannot trust Mr. Joiner to pay royalties. Permit me to explain the absurdity of the situation in which we find ourselves. He doesn't know or have accurate enough records to tell how many times he sold the same property. We propose a restraining order on selling any assets or oil and that a receiver be appointed to make inventory to the Court and begin to prioritize claims. Otherwise, the injury is irreparable."

Judge R.T. Brown spoke, "Before we begin testimony, would Mr. Joiner's Counsel make his position on this request known to the Court?" Judge R.T. Brown looked to a relatively young lawyer who had earlier been announced as Alfred Coleman from Dallas, Texas.

"Your Honor, some of these suits were filed before the Daisy Bradford Number Three struck oil. If you had appointed a receiver at such time, we couldn't have this fight over how to divide the vast wealth. Mr. Joiner is not a receiver. He is an innovator, a discoverer of new wealth. That is to say, Mr. Joiner takes a zero-sum game where there is not enough to divide, and changes the rules to provide for more wealth than anyone realized was possible. Even now, he is making deals, brokering with other oilmen and companies. It took three and a half years to find this oilfield. There are no pipelines, no trucks, no storage tanks, and the roads are impassable. The oil is being collected in huge, open pits in the ground, like lakes. We are using huge tanks set on makeshift carriages and enormous teams of mules to get what oil we can get to market. Please just trust the same man who brought us this bonanza can find a resolution."

Judge R.T. Brown raised his hand to show his palm, while his elbow remained on the bench and pronounced, "I believe when it takes a man three and a half years to find his baby, he ought to be able to rock it for a while. This hearing is abated indefinitely."

Ray Elliott hears Myron Blalock tell the lawyers near him, "I expect we will have better luck sequestering 'Dad' Joiner in the Dallas courts."

Judge R.T. Brown cast a disapproving look at Myron Blalock before announcing, "Watersong vs. Grant et al."

Ray Elliott said, "Your Honor, my name is Ray Elliott and Cecil Grant has sold his land to me and any claims he may have in this lawsuit."

In the gallery to the far right of Ray Elliott stood a man wearing Burberry suit. He had mesmerizing blue eyes. Even from across the room and after thirty years, Ray Elliott recognized Richard Watersong.

CHAPTER 31: WHO LACKS HONOR?

"Your Honor, Wesley Toben for plaintiff and movant, Richard Watersong. Ready, Your Honor. I do object to this Ray Elliott's intervention. Since Cecil Grant had no title and was estopped from asserting a claim, then at best any transfer would only serve as a quit claim, and a quit claim passes no title as a matter of law." The lawyer moved forward to the counsel table with his client.

A young attorney in a navy suit drew Ray Elliott's attention. He knew him, yet he didn't know how or in what context. "Your Honor, Richie Watersong for Respondent, Eleanor Watersong. Not ready, Your Honor. I have not had an opportunity to investigate these claims, nor my mother's interest."

Ray Elliott looked at his feet. How many times had he feared Eleanor or her sons discovering his lie? He had only wanted to spare them the suffering, the shame of Richard Watersong's actions. How many times had he prayed Richie wouldn't hate him? Enough times he had chided himself for praying such a selfish prayer. How could Richie ever forgive him?

Richie looked to Ray Elliott and winked. "We have no objection to the intervention, Your Honor."

The only man not attired in a black or navy suit was Ray Elliott. Despite his best efforts, Ray Elliott's brown suit coat was covered in dust. "Your Honor, I don't have a lawyer and I am not sure I can hire one."

Judge R.T. Brown said, "Mr. Toben, I would not

presume to tell one of the most celebrated trial lawyers in Texas his business. You can strike the intervention of Ray Elliott. However, I submit to you whatever title you establish would not bind Mr. Elliott. Hence the necessity of a subsequent lawsuit."

Wesley Toben said, "I withdraw my objection."

Judge R.T. Brown thumbed another stack of papers. "Gentlemen, I have read the pleadings, and it is well established Mr. Watersong has a substantial likelihood of success and there is no adequate remedy at law were Mr. Grant, or now Mr. Elliott, to permit drilling. So, I will grant the request for injunctions. Do you have any objection, Mr. Richie Watersong?"

Richie answered, "No, Your Honor."

Judge R. T. Brown pushed back only the barest grey lock of what was at one time a full head of curly brown hair. He continued, "The law of capture is working against all of you. Your neighbors are either now or soon will be drilling, siphoning oil from under these two hundred acres. The law of capture makes such drilling legal, however, it diminishes the value of the property at issue. This is where an honest man becomes essential to the administration of justice. I will appoint a receiver, an agent of the court, like a trustee for a trust, acting under the orders of the court to develop the property, such as negotiating a lease. Such a lease will achieve the highest value for the oil, and a royalty on every barrel produced. Further, it will prevent the migration of oil by offset wells. I would like to have everyone agree this is the best alternative until the case can be reached for the final trial."

Wesley Toben volunteered, "Genius, Your Honor. May I volunteer the eminently accomplished businessman, Mr.

Richard Watersong, to serve as receiver."

Ray Elliott said, "Judge, I admit I am no lawyer, but I don't figure you should trust a man without honor to do anything."

Richard Watersong said, "Who lacks honor? The man who is willing to live a lie to protect the woman he loves or the coward who hops a train for fear of facing the truth?"

Ray Elliott took a step back from the counsel table he and Richie were standing behind. The latter was true in its entirety. Did such mean the former statement held any veracity? What did it mean anyway? What other possible lie could Richard Watersong be referencing?

Ray Elliott was lost in thought, contemplating all the possibilities. Moments ago, he would have explained his justification for his lie. The great lie Richard Watersong was dead only served to protect Eleanor and her sons. Still, the indictment against him was true. He was unwilling to live the falsehood. What falsehood had Richard Watersong lived?

Did Richard Watersong mean he had killed Lukas Halten to protect his love, Queen? There were too many possibilities. Why would he ever believe anything Richard Watersong said?

Judge R.T. Brown continued, "The court's receiver or agent will negotiate the best terms and present it to the court and I will authorize approval or ask the receiver to renegotiate the terms. The money will be held in the registry of the court for the ultimate winner of the lawsuit. The receiver will necessarily be paid a fair rate for all of his work. Many of you know the governor is seriously considering imposing martial law to protect the field and to end the lawlessness running rampant. A young man named James Denzel insists independent oilmen can come together to develop the field and prevent waste. He is a good man for the task. However, I won't appoint him unless all of you agree. Mr. Elliott?"

Ray Elliott realized James Denzel never let on that one of the reasons he was flying to East Texas was to be appointed receiver. Denzel and the governor had known far more than they had revealed in Austin. Ray Elliott realized this had been saucered and blown, so there was no point in standing in the way. He nodded. "Agreed, Your Honor."

Judge R.T. Brown asked, "Mr. Richie Watersong?"

"Agreed."

Judge R.T. Brown asked, "Mr. Toben?"

Wesley Toben looked at Richard Watersong and then conferred with him. Then Wesley Toben asked, "You Honor, what if I object to the Court's proposal?"

Judge R.T. Brown answered, "By all means, do make your objection known, Counsel. I will grant your injunctions and no one will drill on the contested land. However, everyone adjoining you will remove the oil under what you believe is your property, like your first girlfriend drank your sarsaparilla thorough her straw before you so much as got a taste."

"We agree, Your Honor."

Judge R.T. Brown pronounced, "Wise decision."

Richard Watersong and his attorney made for the door as soon as the hearing ended. Richie stopped outside the courtroom, and then turned to face Ray Elliott in the hallway.

Ray Elliott said, "Richie, I never should have lied. I

thought–"

Richie interrupted him. "You thought you would restore hope for a kid until he was old enough to handle the truth. There is no need to explain or apologize."

"I hope your little brother shares your opinion." Ray Elliott grinned.

"He died in the war in France." Richie added, "I am not sure Mother ever got over it. She begged him not to enlist."

Ray Elliott's countenance had fallen at the news and the mention of Eleanor. "How is your mother?"

"You haven't seen her in all these years, have you?"

Ray Elliott looked at the cold, white linoleum floor. "I can't face her."

"Mother never mentions you. I do know it was easier for a widow to turn the bank here in Henderson around and reopen the one in Nacogdoches than it would have been for a divorcee. She built her father's dream of a community-minded bank, survived the Crash. Now, she is battling Richard Watersong in courts both here and in Nacogdoches." Richie turned to acknowledge a thin man with a furrowed brow walking toward him. "Good morning, sheriff. I want you to meet Ray Elliott. Sheriff R.E. Gault. Excuse me, gentlemen, I have to be in court in Tyler."

Sheriff Gault extended his hand, and Ray Elliott shook it. "I know who you are. Captain Elliott, I been waiting for you."

CHAPTER 31: JOY

Ray Elliott said, "I don't understand, sheriff."

"I wired Austin a week ago. Finally, today the adjutant general phoned me you were here." Sheriff Gault had both his hands in front of him in a pleading fashion.

"It's complicated. I'm here on personal business. I tried to retire—"

Sheriff Gault interjected, "Adjutant general tells me you can retire after you get this oilfield in line. Follow me captain."

Sheriff Gault walked away, then turned at the stairway. Ray Elliott hadn't moved. "Get this oilfield in line," he was getting roped into something else. It was like he was a puppet for the governor, the adjutant general, James Denzel, even the dearly departed Cecil Grant. He had no say in his life anymore.

Sheriff Gault looked at him. "Been a killing, ranger."

Ray Elliott satisfied himself this was his own decision. After a moment, he stepped toward the sheriff. On the way down the stairs, the sheriff began reciting the events with a pleading tone.

Two imported hoodlums hijacked a truck of oilfield tools, and then two more imported hoodlums hijacked them. The second set killed both men from the first set and stole the load. Even in the new wild and wooly community of Joinerville, two hi-jackings and murders garnered attention.

Ray Elliott asked, "Got any leads on them?"

Sheriff Gault answered, "We got them over in the jail. I want you to help me interview them. They each blame the other one. Prosecutor wants me to figure out which one pulled the trigger or if each shot one."

"Do you have the weapon?"

Sheriff Gault nodded to him. "They used a shotgun, old Winchester pump we found between the seats of the truck. There were two shell casings on the side of the road near the bodies. The shotgun had been reloaded, because it was full when we found it. The first one's name is Sam Jackson."

Ray Elliott and Sheriff Gault walked into the sheriff's office where a young, dark-haired man of no more than twenty sat handcuffed. The young man didn't wait for introductions.

"I didn't shoot nobody. I was trying to heist the truck and this nut job goes off and starts the shooting."

Ray Elliott began questioning, "Sheriff tells me you are a member of 'The Line,' while word on the street is our other suspect is a member of a different criminal crew out of Houston. Why would two rival gang members work together?"

"The sheriff claims I said I was in The Line, but I didn't. I just asked for a lawyer he says works for them."

Ray Elliott looked at Sheriff Gault in a disapproving manner. "I didn't know you asked for a lawyer. I am ending the interview." Ray Elliott gave Sheriff Gault a disapproving stare.

Ray Elliott and Sheriff Gault now proceeded to the next suspect in a cell down the hall.

"My name is Ray Elliott. I am a ranger. I'm here to take your statement. You have a right not to talk at all. Do you want to talk to me?"

The young man was dressed in a threadbare pair of dirty coveralls. "I'm Marcus Hunt. Man, all I can tell you is that cat is crazy. We were just going to do a little work. He flips out and kills these guys. I was scared to death he was going to shoot me."

Ray Elliott figured the remainder of the statement was lies. The person was minimizing his prior criminal history while walking the narrow line of blaming the other person and distancing himself. Ray Elliott wasn't sure the first part of the story necessarily had any veracity either.

Ray Elliott and Sam Gault stood outside the jail. They discussed the quandary.

"We worked the shotgun for fingerprints. There were a few muffed and partial prints and what looked like part of a palm, but nothing comparable," relayed Sheriff Gault, looking across the big grass lawn back up the hill toward where the old courthouse had been demolished.

The two men began walking south-eastward toward the large statue of Thomas J. Rusk standing on a granite pedestal in the center of town.

Sheriff Gault said, "We are in so far over our heads here. It never occurred to me people would hi-jack trucks."

Ray Elliott leaned against a pecan tree. "Hi-jacking is a big problem in boomtowns. It starts with tools, necessities like dry goods and groceries. Later, they steal tanker trucks full of oil, and then they just steal oil from the wellheads selling it to little fly-by-night refineries. Not to mention the gambling, prostitution, and robbery. All comes with a mass of people descending on a small place."

Ray Elliott looked out over the busy downtown, realizing it had been forever changed in a short period. For a century, a five-hundred-pound cotton bale defined worth. Today, forty-two-gallon drums of oil measured wealth.

Ray Elliott asked, "So no fingerprints?"

Sheriff Gault answered, "Muffed or smeared. Like I said, nothing."

Ray Elliott raised his hand in a pleading motion. "But you said it was a shotgun. Don't you have the spent shell, the hull, and the shell reloaded?"

Sheriff Gault nodded as Elliott made a motion like he was loading a shotgun.

Ray Elliott continued, "You see, he is going to set his thumb on the brass base of that shell. It's perfect. I have had more luck with shell casings, especially shotgun hulls than the actual guns. They are moving their hands around the gun at different points in time, muffing the print, while the shell they usually just push in and load."

It was a short walk back into the sheriff's office where the evidence was placed on a desk. Ray Elliott generously applied the fingerprint powder. He brushed powder onto the waxed paper cases of the shotgun hulls to no avail. This was not a surprise to Ray Elliott; rather, it was a necessary elimination.

He began to apply powder to the brass ends of the shell casings. He was gratified as the ridge line of a fingerprint pattern emerged. Ray Elliott realized he was seeing a usable print. He was viewing or trying to view the distinctive features directly on the brass before he realized he was holding his breath, excited by the discovery.

His meticulous process eventually revealed two prints. One was a most likely a thumb lifted from the brass of one spent shotgun shell, and another print from an unspent shotgun shell. He had bent the names over from the known fingerprint cards of the suspects, although he had no bias for either hi-jacker.

Ray Elliott announced his findings to the sheriff. "Mr. Marcus Hunt is your loader. Since his thumb was on both a spent and unspent shell, most likely he's your shooter."

Ray Elliott did not enjoy his evening in the Grant home. What did Richard Watersong mean? After so much hoping his lie was true, and the man was dead, it was surreal to see Richard Watersong and hear his voice. He repeated the words, and the voice echoed in his mind. "Who lacks honor? The man who is willing to live a lie to protect the woman he loves or the coward who hops a train for fear of facing the truth?"

What lie had Richard Watersong lived to protect the woman he loved? Ray Elliott couldn't imagine even in Watersong's deluded mind the man had ever put another human being ahead of his own selfish desires. He suspected the comment lifted the veil over the man's reasoning. Still, the meaning eluded him.

A sleepless night turned to a cool morning. Ray Elliott dusted his suit again so he could dress for Cecil Grant's funeral.

Mt. Hope Baptist Church was in dark letters on a white background. Ray Elliott dismounted, rolled his gun belt and laid it in a cantle bag. He removed his hat.

Ray Elliott entered a church alive with singing. There were four men at the front of the congregation standing before a large choir. Suddenly, the music stopped and everyone looked at Ray Elliott. He was reminded of the old joke about if there were one more then there would have been two. Everyone else in the church was black.

A man rose from the edge of the front pew and turned to face Ray Elliott at the back of the church. Every parishioner was dressed in their finest suit or dress, making the church appear like a kaleidoscope of colors as all the parishioners turned over their shoulder to face Ray Elliott.

The approaching man was wearing a long frock coat, more fashionable in the last century than the current. He reached Ray Elliott and shook his hand vigorously. "I am the pastor, Brother Alton Silver, and my wife is the first lady Martha Silver. You know her better as Junior." He turned his head back toward the front pew and Ray Elliott saw Junior and Martha's familiar faces. "We are proud you came." Then he whispered under his breath, "I know it means a lot to Martha."

Brother Silver nodded at the choir and one of the men at the front of the church began to sing, "Take Me Home Tonight, Lord."

It sounded like a funeral song, a sad dirge about dying in one's sleep. Then the other men joined in the chorus singing, "It's alright." The soloist began to describe meeting his savior.

The pace of the music quickened. It sounded like jazz to Ray Elliott. The song referenced golden streets and massive mansions. The entire choir joined into a joyous celebration of praise for the homecoming of the parishioner. The sound bounced through the sanctuary, reaching crescendo after crescendo of delight. It was as if everyone were basking in the presence of the Almighty.

Brother Silver yelled out to the congregation, "And all God's people said Amen, Amen, Amen, Amen." He continued until "Amen" became a chorus for the congregation. It was as if extreme happiness was raining inside the church. Ray Elliott thought about how he never saw Cecil Grant have any joy in life. It was a pleasant thought to know Cecil Grant had found joy in death, a heritage no Richard Watersong could steal away; a true and lasting promise to a good and faithful servant.

The service continued all morning. Virtually every member of the congregation spoke about Cecil Grant. The Grants were beloved. Ray Elliott learned Martha Grant was a midwife. She had delivered two generations of the church's parishioners while Cecil Grant had ministered to souls as a deacon.

Sometime in the afternoon the service ended. Thereafter, a series of saw horses were hastily erected with large two-by-twelve by ten-foot oak planks. The fare was much the same as any white church. Although there may have been more of the hog on the table, hogshead cheese and pickled pig's feet were not just interesting to Ray Elliott; these quickly became favorites.

Brother Silver stopped Ray Elliott near the end of the day. He presented him a Bible which had the cover wore off. "Martha wants you to have Brother Cecil's Bible."

The gift was so great, Ray Elliott had no words to express himself. He took the Bible. His throat constricted and his eyes started to water until he successfully fought back the emotion.

Brother Silver added, "The family and the church want you to have it, too. We all know what you are doing for Martha."

On the ride back to the Grant farm, Ray Elliott thought about how great it must have been to have had a truly successful marriage like Cecil and Martha. It was more than happiness. Happiness was like an emotion which could end. It was more like the joy which overcame the congregation.

Ray Elliott realized he was wrong about Cecil Grant. Despite the man's suffering, Cecil Grant had nurtured a joy rising from the soil of faith, watered with grace, and fed by the Bible in his hand now. If he only had faith like Cecil Grant, then the task before him wouldn't seem impossible.

He readied himself for bed, placing the Bible on a little table, then his pistol, and finally, his watch. The Bible presented a new addition to the ensemble.

The pistol wasn't the same as the Scofield he had used to kill Dock Baxter, But it served as a constant reminder, nonetheless. All these years, an uncomfortable chunk of steel on his hip reminded him of firing into the man's skull. He had been cold at the time, so sure it was necessary. Throughout all these years, he'd forced an end to the ensuing debate within his warring breast by conceding it was necessary, and yet, near every night when he took the pistol off the question struck him again. Had it truly been necessary?

He opened the watch, viewing the likeness, before closing it and turning it over on the table top. Such had become his custom, for any joy he took in the beautiful woman's likeness only served to remind him of the lie. A lie, albeit told with the best of intentions, which in the end had only caused further pain to Eleanor and her sons.

Tonight, he lifted the new object he had added. Ray Elliott held the Bible and assured himself, he would not fail Cecil Grant. There existed an unspoken promise.The Bible wasn't going to bring grief to him the way the other items made him suffer. He thumbed through the dog-eared pages and underlined passages.

If the measure of a life was by how much a person loved, then Cecil Grant had left a powerful legacy and Ray Elliott's time in this world had been wasted. He tried to console himself with excuses, like he had not had the opportunities at a lasting happiness. It was a lie. He had squandered his chance with Eleanor, and there had been other chances. Eleanor, he would have to face her sooner or later. What would he say?

CHAPTER 32: QUEEN COMES HOME

Queen looked out the window of the Redlands Hotel in Nacogdoches. She looked over the red brick streets across the intersection of Main and Church Street. Her eye caught the opera house, and she remembered the building from her youth.

Her mere presence in the room was a testament to the power of money. Money overcame Jim Crow segregation to get her the best accommodations. Yet, the same money, even in the midst of the depression, made her more objectionable to her family, a symbol of the disgrace her adulterous relationship had brought her family.

Her father had died years ago. Now Queen had failed to get back to Nacogdoches before her mother passed too. Richard Watersong was a pariah to her family and many others.

He had preyed on people of color by making them pay back the same loans many times. Most believed he killed his father-in-law and blamed a poor black man, Dock Baxter. Then he'd tried inciting the community to lynch the innocent man. Folks, both black and white, held a high opinion of Eleanor Watersong and her father, necessarily leading to Queen being characterized as the home-wrecker who ran off with a thief.

Queen turned her gaze to the west. She could only glimpse the bank building, almost hidden by the slow curve of the main street. The telephone rang, and she answered it. She immediately recognized Richard

Watersong's voice.

"Queen, I am so glad you tried to call me. I am driving to Nacogdoches from Dallas tomorrow. Can I see you?"

"Richard, I wanted to say goodbye."

"Good. I will send a wire to the staff to have the house ready. Maybe in a few weeks I can join you." There was a lift in Richard's voice, an excitement she had not heard in years.

She said, "I have missed you. Maybe I have been too hard on you. You have always kept your promises. I release you from them."

Richard Watersong said, "Lately I have been thinking. I made mistakes, a lot of them. I don't know what I thought I knew. But I know I love you."

There was a thud in the next room and she realized she needed to check on the twins. "Goodbye, Richard." She placed the receiver back on the pedestal.

The twins were fighting over a matching pair of toy panda bears when Queen interrupted them by stepping between them. They were seven years old. Walt could not talk, was prone to fits, and his attention could never be fully fixed on anything, even for short periods of time. Elly's behavior was better. Still, since birth she had been plagued by small seizures. Doctors could not determine a cause of the maladies.

Queen told the children, "Get ready. We are going to go bye-bye. We are going to go see a nice lady who will keep you for a while."

Elly asked, "Who is the lady?"

Queen answered, "She is an old friend of your mother. You will like her, Elly. She is a pretty lady and has long red hair."

Elly asked, “Can I take my bear?”

“Of course, you can. You both can take your bears. Now Walt, what is your bear’s name?”

“Mine is Alice,” Elly blurted out.

“Elly, I want Walt to use his words. Walt?”

Walt’s speech was unintelligible. Queen convinced herself she had developed a certain ear for Walt’s utterances. Still, she rarely made anything out. Often, she wondered if he ever said anything decipherable or whether she wanted to communicate with him so badly, she deluded herself. This time she was certain.

Elly said, “Richard.” It was an obvious reference to the late older brother.

Queen began to tear up but stopped herself. “That, that’s a good name, Walt. Now get our shoes on, so we can go.”

As she helped Walt with his shoes, her mind drifted through her options again. Her sisters treated her like a leper. They refused to acknowledge her children, calling them, “That white man’s children.”

Queen knew the real objection had nothing to do with prejudice. It was a reaction to the evil this particular white man had visited upon black folks, more, the wickedness he visited upon all who crossed his path. In a way, she couldn’t fault them.

Over the last thirty years, Queen had watched Richard Watersong change from a greedy man to an evil man. She wanted to be free of anything reminding her of him. As hard as her heart might be to her husband, when she dressed Walt and Elly, her heart couldn’t help but melt with love for them.

Queen had never recovered from the murder of her

eldest. She held her husband accountable. A part of her knew he had loved their son, too. Still, another part of her remembered the man who hired a swamp witch to kill the baby before it could be born.

She couldn't go back to Cuba. She hated her husband, Richard Watersong. The death of their son transformed Cuba from a tropical paradise of wildflowers to a purgatory of a thousand gut wrenching remembrances of her son.

She had seen far too much of Richard Watersong in his namesake, and each time it had pained her heart. It was more than a fear the boy would choose his father's wicked lifestyle.

She had always held a fear her husband would poison the boy against her. The fear had consumed her until she found her only respite was inebriation. After all, Queen had committed an unpardonable sin. She had never been able to forgive herself.

Queen and the children had to use the back door for entry and exit. Money couldn't entirely remove all barriers. Instead of the brick main street and a direct walk to the intersection of Pecan Street, Queen and the children navigated a series of allies.

The streets were muddy, indented with huge puddles. The mucky water was cold and full of grit. Queen fought to keep first Elly and then Walt from playing in the mud.

They walked under clotheslines of wash hanging and black children playing stick ball. Elly wanted to stop and talk to the children. Queen pulled her by the hand, not knowing how to tell Elly she would be rejected once the children's parents told them not to play with her.

Queen wanted to pray before she opened the door to

the bank. She couldn't. How could a just God hear her prayers, especially here? She pushed the door open with one arm while she held Walt's hand. Walt in turn held Elly's hand. Queen felt a chill in her spine and shoulders before it came over her entire body. She was struck by how the bank looked exactly the same as it had when she and Richard Watersong left for New Orleans, so many years ago.

The young clerks at the counter may not have been alive near the turn of the century. Still, their eyes fixed on her, convincing Queen they all knew her story. The sense of shame was overwhelming. How odd she felt the flush of it now, now that it was too late, now when it didn't matter. Why didn't she feel it as a girl?

"May I see Mrs. Eleanor Watersong?" Queen asked.

"I will see if she is in her office," answered a young clerk in a dark waistcoat and trousers.

Queen held each child's hand, aware she had stopped all business in the bank and all eyes were gazing upon her. In a moment, the young clerk returned and stated, "Mrs. Eleanor Watersong will see you in her office, ma'am."

Eleanor rose to meet Queen, then quickly turned her head to the side. She tried to turn back a little too deliberately. Although as sober as Queen was capable, the odor of alcoholic beverages from her breath was pungent. Queen thought to herself the odor must be especially strong to a lady.

The women's eyes met, acknowledging each other, yet before Eleanor could comment, she noticed Walt and Elly moving from behind their mother's dress.

"Please introduce me to the children, Queen." Eleanor's countenance revealed she was forcing down the initial shock of seeing her husband's paramour and his illegitimate children in her office.

Queen's heart-shaped face released the stern countenance which had become normal and smiled. She rubbed the back of Walt's hair. "This is Walt."

Eleanor bent down to the child's level. She said, "Did you know I had a Walt?" Even before the question she had inadvertently invited, her eyes began to tear.

Elly reached her hand to Eleanor's hand. "What happened to your Walt?"

"He went to be with Jesus." Eleanor turned her face away and rose, looking for something to wipe her tears.

Elly said, "My other brother went to be with Jesus too. She does have bright red hair, Momma, like you said."

Eleanor composed herself with a soft laugh. "I am afraid the red comes from a bottle these days, Queen." Eleanor lifted a dainty milk glass candy dish off her desk. She leaned back down to give Walt a piece of divinity. She handed him one of the creamy white balls.

Walt rejected the pecan topped delicacy and swung back behind Queen.

Elly said, "Walt don't talk."

Queen interjected, "He's just shy."

"You're not shy, are you Elly? I miss my kids. Would you give me a hug?" Elly threw her arms around Eleanor with such force Eleanor had to brace herself.

Walt began to throw a fit on the floor. The antic was so unexpected it clearly took Eleanor aback. Queen grabbed him in a bear hug and gradually the noise dissipated.

Queen looked around the office to determine if there was anything Walt's fit might break. She realized it was

Richard Watersong's old office. Well, of course it was. How odd she had not realized it sooner? This was where she had made the fateful decisions which set her life on such a shameful path.

There was nothing left of Richard Watersong in the office. The décor was entirely Eleanor. The walls were adorned from photographs of her sons in graduation and wedding ceremonies to the civic awards from women's temperance and suffrage organizations.

Queen straightened her back and pooled all her courage to the sticking point. "I came to apologize."

Eleanor leaned back up and faced Queen while the children played with their teddy bears. "Queen, I forgave you many years ago." Eleanor's face grew sterner. "And then I forgave myself for choosing a faithless, wicked man."

Queen said, "You will never know how sorry I am or how much I have truly wronged you." She began to cry and Eleanor put a hand on her shoulder before finally holding Queen. "This means so much to me, Eleanor."

Eleanor said, "Call me Ellie."

"Ellie, could I impose on you to watch the twins for just a little while? My parents have passed and I can't count on my family. I only need run a couple of errands."

Eleanor gave the children an apprehensive look. "What kind of business?"

Queen answered, "Short, very short. I need to talk to an attorney no more than an hour, I promise."

Eleanor looked at the children. Walt had tired himself to the point he had curled into a ball while Ellie was pushing one panda bear into another. When Eleanor looked back to Queen, she was down the hall like a shot.

Queen didn't pause, but she slowed to read the sign she had seen so many times in her youth. *A heart at peace gives life to the body, but envy rots the bones, Proverbs 14:30.* The sign had been above her when she worked at the bank. She thought it curious how she never paid attention back then. The whole time her bones had rotted with envy for the woman whom she now entrusted with the only love left in her life.

Queen exited the bank and walked along the same path Dock Baxter had taken over twenty years ago to the stables. She walked through the old Spanish style square, turning south on Fredonia Street. The footbridge over Bonita Creek had been replaced by a bridge capable of supporting vehicles.

With every step she thought about the path she had chosen all those many years ago; how many opportunities to deviate, to step off line, and change her stars.

The brown grass crunched under her feet as she neared the creek. The leaves of the oaks along the creek had turned orange or fallen away, and the blooms had not yet formed on the dogwoods and crepe myrtles. Only the dull evergreen of the pines provided color. She kicked off her shoes and felt the stick of the tough brown grass under her feet.

The words from so long ago "Some women should not be mothers." The words had crushed her even though she denied she was with child. She had wanted the child with every fiber of her being.

The stable was no longer there. She found it was replaced by an auto repair garage. Gone were the horses, the hay, the corrals, and water troughs. Gone was the sweet smell of hay and the sour horse manure from the cart where the stalls were mucked.

The old horse barn was now full of automobiles and they were stacked in the yard, including wrecked vehicles stored where the corrals had once stood. She walked to the front of the building and took a seat on a bench next to the wall.

After a time, a young man wearing greasy overalls walked from one of the large open doors and approached her. She was dressed in an expensive lavender dress and a small flat matching hat, but years of hard living had brought a demise to her potent beauty.

"You can't sit there. The bench is for my customers. Not proper to have a colored person sit in front of my business."

Queen apologized, "I'm sorry. I remember many years ago when this was a stable. I just wanted to sit here for a minute. Perhaps you could rent the bench to me for just a little while?" Queen extended a twenty-dollar bill to the young man.

The young man smiled as he grabbed the money. "I expect a little while ain't gonna hurt nothing." He turned to go back to his work.

"Thank you. I need to rest a moment." Queen looked back into a dark, cloud-filled sky. She removed a little bottle from her purse. Queen removed the cork from the small, clear bottle of a transparent fluid and greedily drank it down.

She traced shapes on the clouds of all the moments in life she wanted to change. She was mesmerized. Then she snapped back into the moment. Her body didn't move. She could no longer feel her feet or her hands and then she looked back into the clouds, expelling her last breath.

Eleanor had found a pencil and paper for the children. She sat down on the floor of her office with them. Elly placed her teddy bear in a chair and took the pencil and paper. Walt now chose to play with Elly's bear.

Elly asked, "What are we going to eat?"

"I don't have anything but candy. Your mom should be back soon."

Elly said, "No. She is not coming back for a long time."

Eleanor snapped her head toward the child. "Elly, of course she is coming back."

"No, she told us it was like a story. We were going to meet our fairy godmother who would take care of us."

Eleanor felt a coldness in the pit of her stomach. For years she had suffered from this woman's hand. Yet all the hard feelings had long since poured over and past her. Eleanor replayed the conversation with Queen in her mind. She reached the telephone and called the police.

CHAPTER 33: JUST AS I AM

Ray Elliott got roped into helping Sheriff Gault again. He had done so for weeks, killing time before the trial over the Grant farm. Thirty years of chasing outlaws had rendered farm work even more monotonous than it had seemed three decades ago, and he had found it drudgery then.

The sheriff's Model T Ford was bouncing over the poor road as fast as they dared without blowing out a tire. Before noon they were nearing Kilgore and began crossing camps of squatters. Some families slept in cars while others had hung quilts over a barbed wire fence and then onto stakes to make a tent shelter.

As he neared tall derricks in the distance, the tents began to appear better ordered. They were flanked by batten board buildings with signs denoting the "Magnolia Camp" under a board with an arrow pointing north, "Gulf Camp." He found himself on the wide, muddy South Commerce street facing the train depot. The street was almost impassable. What wasn't covered in trucks was covered in wagons with their long rigs of mule teams, while the remainder of the earth was littered with drill piping stacked in neat rows. Everywhere was the deafening noise of the boilers turning the rotary tables of drilling rigs.

In response to Ray Elliott's many questions, Sheriff Gault gave him a brief lecture setting forth the current lay of the land. "Back at the end of the summer, there probably weren't five hundred people living here. There are several thousand now. Malcom Crim and Roy Laird are organizing an incorporated town. It started with the Lou Della Crim Well. The drilling really took off after the Lanthrop Well."

Ray Elliott said, "Denzel told me about the Crim Well. The Lanthrop was still in progress."

Sheriff Gault continued, "The Longview Chamber of Commerce put up ten thousand dollars for the first Gregg County well. Ever since then, oil folks figured no matter where you drill, from the Lanthrop down to Joinerville, you can hit a gusher."

Elliott asked, "How are you fixed for law?"

"It's us and a couple of rangers. The deputies for both Rusk and Gregg County are quitting to go drilling. If you got a speck of ground, you can drill a well. Own an acre, you might drill three."

The two men got out and walked further up Commerce Street. They turned east and arrived at the First Presbyterian Church. Ray Elliott possessed considerable boom town law enforcement experience. One of the many failures of infrastructure in a place booming from five hundred to ten thousand people were jail facilities.

Trotlining citizens accused of crimes was not uncommon in boom towns. However, nothing prepared Ray Elliott for the scene inside the church.

At the front of the many pews of shackled men was a powerful looking figure dressed in a silver suit, white shirt, and black bolo tie. He wore a leather two-gun holster rig with silver accents holding a pair of nickel-plated Colt 1911s, topped by a Cinco Peso badge on a bright white, starched shirt.

The glamourous looking man standing between the alter and the pulpit winked to acknowledge his old friend's entrance. Ray Elliott nodded back.

The finely adorned fellow said in a loud voice, "Three stabbed, one shot through the leg, and one through the shoulder. You forgive me, preacher and ladies of the choir for speaking plain. I understand young single men working fourteen-hour days doing hard dangerous work. Of course, you would stand in line for hours to smell the perfume and feel the embrace of a woman. It's why there is Miss Magdeline's dance house. But then you go and question some gal's honor, or you get jealous, or you try to take liberties, all of which causes the others to fight you until I get there and got no way to know who started what or when."

There was a low rumble as the men began muttering to defend themselves and make excuses. The speaker raised his voice over the crowd and it reverberated through the church. "Stop it. You're all guilty. Here's what we are going to do. These good church people are going to take each of your names and descriptions down in my book. Only after you listen to this fine parson and come to Jesus at the altar, will you get released. I ever arrest any of you again and we are going to find us a real jail and you'll find you didn't really get off easy today. Agreed?"

The response was less than unanimous, which lead to an additional lecture. "Some of you are not happy with the way the rangers are keeping the peace. I hear you whining about how bad rangers treat folks. Wrong thinking; wrong thinking for law enforcement purposes, the governor is on the verge of declaring martial law. Boys, soldiers break batons over your heads until there is order. There won't be any Miss Magdeline's or Ms. Candace's Ballroom or anywhere else except for the soldier boys. Y'all will wish you appreciated ranger justice then."

The speaker stepped to the back of the church where Sheriff Gault and Ray Elliott awaited, while the pastor and choir began the hymn, *Just As I Am*.

When he reached the entranceway, Ray Elliott greeted the man with a solid swat across the shoulder, "*El Solo Lobo*." The phrase was a moniker for famed ranger Lone Wolf Gonzallas. Ray Elliott grinned. "I feared seeing you between the altar and the pulpit. You get too close to either one and the Lord will smite this place with lightening. I could almost see the sparks from all those shackles. Be a fine story. Make us the only rangers in the State Cemetery smote to death by the Almighty."

Lone Wolf smiled. He slammed his hand across Ray Elliott's coat, knocking more dust from the garment. "If the adjutant general is going to dig you old timers up and put badges on you, the least he could do is buy you a new suit."

Sheriff Gault joined in the revelry. "If you two are half as ornery with the outlaws as you are with each other, then we'll have this place cleaned up in no time."

Lone Wolf said, "Got to give Elliott a hard time. Haven't seen him since Sherman." His face turned somber. "If you would have given me a chance, I would have holed up in the vault with you."

Ray Elliott took a more serious tone. "I know you would have. Why I didn't give you a chance."

"I'm being serious. If I had ever thought they would really drum you out of the service, then I would have resigned." Lone Wolf nodded. It was obvious he was seeking some acknowledgement of the sentiment.

Ray Elliott's smile reappeared. "It's harder to get out of the ranger service than you could ever know. I must have resigned five times already. The governor and the adjutant general just act like I didn't do it."

All three men laughed. Sheriff Gault stated the obvious. "Even big muckedy-muck Ranger Captains get voluntold."

Over his shoulder and past the foyer door, the sanctuary filled with a sermon. The prisoners shared their sins and professed Jesus. People, mostly men, had journeyed from all over Arkansas, Louisiana, Missouri, Mississippi, and further in hopes of earning enough to beat the Depression, for money to hold on to their homes, or to buy doctors for children suffering from diseases like polio. After they arrived, some lost their way in the ups and downs of the oil business, squandered the money they coveted, and turned their backs on the obligations which drove them here.

Ray Elliott congratulated Lone Wolf. "You reminded them of the men they came here to be."

"The real test is whether they can straighten up and fly right for a little while anyway. Let's go over to the depot: the Gregg County sheriff is there. We can draw up a plan to pull this place together."

Sheriff Gault asserted, "We get order in this field..."

Lone Wolf said, "We can stop the hi-jacking, the robbing, and the killings. What we can't do is limit production. The governor wants to set allowable production per well and there is no way we can do it."

The lawmen met to formulate a plan. They set a target for the number of deputies to request each Commissioners

Court provide. They also determined the number of rangers to request from the adjutant general, and other resources from the governor.

The plans included coordinating with adjoining counties, forming local police departments, jail facilities, and new technology such as patrol cars with radios. They also proposed initiatives for encouraging merchants and companies to provide private security.

Sheriff Gault was scribbling down the final notes from the discussion when Ray Elliott and Lone Wolf stepped onto the long, narrow porch of the depot.

Ray Elliott said, “I never will forget seeing you in front of that courthouse with a gun on each hip, a Thompson in one hand and a shotgun in the other.”

“You know, if we had been authorized to shoot at their legs, you never would have had to go into the vault and there would be a whole lot of folks dragging around Sherman.” Lone Wolf looked away.

Ray Elliott said “Might have been only the start. You know as well as I do once you stop firing over their heads and start firing into a mob, you better be ready to kill them all. I don’t know if I was ready to kill anyone. How many people needed to die in Sherman to get a guilty man a trial? But sometimes I think—” He paused. “Best I never know.”

Lone Wolf walked away while Ray Elliott watched the derricks rising over the world’s richest acre.

CHAPTER 34: RECOVERING HONOR

Ever since the first day they were in court, Ray Elliott had wanted to have a discussion with Richie. He was proud to see the young man make a successful lawyer. More, he was moved by the fact Richie held no animosity toward him.

After all, he had lied about the boy's father being dead. Out of context, it seemed like a pretty rotten thing to do. He found excuses to call Richie and set up a meeting. Before he would call though, he would find another excuse to put it off until tomorrow, the next day and so forth.

He was trying to admit to himself he really wanted to see Eleanor. There was no doubt he didn't have the courage to see her. Odd how the same man who stared down blood thirsty lynch mobs and cut-throat outlaw gangs couldn't face one woman. Somewhere he had heard parties to a lawsuit should only communicate through their attorneys, hence Richie.

While working the oilfield with Lone Wolf and Sheriff Gault, he was informed there was a meeting in Longview to discuss calling for martial law. He borrowed Lone Wolf's convertible after a series of instructions and admonishments.

Ray Elliott pulled into a parking spot on the corner of Green and Methvin Streets in front of the newly built Gregg Hotel. A sign labeled 'East Texas Chamber of Commerce' led him to the dining room. He passed ivory walls, grand chandeliers, and velvet rugs along the way to a dining room with walnut paneling, bright silk drapes, and mahogany tables and chairs.

Ray Elliott's suit had been dry cleaned, yet he still chided himself. It was out of date and this room was full of well-dressed men and women. He didn't see Richie. It was a big room. A hand waved from across the way; it was James Denzel.

Ray Elliott intended to make his way over to greet the man. However, he didn't want to interrupt the speaker and draw attention to himself.

Much of the speech was Greek to Ray Elliott. Words like woodbine, sandstone, pounds per square inch, and permeable rock meant nothing to him. He was able to decipher there were two competing plans before the regulatory authority, the Texas Railroad Commission. The goal of these plans was to stop the free-fall of oil prices before it was cheaper than water.

The speaker claimed neither plan was an option unless the governor declared a state of lawlessness. He contended such existed and was so severe it amounted to insurrection necessitating a declaration of martial law. Otherwise, producers would continue selling oil in excess of the amount allowed, a commodity referred to as "hot oil."

After two more speakers, Denzel took the floor. "Price controls will always fail and martial law is unconstitutional. The answer is organizing independent oilmen. Convincing independent oil producers to support reasonable regulation for the long-term viability of the market and the formation is the only answer."

Ray Elliott didn't notice Richie at his side until a hand tugged on his suit sleeve. "Richie, I didn't see you come in."

Richie spoke in a quiet tone, motioning toward Denzel. “Sharp fellow, tells me he has already got two producing wells on the Grant farm and is drilling two more now.”

Ray Elliott whispered back. “True. He calls them offset wells. He told me he has an idea for a refinery out there. He needs more money and wants us to get this trial finished.”

Richie said, “Good choice if you have to have a receiver.”

“Why is it taking so long to get to trial?”

Richie snickered a little. “This isn’t long. It was filed last fall and we will probably reach trial sometime this summer. I think I saw an order setting jury trial for August. For a big lawsuit, a year is short.”

Ray Elliott appeared as though he had been deflated. Richie asked, “Cecil Grant didn’t explain that you were going to have to give up a year of your life to protect Martha and the grandkids, did he?”

Ray Elliott looked around the packed ballroom. “Let’s step outside.”

Once they reached the sidewalk, Ray Elliott said, “How do you know?”

“What, that you didn’t really buy Cecil Grant’s interest? You are only trying to keep a promise to a dying friend.” Richie shook his head. “You lawmen really don’t follow gossip at all, do you?”

Ray Elliott looked at Richie. His intentions and secrets were laid bare by Richie in such a cavalier manner.

Richie continued, “I followed your career, since law school anyway; not difficult, between catching murderers, putting down riots, and chasing outlaws.”

Ray Elliott looked at his boots. He was embarrassed:

embarrassed to be so transparent when he thought he was deceptive, embarrassed by a career which put him in the headlines because it was easier to list him than the entire company or all the local officers.

"I hated you for years. I was in law school in Waco when I searched the newspapers for myself. I had heard rumors, even stories Queen had sent letters back to her family about my father being alive and living in the Caribbean or South America or Panama with her. I found the New Orleans Picayune article describing his embezzlement."

Richie's voice was breaking with emotion. He paused a moment and Ray Elliott looked away to give the young man room. He continued. "How he had been seen in New Orleans with his colored mistress. I was devastated. He was my hero who died trying to avenge my sainted grandfather. Then I put it together. I knew what you did and why. I think my mother knew, but I never asked her."

Richie fought back emotion. "I suppose I started researching your career because I needed to be proud of someone. I needed to believe men could be noble."

Ray Elliott interjected, "I was a liar, and then I couldn't live with it. Richard Watersong called it right—without honor."

"Honor is choosing to make the world more just. It is the only thing we can do to evidence we were here. Richard Watersong stole from my family, murdered my grandfather, and left my mother for a child. You tried to make it better; makes you noble. The fact you couldn't live the lie makes you moral."

Ray Elliott fought back his own emotion. "I have thought a lot about why I really wanted to see you and your mother. I believe I have been afraid to admit it to myself. I have kept people away, scared to disappoint them the way I, the way I–" Ray Elliott struggled for a way to continue before he finally stopped. He changed the subject. "Do you intend to out me about protecting Martha?"

"No, but Wesley Toben, Richard Watersong's lawyer, will bring it out. It proves you took subject to Cecil Grant's encumbrances. Lawyers would say you are not a good faith purchaser for value, so you are exactly like Cecil. Lawyer didn't explain this to you?"

"I don't have one."

"You need one. Your only hope is tacking onto Cecil Grant's claim for adverse possession. I assumed someone had counseled you and it was why you lived on the Grant farm. You and Cecil Grant have been in continuous, peaceable, and adverse possession for more than twenty-five years; not bad when I say it out loud." Richie beamed with pride.

"Why are you telling me this? Doesn't your mother's title depend on a community property claim based on Richard Watersong's foreclosure?"

"Mother's orders are simple. Do not let Richard Watersong win."

"Not smart business is it?"

"Mother takes the long view. We are in litigation in Nacogdoches, the Texas Supreme Court, Dallas, Rusk County, and a half dozen other claims and disputes which haven't risen to lawsuits. You realize Richard Watersong is literally the living dead. There are cases of reappearance after people have been declared dead. However, no one ever turned out to be alive who had the legal wherewithal to set aside a presumption of death. There is no precedent for this mess." Richie shrugged.

Ray Elliott's tone was more upbeat. "All I want is to see Cecil pass on his family's legacy to Martha and the grandchildren. Sounds like we are on the same side. Why don't you represent me?"

Richie said, "Because it is a conflict. Mother can waive it though. Ask her."

CHAPTER 35: ELLIE

Ray Elliott had bought a new suit. It was as grey as the hat he held in his hand. He knocked on the door again.

The door swung open. A stooped black lady in a housecoat holding a cane appeared. "What you want?"

"My name is Ray Ell–"

She interrupted, "I know your name. We heard you were back. What do you want?"

"I would like to see Mrs. Watersong."

She turned and yelled inside the house with deafening force. "Elliott's train done pulled back into the station."

Ray Elliott concluded, "You're Yolonda, aren't you?"

"Yes, I am. I told her not to throw herself at you. She would scare you off. Still, you got no business running out on my Ellie."

"I didn't think you would still be keeping house." Ray Elliott didn't really know what to say, so he had blurted out what was going through his mind.

"I just live here. We have had a housekeeper for a long time."

Ray Elliott no longer knew what to say. He had rehearsed what he would say when the door was opened and none of this had seemed foreseeable. He feared being the butt of any more jokes so there was a long uncomfortable silence.

Finally, he asked, "Is she coming down?"

Yolonda smirked. "Ellie is not up there. She took Walt to see a doctor in Lufkin. She is always trying doctors for the boy."

Ray Elliott didn't know this Walt's connection to Eleanor. He had expressed no romantic intentions, so maybe Richie didn't tell him Ellie had someone in her life. Of course, she had someone in her life. No one just walks back through the door thirty years later and finds the person they cared about has carried a torch for them all these years. He pronounced himself an idiot. "Please tell her I stopped by to see her about a business matter."

"What, did you hear a train whistle?" Ray Elliott turned his back to Yolonda. She said, "I'm old. I had a filter when I was younger. Richie told us you might visit, but we didn't know when. Come in and have a seat; she will be back anytime."

"I really don't think I should."

"Get in here. Being old is not only good for speaking my mind; I can be rude, too. Come in here and let me get you a glass of tea. Ellie wants to see you."

She showed Ray Elliott to a seat in the parlor. Yolonda was slow and walked with a cane. Ray Elliott decided when Eleanor arrived, he would limit his conversation to the issue of unifying against Richard Watersong. The guilt over the lie continued to weigh on him. He had to steel himself to the purpose before him. He would make no apologies, have no regrets, no weakness.

He was lost deep in thought when a little girl came running through the room, swinging a large stuffed animal. It was a giraffe, and she was bumping it into the furniture. Ray Elliott jumped to secure a lamp. He recognized the lamp as one with a multi-colored glass shade like people bragged on having bought in New York or Europe.

The girl stopped as quick as she had appeared. "My red mommy will be mad if you break her lamp."

Ray Elliott decided it was too much to expect the child to be grateful he had saved the lamp, so he moved the next issue. "Your 'red mommy'?"

"I call her the red mommy because we are both Ellies and she has red hair. She is not my real mommy—my black mommy." The child looked up at Ray Elliott with an incredulous expression.

"Your black mommy must have black hair."

The child appeared annoyed. "No."

He concluded it must all make perfect sense in her mind. The investigator saw an opportunity to satisfy his curiosity. He kneeled down. "So, your name is Ellie. Who is Walt?"

The child studied him before answering. "Walt is my brother, but he can't talk."

Ray Elliott reached over in a slow, deliberate manner to pet the giraffe. "Then who is this giraffe?" The child beamed.

There had been times over the years when child witnesses were the key to cases. Parents were always on guard. Children, even children told what to say by parents, could sometimes be lured off script by moving between subjects and establishing a better rapport.

By the time he heard the automobile pull into the driveway, Ray Elliott knew everything the child knew. He listened to stories about Jerry the giraffe, Walt, and Cuba. He also learned about the black mommy and the red mommy. Yolonda had brought him a glass of tea and excused herself after giving him a look like she was well aware of his reconnaissance operation.

The little girl and Ray Elliott were playing with the giraffe on the floor when she jumped and ran to the door. When the door swung open, Ray Elliott was holding Jerry the giraffe and moving himself off the floor to stand. Eleanor was taking off an enormous floppy hat. She placed it on spindle-style rack next to Ray Elliott's hat and stared at her former suitor.

Walt walked through the door, and then turned, running back into the yard. Eleanor reached for the boy and missed. She chased him into the yard and managed to bear hug him. Ray Elliott started to run to the door, then he feared his presence would further upset the child, so he retreated toward the back of the parlor.

Little Elly was able to calm Walt, telling him how nice the man had been to her and how they had played with Jerry. Eleanor asked Elly to take Walt upstairs and change into play clothes.

Eleanor walked back into the parlor. "Train get back?"

Ray Elliott answered, "I thought Yolonda had all the train jokes covered."

Eleanor smiled. "You can't imagine. Thirty years of 'I told you so' and train jokes. Don't you begin to complain about Yolonda."

"I expect it has been tough." Ray Elliott grinned in response to Eleanor.

"Well, as long as you understand it has been tough. My husband killed my father and ran off with a child maid. I raised two sons by myself. Kept two failed banks afloat. Built those failed banks into a financial juggernaut in a world which has no respect for businesswomen. Then I survived the greatest run on banks in history. All while living with the shame my husband chose a girl over me.

Which wasn't a bad enough slap to my ego, because my lover chose a fast-bound train over me? It has not been tough you–you–ignorant fool."

"I am sorry, Ellie."

"Well 'sorry' makes it ok, because I didn't add the part about how thirty years later, the former child maid shows up with two special needs kids." Eleanor changed her tone to a whisper, "One can't even talk because he is so messed up. Then their alcoholic mommy walks out into town and drinks poison after promising me she was coming back." Eleanor was in tears. "I think I hate her so much more for what she did to these children than what she did to me."

Ray Elliott stepped forward and pulled Ellie to him. The most ignorant idea of his life came over him. He had lied to Eleanor, failed Eleanor on every level, and unintentionally mocked her as a woman for thirty years. Yet if he kissed her, somehow, in an inexplicably ignorant way, it could still be alright.

Ray Elliott leaned Eleanor back and rested her on his hand. He leaned closer to kiss her with all the passion for her he had denied.

She pushed him away. "No. You cannot walk into my life after thirty years, you fool."

She sat back into a chair while he stepped backwards toward the wall. Ray Elliott said, "I came here about a business matter."

Eleanor looked away, composing herself. "What is the business matter?"

"Here is the deal. I am only here for Martha. I made a promise to Cecil Grant. If the land is as rich as James Denzel tells me, then she can live well on much less than the full two hundred acres. Permit your son to represent us both in common and I will make sure you have the lion's share."

She sneered. "Why didn't you start with your business proposal?"

"I thought you wanted me to kiss you."

"I did thirty years ago. Now I don't know. I am mad. You have no right to expect me to get over thirty years of mad in a day."

"I don't have any right to anything, Ellie."

"Just when you are hopeless, you do something to make me think you are worth believing in again, like sticking up for the Grant family." Ellie stood, then reached up to Ray Elliott and kissed him.

"If you want to be useful, you can take Yolonda to the doctor this afternoon."

Ray Elliott stammered.

Eleanor's demeanor turned colder. "I am fifty-three years old and have to raise seven-year-old twins, one of whom can't speak. In addition, Yolonda is in pain all the time from arthritis. She is losing her eyesight and takes a lot of care. She is not a joy."

Ray Elliott nodded.

"I'm not a young widow to sit with you on a courting couch. If you are going to keep time with me, you are going to make yourself useful." Eleanor's hazel eyes softened and faded, appearing to have replaced the light green with more of a light blue hue, matching her dress.

No one spoke to Ray Elliott like Eleanor had: not the adjutant general, and not the governor. He considered walking out and then he saw her face and eyes soften. She wasn't really chewing him out or belittling him. She was a proud woman, and this was her way of seeking help.

"Can't Queen's family take the children?"

Eleanor shrugged and looked around before answering. "Richard has no use for his children; besides, I wouldn't let Richard near those precious babies. Queen's sisters disowned her over Richard. They are unequivocal about not raising Richard Watersong's children. No one can take two more mouths to feed, especially one who needs so much care, in the midst of this depression."

With considerable hesitation, Ray Elliott opened his arms, but she declined his embrace. "I miss my Walt. Richie really doesn't need me. He was always independent. Walt was my baby. I blame his death on Richard. I think he wanted to prove himself, to make up for the way everyone gossiped about his father. Walt wanted to be a hero. "Eleanor was quick in composing herself. "Join us for lunch. I have some potato soup and corn bread."

Lunch was an experience. There was an outburst of anger by Walt. Elly sulked because she wanted something else. Yolonda was disagreeable. Poor Eleanor kept them all in check and played the gracious hostess.

Lunch was a circus, yet Ray Elliott found a comfort in it. Amongst the chaos was the power and warmth of Eleanor's love holding them all together. Ray Elliott got the directions and information for the doctor's appointment. Yolonda was less than enthusiastic about his company, and she let him know it. Yolonda asked Eleanor in a loud voice, "What if he sees a train and takes off like a dog chasing a car."

"I have escorted bandidos to the gallows, rapists and killers to prison. I figure I can get one cantankerous old lady to the doctor and back."

Eleanor interjected, "Yolonda, it is a beautiful spring

day. You always used to talk about azaleas starting to bloom. I saw some this morning."

Yolonda ignored the comment. She turned to Ray Elliott. "I used to like you before you became a hobo."

"Lucky me."

CHAPTER 36: TRIAL BEGINS

Wesley Toben held a piece of paper with his right hand and pointed at it while walking up and down the jury rail. He walked the short distance twice in silence before he spoke.

"This is a conveyance. There are thousands, probably tens of thousands of these sheets of paper in the county clerk's office below us on the second floor. You likely have one for your home, family farm. All over our county are drilling rigs run by hard-working people proud for work to feed their families."

He swung the paper back up near to his head. "Those rigs turn because somewhere there is a piece of paper which conveyed an oil and gas lease and another piece of paper conveying the capital to finance it."

Wesley Toben had lowered the paper. He paused and raised it again. "You see, the words on this paper and those like it are the bedrock of private property. Those words have created the greatest economic engine in the history of man, because for thousands of years, unless your first name was pharaoh, or king, prince, duke, count, baron, or something similar, words on paper held no meaning for you. Only in America could John Doe own land. It didn't matter whether John Doe's parents were royalty or the lowest of beggars. It's why our ancestors beat a path here."

Wesley Toben walked toward the counsel table where his client Richard Watersong was seated. He turned abruptly and raised the paper again. "If my name is on this paper, then I own the property. You may not like me. In fact, after having to miss work yesterday and today, I expect you don't. It may be worse; maybe you find out I am a faithless husband, a thief only saved from jail by the statute of limitations. I expect we pull those tens of thousands of papers downstairs and you will see some adulterers, some thieves, some folks we wouldn't have to supper, and yet they are all still owners."

He stopped and paused again. "The people who built this nation understood that if the law determines these papers only mean what they say if you happen to be one of the good people, the special people, then we might as well go back to kings. I mean, those were supposed to be the people chosen by God."

He looked again at the paper in his hand. "You see, if the words on this paper mean nothing, then the words on all those other papers mean nothing."

Wesley Toben adjusted his documents at the lectern. He said, "You are going to find out a man named Cecil Grant borrowed money against this land many years ago. He failed to pay it back and lost the land. We all know it is the way the world works. Mr. Watersong had to foreclose on the note to recover the money Cecil Grant didn't pay back. Richard Watersong allowed Cecil Grant and his family to live on the property."

Wesley Toben paused before continuing. "There wasn't much Mr. Watersong could do with the land until oil was discovered, so he was magnanimous and let the Grants live there. Cecil Grant repaid him with treachery and fraud by deeding the property to a man named Ray Elliott. It was a gambit to clean the title, and I will show you with my first witness how badly the plan failed.

Richard wants to put this land in production so it can help lift us out of this terrible depression. He has already been delayed by a year while this lawsuit has been pending."

Wesley Toben stepped back to the counsel table and raised his tone and the paper again. "Ask yourself how we got in this Great Depression. There was nothing to back up the words on papers. People panicked, because if these words mean nothing on this page then they mean nothing on all the other pages, causing the market to crash, private property to fail, and our nation to face the greatest threat to its existence since the Civil War."

Judge R.T. Brown leaned forward over the bench. "The defense may make its opening statement."

CHAPTER 37: THE FIRST WITNESS

Richie rose, buttoned his top button, and smiled at the jury. "May it please the Court, ladies and gentlemen of the jury."

Richie walked to the side of the lectern and moved up the rail along the jury box. "A rose by any other name would smell as sweet. We all know Shakespeare's words. Juliet is explaining the fact Romeo is a Montague is meaningless." Richie was aware of the fact Montague was an alias for Richard Watersong, so he stopped on the word and stared in his father's cold eyes as he said it. The father cast only the shell of his robust appearance from a year ago.

"The law is not stupid. There are places in this county where the population went from several hundred to many thousands of people overnight. Men and women striving to escape the hopelessness of depression were thrown together in Kilgore, Overton, Joinerville, a half dozen oil company camps, dance halls, cafes, stores, and everywhere else. Somewhere, love will blossom and there will be a proposal of marriage. We know many won't go buy a license and don't have money for a formal wedding. They will get a jackleg preacher to exchange vows, or they might not. What they will do is build a life together. They will forge a union through good times, bad times, perhaps build a family, bringing children into this world. In short, the same way our ancestors who moved here built strong families without necessarily always having a marriage certificate."

He paused, facing the opposing lawyer before turning back to the jury. Richie made his point. "Texas law tells us what I have described is a marriage with all the rights and duties of any marriage. Why? Because God makes roses; we just name them."

Richie continued, "Another example: the first Texans had to convert to Catholicism to own land. It was what the Mexican government required. Most of our ancestors were Protestants. A fair number of good Baptist and Methodist were not going to convert, so they settled here in these Redlands. Folks who carved farms out of the wilderness put the land to use for the benefit of everyone. The law devised a series of rules which permitted their claims on their own farms to be accepted as legal title."

Richie stopped at the lectern. "One of those laws established title if someone claims land for twenty-five years. Other laws have lesser years if improvements to the property were made. Cecil Grant believed he repaid the debt, so he surely believed it was his land, like his father before him. Cecil Grant conveyed the land to his old friend, Texas Ranger Captain Ray Elliott, to protect Cecil's wife, Martha, from crooks and land swindlers."

Richie made a gesture with an open hand to his mother and pointed. "In the alternative, meaning if you don't agree with me, then I submit that any interest you find for Richard Watersong is the community property estate of my mother, Eleanor Watersong. I am sure you were wondering during jury selection how my family reached this odd state of division. Well, it all starts with murder."

Wesley Toben jumped to his feet. "Objection. Your Honor, may we approach?"

Judge R.T. Brown motioned the attorneys to the bench.

Wesley Toben spoke in a near whisper. "Your Honor, defense counsel had to spend much of his life without a father, admittedly, because my client embezzled and ran off in an illicit affair. I have no objection to those matters, even though they were thirty years ago. However, I have been advised defense counsel has formed a delusion about his father killing his grandfather, even though a man named Dock Baxter was charged. In fact, there is no doubt Dock Baxter would have been convicted had he not been killed by Mr. Ray Elliott."

Richie responded, "Courtrooms are about truth, and the truth is Richard Watersong is a killer."

Judge R.T. Brown said, "I knew Lukas Halten. I have heard all the rumors and salacious gossip. We won't have rumors in this courtroom. You will approach and we will have a hearing prior to any questions about Richard Watersong murdering Lukas Halten."

Richie said, "Yes sir." Richie stepped back to the lectern. "Well, you will hear from a number of credible witnesses about how long Cecil Grant's family worked their farm. You will hear from a hero Texas Ranger Captain. You will hear from one of the most successful businesswomen in Texas—a host of imminently credible people."

Richie pointed to Richard Watersong. "And you will hear from someone who is not. After you have heard the evidence, you will agree with all the people in this county who have called this property the Grant place for near three quarters of a century." Richie returned to the counsel table and sat next to his mother. Ray Elliott was seated to her left.

Judge R.T. Brown announced, "Counsel, you may call your first witness."

Wesley Toben stood, pausing before turning to the gallery. There was a substantial crowd. Directly behind the defense table sat Martha Grant and her family. Wesley Toben ignored her and projected his voice toward the back of the room. "Plaintiff calls Ray Elliott."

Ray Elliott walked to the witness stand. Judge R.T. Brown advised the jury. "All the witnesses were sworn, and the rule invoked prior to opening statements."

Wesley Toben said, "Please tell the jury your name and a little about yourself."

"My name is Ray Elliott. I was a lawman. I am in the process of retiring."

"Are you retired?"

"It's complicated."

"Your lawyer called you a 'hero Texas Ranger Captain.' Tell me, are you familiar with Jack Coffee Hays, RIP Ford, or Leander McNelly?" Wesley Toben paused to watch Ray Elliott nod his head. "And I could name many more, couldn't I?"

Ray Elliott said, "Yes, all heroes, all great Ranger Captains."

"Your lawyer has you in esteemed company, doesn't he?"

"Apparently."

Wesley Toben said, "These days, each captain commands a company of rangers; so, tell the jury, which company is your command?"

"I am not assigned to a company at this time."

"You're not retired and you don't have a company because you were removed from command after Sherman.

Tell the jury in your own words why you were taken out of command."

Ray Elliott looked at Eleanor, then he turned to the jury. "I failed to protect a prisoner from a mob."

"You couldn't protect a prisoner from a bunch of farmers. They literally blew up the courthouse, lynched the prisoner, who was dead already by the way, then they burned an entire colored neighborhood on your watch, and you didn't get a scratch, did you?"

Ray Elliott paused, lowering his head.

Wesley Toben continued, "It's all true, isn't it?"

"Yes." Ray Elliott looked to Eleanor. She showed the same steely public persona which had built her banking interest.

Wesley Toben said, "Sherman was a disaster, and it made the front page of the New York Times as well as many other newspapers. So, are you really a hero?"

"No; I'm no hero."

"In fact, you have as much as conceded you bear the responsibility for Sherman, haven't you?"

"It was my command."

Wesley Toben said, "There was another time, much earlier in your career when you were charged with apprehending another prisoner, a Dock Baxter, correct?"

"Yes."

Wesley Toben said, "I found a notation in court records in Nacogdoches stating you shot Dock Baxter. Doesn't state he was armed, was running, or was trying to harm you. So why did you shoot him?"

"It's complicated."

"Like you are a captain, but not really a captain, complicated?"

Richie said, "Objection, side bar."

Judge R.T. Brown said, "Sustained."

Ray Elliott said. "Two good men were killed trying to protect him. I made Dock Baxter a promise."

Wesley Toben repeated the phrase. "You made 'Dock Baxter a promise.' Or was it because he was the man who killed your lover's father?"

Richie objected. "Your Honor, these questions are not relevant. This is a trespass to try title suit."

Wesley Toben welcomed the opportunity to respond. He addressed the judge, but turned to face the jury. "Your Honor, it explains why Mrs. Watersong and Ray Elliott are aligned. It also shows the extent of the bias, that is to say, the obvious animosity against Mr. Richard Watersong. For thirty years, Ray Elliott has carried on an illicit affair with my client's wife. He will not only perjure himself for her, your Honor; he will literally kill for her."

Judge R.T. Brown lowered the gavel onto the pedestal. "Stop. We are going to discharge the jury for the day. Jurors, we have some matters which the court and lawyers need to address; then we will reconvene in the morning and I will direct you how much, if any, of this line of questioning to consider.

The jury was excused. Once they exited, Richie renewed his objection.

Judge R.T. Brown stated, "The jury is gone for the day. Right now, we are going to wade through this morass until I can decide how far to let it go. Continue Mr. Toben."

Wesley Toben asked. "You and Eleanor Watersong have committed adultery, haven't you?"

Ray Elliott looked at Eleanor. She continued to maintain a rigid demeanor, yet he could see the tears in the corners of her eyes. The pain she was enduring was too much for him to watch.

The pause caused Judge R.T. Brown to direct the witness. "Mr. Elliott, I need you answer the question. The jury is gone, so take your time and let me know the truth.

Ray Elliott looked to Judge R.T. Brown "We never saw it that way and still don't. I never killed for Eleanor. So, you Mr. Toben, are a liar. The biggest mistake of my life was lying for her. I couldn't live with it. Lying caused me a thirty-year exile from her." Ray Elliott turned and looked at Eleanor. The public demeanor was gone. Slow tears were trickling from her hazel eyes. "Thirty years without the light in those beautiful eyes in my life. It's my intention to marry her if she will have me?"

Judge R.T. Brown shook his head. "Gentlemen, I would like to see briefs on this matter by seven thirty so I can be ready to decide when the jury gets here at nine. As for you, Mr. Elliott, I appreciate your candor on such a delicate matter. As for your intended proposal, I suggest you seek guidance from a higher court. We are in recess in this case."

PART V

Will a Verdict Restore Honor?

CHAPTER 38: A MATTER OF HONOR

Richard Watersong had turned the hot August night into a cool breeze with the Duesenberg. He was driving fast, far too fast for the poor rural roads already burdened by the weight of moving drilling rigs and vessels of oil.

He had paid to have the car shipped from Cuba. It reminded him of his son, the Richard who grew up idolizing his father, not hating him like Richie did. The son Queen never forgave him for putting in danger. To hear Richie in court accuse him of wantonly murdering the boy's grandfather in such a matter-of-fact tone was beyond outrageous.

There was no point in bench conferences that the counsel tables and likely the jury could hear almost as well as open court. He had heard all of it, and it kept playing in his head. Richie was a walking ledger balance of what he had lost, what he had traded, what he could never have again: the love and respect of a son.

When he left Texas thirty years ago, Richard Watersong had not held much hope Richie and his brother Walt could forgive him. It was the loss of the boys and Eleanor which had motivated him to name his Cuban children by the same names.

The long-bodied Duesenberg fish-tailed around a turn, and Richard Watersong turned the wheel with all his might. His might seemed less and less these days. Still, he didn't slow; instead, he accelerated after the turn. When he saw the shack of a house, he congratulated himself on a feat of navigation. He was pondering how much this hovel looked like so many others to engender such interest.

Richard Watersong was startled by how close to the structure he had driven. Locking his brakes up hard, he barely avoided the porch. He killed the motor. Then he reached over to the passenger seat and raised a Colt pistol before opening the automobile door and standing.

When he looked back up at the porch, there was Ray Elliott standing in his trousers and gun belt. “I expected you to be with my wife.”

Ray Elliott snapped, “I always expected you would come, though I figured you would have about a dozen white cappers with you.”

“Maybe we have always misjudged each other. I thought we could talk.” Richard Watersong stepped away from the car.

Ray Elliott nodded his head at the pistol in Richard Watersong’s hand. “Take you all seven shots to talk?”

Richard Watersong looked at his pistol. “You were too modest in court today. Though I agree you’re no hero, I expect you could draw and kill me even with a pistol in my hand. I deduced this was self-defense.”

“Is it like it was self-defense when you killed Lukas Halten or do I get a better chance?”

Richard Watersong shook his head. “I didn’t kill Lukas. Lukas saved my backside more than once. To protect Eleanor from the shame of a thieving husband, he was close to negotiating a deal on the money I stole at the Henderson bank. He had all the customers paid off except one lumber company. Oh, he was prone to bluster, yelling, mostly promoting his own idealistic dreams; still, a better man never lived."

"Who do you expect me to believe killed him?"

"I heard a man on the witness stand today mention a promise and say, 'It's complicated.'"

"Didn't come off like much man on the witness stand."

Richard Watersong stepped closer and leaned against the Duesenberg. He had to smile. "I paid Toben a lot of money and fed him a considerable amount of misinformation. I am glad to hear it paid off. Now I have seen all of this trial I want to see. How about you and me settle it before Ellie has to testify?"

It was difficult to see in the near darkness; only moonlight illuminated them. The delay in response told Richard Watersong he had struck a weak spot, as intended. He plunged the sharp words deeper. "Ellie is not like you. She was born and raised here, an heir to the high and mighty. Her father's memory is near sacred in this part of the world. Toben and I have plenty to ask her. Folks always want to the see the respected and powerful brought low, especially a fine, Christian lady like Ellie."

Ray Elliott moved his hand closer to his Colt forty-five, avoiding anything which might give rise to motion in the dim moonlight. "For years I blamed you for having to kill Dock Baxter. If I had found you, then I would have killed you."

"You gunned down an innocent man in cold blood and you blame me." Richard Watersong stared into the darkness where Ray Elliott stood. "I have reached a point where I will take a life when it is expedient. No longer am I squeamish. Still, it has to serve a purpose and I have to be able to get away with it." Richard Watersong raised his pistol higher, pointing at the dim outline of Ray Elliott's head. "You, on the other hand, don't factor whether you can get away with it. When someone reaches the point you decide they need killing, they are dead. You put no more thought and hesitation than killing a mosquito. You could have easily claimed self-defense or attempted escape for Dock Baxter."

There was a pause in the conversation until Richard Watersong laughed. "You see my point. My gun is aimed at you and the sole thought in your mind is whether you can survive long enough to kill me. Whether you live beyond this moment is not a variable in your equation."

"We are both alive because I figure this is a negotiation. You said you wanted to talk." Ray Elliott added, "If we are going to die, then I would as soon do it before I get eat up by mosquitoes."

Richard Watersong said, "Let's say you win. A colored feme sole, which is what the law calls Martha Grant, is easy pickings for predators chasing oil money and you are not always going to be around. We both know you may step on a train one day. I will have the lawyers draw up a trust for Martha. Most people can't make a thousand dollars a year. I will pay her five thousand for fifteen years; that is seventy-five thousand dollars."

Ray Elliott relaxed his hand. "Mr. Denzel believes this place is worth a lot more in the long run. He says the field may produce fifty years, maybe more."

"Might be a hundred, might be five, might be the governor declares martial law and ends production tomorrow. Point is, you can keep your promise to Cecil Grant. I make a little more money. Ellie never has to go on the witness stand. Sound like a deal?"

"I will have to talk to Martha."

"It is going to be a long trial." Richard Watersong let his gun hand fall to his side and turned toward the door of the Duesenberg.

Ray Elliott asked, "Why didn't you offer this deal a year ago?"

"You mean, why did I wait until after I humiliated you on the witness stand? You needed to know what every day would have been like if you hadn't stepped on a train." The massive engine cranked to life. Ray Elliott was blinded by the lights and then the Duesenberg was gone into the night.

Ray Elliott stood in the darkness. Why didn't he fire? Likely Ellie and Martha would have been better off. At last, Richard Watersong would have been dead. If he only feared Richard Watersong had the drop on him, then why not lay in wait for the man and kill him?

He did not want to believe it was because of Richard Watersong's words, "Who lacks honor? The man who is willing to live a lie to protect the woman he loves or the coward who hops a train for fear of facing the truth." Ray Elliott was sure he was somehow just overlooking the answer. It had to be right in front of him.

CHAPTER 39: VALUE

Judge R.T. Brown's intention to have a ruling prior to the jury returning at nine failed to come to fruition. Instead of arguing the issues, the parties took the opportunity to discuss the settlement proposed by Richard Watersong the previous night.

Eleanor was not present in court today. Richie said his mother's hands were full with Walt because any change in the child's routine provoked uncontrollable fits. Additionally, Yolonda's health was poor. Eleanor had great difficulty finding anyone she trusted to stay with them.

Ray Elliott suspected yesterday was too much embarrassment for Eleanor. He thought about the proud, almost haughty bearing of Eleanor in her youth before scandal, tragedy, and struggle shaped her. She had already suffered too much humiliation for a proud woman. She had said little as they left the courtroom. She avoided being alone with him.

Ray Elliott considered himself the stupidest man on Earth. Having finally admitted to himself his feelings for Eleanor, he couldn't think of a romantic way to tell her.

Instead, he focused on his plan for settlement. He focused on the practical, the tangible, the immediate problem before him. Ray Elliott left the details of the negotiation out of his synopsis, specifically that such occurred during what most would call a Mexican standoff with loaded forty-five caliber pistols between himself and Richard Watersong. Richie considered the offer a positive development. Without Ray Elliott stating Eleanor would be able to avoid testifying, Richie had picked up on the fact.

Richie became an ardent supporter of reaching a deal. He surmised Richard Watersong had not yet made his best offer. He called it an encouraging turn of events.

Martha listened to the discussions about settlement. Ray Elliott suggested Richard Watersong had established a value for the property. He wasn't sure how he had done it and Richard Watersong would not tell them the truth. It was the only explanation for his offer. Richard Watersong never risked cheating himself. He only cheated others. Still, the negotiation could lead to a fair settlement.

Ray Elliott held out hope. He couldn't be sure whether he was deluding himself. He couldn't cheat Martha or go back on his word to Cecil, but he so wanted to protect Ellie from the witness stand.

Martha said, "Cecil's father was born a slave. He used to say, 'President Lincoln freed people, but it was Grant made it so.' Why we are Grants."

Richie said, "Cecil would want you taken care of. You could buy much more land somewhere else, plenty for your grandchildren."

"The name has become our name, and it stands for something on this little piece of dirt. We have fought so long and so hard and won so many times, I can only think God gave it to us." Martha looked to Ray Elliott.

Experience taught him not to argue with people who believed God had revealed something to them. He had an admiration for people capable of such faith, such appreciation of divine discernment. For himself, it seemed like God was too far distant, too amorphous to speak to him.

When the trial resumed, Judge R.T. Brown ruled in favor of Wesley Toben. He authorized the cross examination of Ray Elliott in its entirety. Wesley Toben lambasted Ray Elliott most of the day. However, he never delivered the coup de gras; rather, he was a cat toying with a mouse.

Near the end of the day, Ray Elliott found a second wind. He overcame the shame crushing emotion from his demeanor. Then he shortened his answers and stopped trying to explain. Ray Elliott buoyed himself with the knowledge Richie could later address in argument the half-truths Toben was using to mischaracterize his actions.

Ray Elliott looked to Richie. He could see the yellowing fire in Richie's hazel eyes. The flame burned bright.

Near the end of the day, Ray Elliott was permitted to step off the witness stand. Wesley Toben called James Denzel. On the final break of the day, Richie told Ray Elliott this had to be an attempt to promote a settlement by Richard Watersong.

The value of the property had little to do with ownership. The real reason to call Denzel was to permit the parties to reach a consensus on value. The reasoning made sense to Ray Elliott.

Wesley Toben established James Denzel as an expert in the oil business. Denzel had grown up in modest circumstances in East Texas, was educated at the University of Texas, and made his fortune as a young attorney in the oilfields in Louisiana and El Dorado, Arkansas. He later turned his attention to oil plays as the business presented in West Texas before pursuing this Black Giant in East Texas.

"How many wells have you drilled in your capacity as receiver of the real property in question?"

"I have four wells, all designed to offset wells on adjoining property." James Denzel anticipated the next question. "All good producers."

Wesley Toben asked, "Why not more? Because the way I understand it, every barrel you fail to capture, your neighbor likely does."

"There are a number of reasons. First, the infrastructure is insufficient to get more oil to market. We are having to store oil in open pits and move it by mule train. More oil will only slow our supply chain, not speed it. Secondly, we don't know yet whether many wells close together damages the formation, ultimately reducing how much oil can be recovered. Third, the railroad commission is already limiting wells to 'allowables' per well and adding spacing requirements on new wells. The greater the spacing, the greater the allowable production. Knowledge and reasonable regulation are overcoming the incentive for waste."

Wesley Toben asked, "Is what you are doing really best for the ultimate owner?"

"Yes. There is no more money to be made. What you describe is damaging the surface of the property, as well as the formation, and causing further price deflation. Producers aren't policing themselves like I had hoped they would. So sooner or later, the government will declare martial law."

Wesley Toben turned to his opposing counsel before asking James Denzel the ultimate question, "How much is this property ultimately worth?"

James Denzel said, "In the short term, the market will

depreciate to nothing. The glut will cause new uses, more markets, and additional products. Long term, the field will fuel an economic engine capable of pulling this nation out of depression."

Wesley Toben's face showed his disappointment. James Denzel acknowledged the failure. "You are presenting me with the same problem faced by Dad Joiner and H. L. Hunt. The long-term value is enormous, tempered by the short-term difficulties which may or may not be likewise enormous."

James Denzel looked at the disappointed and bewildered parties and jurors. He explained, "Value is fluid. For example, in the law, we know there is no such concept as lost production because the law holds the oil is still in the formation, subject to production. However, if I am an oilman with loan payments, bills, and payrolls to meet while my equipment experiences a mechanical breakdown prohibiting two days of production, two days may cost me my company, my leases, and my assets."

He added, "I will give you another example. If I produce an enormous crop of tomatoes which vastly exceeds my ability to pick and transport them to a railhead, I may still go out of business or, sell out for nothing. The new owner may invest in harvest and transport only to glut the market and likewise, the new owner goes out of business. The glut causes people to find additional uses for tomatoes. Perhaps instead of by themselves or in salad, someone develops a factory for ketchup and other sauces. The final owner may reap the benefits of all the failed owners. You see, my point is at any one time, the value of the commodity is not a fixed number. I tend to believe it is high; how high is speculation?"

Wesley Toben said, "Why they say pigs get fat and hogs get slaughtered?"

James Denzel smiled. "Right. A million dollars in the bottom of a hole is not necessarily a million dollars. It is like the old saying Shakespeare was referencing in Richard III. 'For want of a nail the shoe was lost. For want of a shoe the horse was lost. For want of a horse the knight was lost. For want of the knight the castle and so, for want of a nail the kingdom was lost.'"

Ray Elliott surmised one number was as good as another; so much for experts. It made more sense for Martha to take the money, yet he would stand behind whatever decision she made. He turned and looked at her, confirming his supposition.

Before leaving the courthouse, Richie told Ray Elliott about phoning Eleanor. Eleanor had agreed with Ray Elliott and Martha, especially after she was advised Denzel couldn't provide an accurate estimate on the value of the property. Richie also said Eleanor believed her place was with Walt. She would not be coming back to trial unless subpoenaed.

In Ray Elliott's opinion, a telephone was a poor medium to discuss anything, except when compared to not talking at all. He made up his mind to use the Sheriff's telephone to call Ellie and find out for himself where he stood.

CHAPTER 40: INVASION

Ray Elliott discovered Sheriff Gault was in an uncharacteristic good mood. He was standing in front of a Ford Model A. The automobile was black with a white star on the driver's side door.

Ray Elliott eased out a long breath evidencing his approval when Sheriff Gault raised a finger. "Wait a minute; look inside the cab, in car two-way radio."

Ray Elliott opened the door. "I heard they had these in New York."

Sheriff Gault laughed. "New York, New York and Rusk County Texas. I took the train to Dallas to get this one. In a month, we will have another one."

Ray Elliott debated whether to suggest Sheriff Gault replace the old six shooter on his hip. It was 1870s technology rendered well out of date by new semi-automatics like Colt's Model 1911 forty-five caliber pistol. Still, Ray Elliott knew Sheriff Gault was lightening quick with the ancient implement. Sheriff Gault was known throughout East Texas for presenting trick shooting exhibitions to schools, at picnics following cemetery work days, and church homecomings.

Despite his advancing age, Sheriff Gault's size naturally commanded attention. His narrowing frame was still tall and broad at the shoulders.

"No one down in Austin can be critical of the work you're doing here." Ray Elliott intended to compliment the sheriff, though he immediately regretted his remark.

"All I saw in Dallas newspapers were headlines about lawlessness in the East Texas Oilfield, not the hi-jackings and robberies you and I are investigating. No, a bunch of crying about folks violating allowables and railroad commission proration rules. They call that lawlessness? I've never known hot oil to kill anybody." Sheriff Gault turned and spat a wad of tobacco.

Ray Elliott made a second attempt. "A real lawman protects people from killers and murders, not enforcing rules for big oil and bankers in Dallas, Houston, and New York."

"Exactly. Old boy who can't pay his people because oil is cheaper than water, so what else can he do? He sells more of the only thing he has, oil." Sheriff Gault shook his head in an animated manner. Then he continued, "Newspaper editorial wants more rangers and the national guard. No offense ranger, but these folks did not elect you or a bunch of soldier boys to keep the peace."

Ray Elliott nodded. His years in the ranger service taught him to avoid any comment or action a local sheriff might take as belittling or demeaning. He would never be the state police, supplanting local elected law enforcement. He conveyed to his troops a servant model of law enforcement. Sheriffs universally reflected their communities. Honest sheriffs reflected generally honest communities and vice versa. Experience taught him some of the most corrupt sheriffs were reformers compared to the communities they served. Ray Elliott said, "Well I'm sure they are not talking about an invasion."

Sheriff Gault stared at him. Then he invited Ray Elliott into his office. As they walked through the outer entrance, Ray Elliott saw the shiny radio dispatching equipment.

The newness of the radio set made it ripe for examination. Ray Elliott reached for the microphone.

Sheriff Gault raised his hand, "What are you going to say?"

"Don't know, just thought I would try it out."

"The first words should be something auspicious. You know, dignified." Sheriff Gault took the microphone and set it back on the table next to the massive radio box.

"What are going to be the first words?"

Sheriff Gault raised his index finger to his temple. "Still pondering on it. I got a deputy to work this transmitter early in the morning and I am going to drive up toward the north end of the county in the new patrol car and see what we run across. Either he will get a phone call or I will radio him."

Ray Elliott said, "Probably the latter. Not many folks have a phone yet, which is why I am here. Can I use your phone?"

Sheriff Gault waved his arm toward the wall mounted telephone unit. Ray Elliott picked up the receiver and looked at Sheriff Gault.

"Oh, you need me to leave."

"Yes." The sheriff was outside by the time the response was spoken.

In a moment he heard Ellie's warm voice. "Hello."

"Ellie, I didn't get a chance to talk to you yesterday."

"I thought you said a lot."

Ray Elliott chuckled and then he was embarrassed because he decided his nervousness made the chuckle a little too raucous. He had spent a great deal of time with Eleanor since the spring. Despite the many hours together, he couldn't tell whether Eleanor was being serious or making a joke. "Will you come tomorrow?"

"I was up all night with Walt. Being away from him has made him worse."

Ray Elliott saw no way to avoid the awkward subject between them. "Well, I did say a lot yesterday, and you didn't say anything."

There was silence on the line before Eleanor spoke. "What am I supposed to say? Part of me wants to say you are thirty years too late. Part of me wants to build a life with you." There was a shriek in the background which corresponded to Walt. "But all of me is committed to these children. Good bye Ray."

The line went dead. Ray Elliott stood stunned for a long time. He didn't notice Sheriff Gault return to the room.

Sheriff Gault said, "You want to walk over to the Southwestern Hotel and have some dinner?"

"I figured your wife would be waiting on you."

"I get tired of good food."

Ray Elliott said, "I appreciate the offer. I got another big trial day tomorrow. I best get home." He walked out, unsure of anything.

Once back at the Grant homestead he sat on the porch and opened his watch. The lazy red sun descended into the horizon like it was melting in a fire. The slow process and long August days gave Ray Elliott ample time to reflect on his failures, missed opportunities, and a multitude of sins.

Sunshine found Ray Elliott seated in the same chair. It took all of his strength to lift himself from the chair. He forced himself to wash his face and confront the dawn.

Twelve miles away from the Grant homestead, Sheriff Gault drove through the town of Kilgore. He turned around at the Gregg County line. The boom town was rising with the dawn. Kilgore was a town now governing itself and establishing its own institutions. Sheriff Gault had turned off Highway 31 and was headed for the red clay dirt of Highway 29 toward Henderson when he heard his dispatcher.

"Sheriff, I got two telephone calls from oil company camps. Armed men are taking over oil well locations: the Bateman, Putnam, and Waggoner leases so far."

Sheriff Gault turned toward the Putnam lease because it was closest. He debated whether to respond on the new radio. This sounded odd, probably just a big coon hunt gone awry; nothing else made sense. He did not want to commemorate panic over a coon hunt by making it the first official communication from a police vehicle in the history of the county, likely all of East Texas.

He drove west onto the lease road and saw no activity. He didn't hear the customary sounds of production. Then he witnessed two uniformed men standing in the light of dawn. They were dressed in identical dark colored shirts and trousers wearing flat wide-brimmed hats.

Sheriff Gault brought his new police car to a stop, swung open his door and drew his Colt six shooter all in one smooth motion. The two weekend warriors were transfixed on the barrel of the old Peacemaker, despite the rifles in their own hands.

"Put those rifles on the ground, boys."

"Mister, we are here by order of General Woosley in command of the 124th Cavalry Texas National Guard. The governor has declared a state of open insurrection exists because of the extreme lawlessness of the Great East Texas Field and the inability of local authorities to restore order."

Sheriff Gault yelled the last phrase back at them. "'Inability of local authorities?' Boys, put those rifles on the ground."

The cavalryman on the right responded, "No sir, the general will have our hides. We don't come under local law enforcement. It is why we have to shut everything down; the locals can't handle it or they're on the take."

The other cavalryman looked at the pistol barrel, then at his fellow solider as if his companion had lost his mind. Sheriff Gault placed his revolver in his left hand, cocking it as he did so. With his right hand, he lifted the large, clumsy microphone to the new police radio.

He keyed the microphone for a long time to be certain his first words were heard, exactly as the instructor in Dallas had trained him.

"This is Sheriff Gault. Send an ambulance to the Putman lease west of Kilgore. A man has been shot and is in grave condition."

CHAPTER 41: REACHING FOR THE TRUTH

The two soldiers looked at each other with puzzled faces. The soldier on the right asked Sheriff Gault, "Sir, who got shot?"

"Son if you don't throw your rifle down, I am fixin to shoot you. I figure every moment we wait on an ambulance counts, cause boy, I'm not one to miss."

The sunshine patriots immediately threw their rifles on the ground.

Sheriff Gault placed his prisoners in the model A. He spoke to his prisoners in a somewhat less gruff tone. "Boys, when I see the official governor declaration and Judge R.T. Brown tells me it's legal, then I will let you go. Just because a fella is the bull of the woods in Austin don't mean we got to all bow and scrape up here."

The wiser of the two soldiers spoke, "It's okay sir, probably better we remain in your custody. When General Woosley finds out we got arrested, then we will get arrested again."

"You soldier boys really didn't get arrested. It is more of a being taken prisoner if that makes you feel any better. Better isn't it?"

"No, sir, it isn't."

"We'll call you guests of Rusk County and leave it at that."

The ride to Henderson was hot and dusty. Upon arrival, Sheriff Gault intended to search out the supreme legal authority, at least in his opinion—Judge R.T. Brown.

If Judge R.T. Brown was still tied up in Ray Elliott's trial, then these soldier boys would have to wait.

Above them in the district courtroom, Judge R.T. Brown pronounced, "Mr. Toben, you may call your next witness."

Wesley Toben said, "Your Honor, the Plaintiff rests."

Judge R.T. Brown stated, "The Defendant may call its first witness."

Richie rose and smiled. Ray Elliott pulled on his sleeve, whispering, "Don't do it, Richie."

Richie turned to the jury. "Your Honor, the Defense calls Richard Watersong to the witness stand."

Wesley Toben rose to both feet in one motion. "Your Honor, may we approach?"

There was a loud clap of applause outside. The clap fell to a dull roar from outside the front of the courthouse. Everyone in the courtroom turned their head, however, the jury couldn't see at all from their vantage point. The counsel table and the judge could make out a group of people.

Judge R.T. Brown motioned for the bailiff, then whispered, "What is the commotion?"

"Earlier, one of the clerks told me the sheriff had captured some Yankee soldiers, and he is showing them off."

Judge R.T. Brown looked intently at the bailiff.

The bailiff whispered, "I don't think they're really Yankees, sir."

Judge R.T. Brown spoke under his breath. "Go get the D.A. Tell him I received a telegram this morning that the governor has declared martial law. Ask him to please get Sheriff Gault to surrender without further incident."

The bailiff nodded and was off.

Judge R.T. Brown announced to the jury, "I am sure you have all followed in the news how the governor has proposed declaring a state of martial law. He has done so. I am certain there will be challenges to the declaration in both state and federal court. Until such times as the courts rule on the Constitutionality of the declaration or he withdraws the declaration, we shall honor such and this trial will continue. I need to recess you for a moment to address a new issue."

The jury was instructed and excused from the courtroom. All agreed it was better to let them satisfy themselves there was no invasion. The average citizens would notice little change other than the presence of armed troops, and most of them would be in the oilfield.

Wesley Toben said, "Your Honor, my client's son has every reason to hate his father. My client ran out on him, choosing a paramour over his own family, admittedly shameful. Be that as it may, my client is no killer. These are delusions formed in the suffering mind of a child who felt betrayed. The murderer of Lukas Halten was executed thirty years ago by Mr. Ray Elliott."

Richie's tone was higher and cadence quicker. "Your Honor, there was never a trial and certainly no confession. There is powerful circumstantial evidence against Richard Watersong. I submit you and other judges have granted arrest warrants on less evidence many times. These events occur close in time. Richard Watersong foreclosed on the property earlier on the same day as the murder. If he lied for thirty years about killing my grandfather, then why wouldn't he lie about stealing a man's land? The jury has a right to know and then decide if they believe it."

Judge R.T. Brown stated, "I am inclined to agree."

Wesley Toben said, "Your Honor, my client asserts his privilege against self-incrimination pursuant to the Fifth Amendment of the United States Constitution and the Texas Constitution Article One Sec—"

Richard Watersong yelled from the counsel table as he rose. "Objection."

Judge R.T. Brown said, "Mr. Watersong, you can't object to your own attorney."

"Why not?" Richard Watersong looked from Richie to the judge and added, "Your Honor, why can't I object to my own attorney?"

Judge R.T. Brown looked to Wesley Toben. "Counsel, are you going to object to your own client's objection to your objection?"

"Yes; I submit such demonstrates the absurdity of the circumstance in which we find ourselves. A son is calling his father to the witness stand for the sole purpose of accusing the father of murdering the grandfather, all purportedly in relation to a trespass to try title suit."

Richie said, "Your Honor, as I stand here, I can see a courthouse lawn of gawkers to view captured soldiers. I submit in this surreal environment the only event which makes sense is my attempt to put to rest an unsolved murder."

Judge R.T. Brown looked to Richard Watersong. "Your objection, sir."

"I want to testify before the jury. I made mistakes, a lot of them. I need to set it all straight as best I can." Richard Watersong turned and looked into Richie's hazel eyes. Wesley Toben moved forward as if to speak. Richard Watersong raised his hand. "You work for me, counselor."

Judge R.T. Brown administered the oath. “Do you swear to tell the truth, the whole truth, and nothing but the truth, so help you God.”

Richard Watersong answered with his right hand in the air. “I do.”

Judge R.T. Brown gestured his arm to the witness stand. “Then sir, after the recess, you may testify.”

Richard Watersong looked at Richie, then Ray Elliott.

CHAPTER 42: The Death of Honor

While the parties waited for the jury to return, Ray Elliott stepped onto the tall courthouse steps to see the commotion on the lawn. He was surprised by someone who was so out of context for him, he literally stepped backwards.

"Yolonda."

Yolonda exclaimed, "Well if it isn't the Caboose!"

"What are you doing here?"

"I came here because I love Ellie. I knew you would come back. After time dragged on, I began to dread it."

"Why?"

Yolonda wheezed and pushed her cane forward. "Eleanor lost her case in Nacogdoches. Court ruled you can't be living dead, so Richard Watersong had to be declared alive no matter how many years it has been. Legally, Eleanor is his wife, like being declared a slave. She can't do anything in business without his approval."

Ray Elliott said, "I understand."

Yolonda raised her cane. "You don't understand. Eleanor is in Dallas today trying to get a specialist to see Walt."

Ray Elliott said, "Good."

"They're not her kids, no kin to her. They are Richard Watersong's kids. All he has to do is show up, and the law says he can take them from her. There is nothing she can do. Between you and the twins, she will choose the children. That's what you need to understand. You leave her be."

Ray Elliott wheeled on his back foot without showing further response. He was cut to the quick, his soul crushed. He told himself the contrary old heifer didn't know anything anyway, though he knew she was right. He walked back to the courtroom.

Richie asked, "Please state your name."

"Richard Watersong."

"You married Eleanor Halten, and your father-in-law was Lukas Halten, wasn't he?"

"Yes."

"Your father-in-law was a war hero who started a bank to help the community?"

"Yes."

"Wasn't he universally loved?"

Richard Watersong leaned back. "Fair to say."

Richie asked, "You and Eleanor had two sons, correct?"

"You are one of them."

Richie asked, "Still, you cheated on your wife with a girl named Queen, right?"

"No."

Richie looked up, lost for a moment. "Are you denying you had an affair with Queen?"

Richard Watersong answered, "Not fair to limit the question to Queen. I cheated on my wife with any woman who would slow down long enough."

The jury gasped. Adultery was scandalous in the Bible belt. Pride in adultery was a bridge too far for anyone in polite society. Richie balled his fist, then in a deliberate motion let it fall on the table.

Richie asked, "You took Queen to Cuba with you and

had three children with her, didn't you?"

Richard Watersong answered, "I had one child with Queen; a son named Richard. He was murdered by thieves in Cuba trying to steal my gold. The other two morons can't be mine."

Ray Elliott dug his fingers under the bottom of the table top. He dug until he felt the wood push apart his nails from his digits.

Richie said, "Before you took off for Cuba, you robbed the bank's depositors blind, didn't you?"

"Yes."

"In fact, there was a warrant for you out of the bank here in Henderson, wasn't there?"

Richard Watersong looked away. "What I was told."

"You were also stealing from the depositors in Nacogdoches and were about to be found out, correct?" Richie composed himself.

"True."

The son accused the father. "Lukas Halten had caught you stealing, hadn't he?"

Richard Watersong shifted in the straight-back chair. "He had at that, Mr. Watersong."

Richie said, "You were in the same room when he was murdered, weren't you?"

"Yes."

Richie rose to the edge of his chair. "So, you had motive and opportunity for murder?"

"Yes."

Richie extended an arm, pointing. "You had your money and paramour ready to abscond in the same moment. All the stars were lined up for you, weren't they?"

"True."

Richie turned to the jury. "So, you cut your own father-in-law's throat, didn't you?"

Richard Watersong looked at the judge then to Richie before turning to the jury. "No."

Richie repeated the answer as if it didn't register. "No. No?"

Richard Watersong stared at his estranged son and repeated in a loud clear voice. "No." He looked around. The courtroom was completely without sound before he spoke again. "It was such an odd set of facts which cost Lukas his life, I promised on my sacred honor I would never divulge the truth. I have thought a lot about the promise and to whom I made it. I lived a lie to preserve my promise, my honor. The whole agonizing thirty years I was dying and witnessing the death of my honor. It was like a poison killing everything I loved."

Richard Watersong stared at Ray Elliott as if they had some bond. In that moment, they did, for Ray Elliott began to understand Richard Watersong. He could never respect the man. However, Watersong did have some code, albeit a dishonorable compass. The unscrupulous bearings guided his Machiavellian decisions. Ray Elliott was reminded wickedness had its own principles.

Richie still appeared dumbfounded. He could only articulate one word. "Who?"

Richard Watersong smirked. "Let me tell you why first. It has taken me years to put it all together. There are a lot of pieces to the puzzle. Queen was pregnant. I did not know it. In hindsight, I know somehow Lukas Halten had found out. It is likely Queen had told someone. Queen cleaned the bank. Like a lot of places, we kept a cask of liquor open for customers. I never saw anyone really get drunk. Like the general stores, we thought it sort of greased the wheels of commerce."

Richard Watersong turned to the jury. "You have to understand this was well before prohibition. It was even before the temperance leagues. Well, Queen developed a taste for it. At first, I encouraged her because the liquor made it easier to have my way with her. You also need to know Lukas Halten. He was an even better man than any of you have heard or known."

Richard Watersong paused before continuing. "He had repaid the investors in Henderson and talked all but one into declining to press charges. Originally, he thought it was only the Henderson bank; probably assumed I was too smart to mess in the trough where I ate. I wasn't. Again, I am putting it together over the years. He had discovered I was stealing from the Nacogdoches Bank, too."

Richard Watersong looked down and seemed to lose his train of thought. Someone cleared their throat and Richard Watersong started again. "You have to understand, Lukas Halten was prone to outburst. He had threatened to kill me for my adultery many times and he hated a thief. Despite all I had done, he would never have hurt me. It would have crushed you, your brother Walt, his grandsons, and disgraced your mother, rendered his baby girl an object of shame in polite society. There was no way he would have harmed me, or anyone else."

Another silence filled the courtroom. Richie added, "Are you trying to convince us Queen didn't know Lukas Halten would have never hurt you?"

Richard Watersong answered, "Not just me. Despite his valor in the war, war was war. He would never hurt a woman or a child or an unborn child. He was a far better man than I."

Richard Watersong's voice trailed off. The corners of Richard Watersong's eyes became moist, holding back tears. "I had a letter opener on my desk; a gift from your mother. It was made of sheep horn and had probably a six-inch blade. He was hitting me with his cane. He wasn't hurting me and I deserved it. Lukas was calling me a thief and an adulterer, going on about how I was destroying your mother's good name and exposing you and your brother to a lifetime of shame."

Richard Watersong composed himself and returned his gaze to Richie. "Out of the blue, Queen began defending me. Lukas, your grandfather, became infuriated, yelling it must be true that Queen was pregnant. She denied it, but he continued. Then he told her, 'Some women should not be mothers.' It was too much, far too much."

Richard Watersong steadied himself and looked back to the jury. "It still doesn't seem real to this day. She drew the letter opener across his throat in no more time than it took to say the words. I didn't even think the thing was sharp enough to cut."

Richard Watersong shook his head. "I took the letter opener from Queen. Dock Baxter was building shelves in the vault room. He walked in the room. I guess he heard the commotion. Well, it was expedient. I have always prided myself on seeing the expedient. In a way, Lukas Halten did, too. If Queen would have left things alone, he would have paid back the money I stole and likely paid her handsomely. She could have started a new life."

Richie said, "So you expect us to believe Queen killed Lukas Halten?"

"I don't expect you to believe anything. I made a

promise to Queen. She is dead now and our son is dead. With her final words, she released me from my promise. For thirty years, I fulfilled my promise to her. At first, I thought I was so noble; then I realized I held it over her, stifling her, crushing her. She was down and I never let her up." Richard Watersong turned from the jury back to his son.

Richie swung his hand toward the jury. "We are supposed to believe you are an innocent man?"

Richard Watersong smirked at the question. "At first, I believed I was innocent. It caused me to resent Queen and wallow in self-pity. I knew what would happen to a colored person even if it were really manslaughter or self-defense. She owed me her life and I never let her forget it. Decades later, I realized it was my fault all along. She was protecting me, protecting our child. If I hadn't plucked the rose from the vine, then it wouldn't have withered."

There was a long pause and the only sound in the courtroom was the irregular breathing of the jurors. They were enthralled.

Richard Watersong placed his hand over his face. "It wasn't long ago when I realized I loved her as much as I was capable of loving anyone, which was far too little, far too late."

He wiped his face with the hand and lifted it. "I never meant to run out on you, son. It was an odd set of events, setting circumstances in motion beyond my control. I was fulfilling a promise, protecting what was really an innocent girl whose only true crime was succumbing to my lust."

Ray Elliott heard Richie whisper under his breath. "Tell it to the Devil."

CHAPTER 43:
A Second Death

Over the next day and a half, Richie called witnesses to build Cecil Grant's adverse possession claim. Community leaders both black and white knew the property as the Grant farm.

Each proved it had been the Grant farm for what the law refers to as, "so long the memory of man runneth not to the contrary." The witnesses told the story of Cecil and Martha Grant.

Their tale was less dramatic than Richard Watersong's. Their love story was a portrait of Christian people scrabbling out a life from a hard, iron ore rock farm in Jim Crow era Texas. Still, there were joys, the birth of children, additions to the home, completing fences, and raising barns. There was the day Cecil Grant became a deacon; the smile on his face and the beaming pride and admiration with which his wife looked at him; the way Martha was the first sight for two generations of children in her community and the lives she saved.

Contrasted against Richard Watersong's life of regret, the Grant story held the quiet beauty of a moral life. What a dichotomy. The rage and violence of a conscience set against one's soul versus the bountiful softness of hearts at peace.

Wesley Toben asked few questions. Thereafter, the judge called a recess.

Richie commented to Ray Elliott about the strength of the testimonials. They attested to a life well lived. Richie was convinced the evidence was moving the jury, but to what extent was beyond his ability to ascertain.

Ray Elliott said, "The Grants are good people, always been good people. I don't know why I spoke up for a black man thirty years ago. He was a stranger to me. I sure am proud I did, though."

Richie said, "Cecil would be proud of you."

Ray Elliott said, "No he wouldn't."

Richie chose to end his case in chief with Brother Alton Silver. The direct examination focused on Brother Alton Silver working with his father-in-law, Cecil Grant, to make valuable improvements to the property. These ranged from small projects like a chicken coop to home additions and clearing additional cropland.

In between the legally necessary elements Richie needed to prove, another story emerged. Brother Alton Silver had been an aimless youth mired in gambling on horse racing, tobacco, and strong drink when he met the Grant family.

"I was pulled to my future wife. They call her Junior in the family and the attraction brought me to Cecil and Martha. Cecil never said a cross word to me. Every time I saw him, he told me he was praying for me. I told him to pray for himself or someone who needed his praying."

Richie asked, "Is Cecil what brought you to the ministry?"

"I had never known people like them. One day, Cecil asked me to pray with him and I did." Brother Alton Silver was smiling and crying at the same time.

After Brother Alton Silver testified, the judge called a recess. The lawyer and the judge began to compose the jury instructions, called the charge. Charge conferences as the hearings were referenced were often contentious. Ray Elliott stood in the hall.

Brother Alton Silver said, “Been praying for you.”

Ray Elliott nodded and turned away.

Brother Alton Silver said, “Cecil asked me to do it. Before he died, he told me I needed to pray for you to give your life to Christ. He made me promise him.”

Ray Elliott sneered. “God don’t want my life. I got a lot more darkness on my heart than any boyhood gambling and tobacco, preacher.”

“God sees your heart even in the darkness.” There was an awkward pause before Brother Alton Silver added, “I will keep praying.”

“I have to get back in the courtroom.” Richie had presented a strong case. Ray Elliott was curious what Wesley Toben would argue. Toben rose to the challenge.

Wesley Toben raised the paper in the air again. He made the same spirited defense of private property and free enterprise. Then, he wrapped the entire bundle of freedom in the American flag.

His response to the adverse possession claim was nothing short of brilliant. “One thing we know for certain is Cecil Grant, God rest the man’s soul, was no thief. I refuse to say he was trying to take from another or claiming anything he did not own. The best evidence of what Cecil Grant believed he owned is his signature right here on this paper. Don’t disparage an honorable Christian man by calling him a thief with your verdict. Certainly, it may be what his family wants for short term oil wealth. In the long run, they would have to live with the guilt and admit they disparaged a great patriarch for a dollar bill. Give meaning to the man’s life, not thirty pieces of silver.

Give meaning to the words he adopted with his signature on this page. For better or worse, it is words we all live and die by."

Richie's closing was not as compelling. He summarized all the elements necessary for his adverse possession laws. However, Richie spent most of his time focused on Richard Watersong's selfishness and misspent life. To Ray Elliott, it would have been wiser to focus on the dignity of Cecil and Martha's years of toiling the land at issue. Richie squandered the chance to tell a positive story of Christian discipleship to harp on the wages of sin.

Ray Elliott realized the young man who had so freely forgiven him and remembered only the good moments of their time together held an open animosity for his father. The father richly deserved the ire. However, experience taught Ray Elliott the hatred poisoned the one who most lived with it.

The jury retired to the jury room to deliberate. Time passed slow at first, then it moved quicker.

Ray Elliott stepped onto the large cement porch in front of the Art Deco style courthouse. He stood over the wide steps moving below him to the lawn. He looked up North Main Street.

"How is it going to come out?"

Ray Elliott touched the hilt of his forty-five. He turned to see Richard Watersong leaning against one of the gritty, concrete-topped brick posts marking the wall of the large stoop. The August sun burned down on them. There was no breeze, yet it was an improvement over the stale, humid courtroom air.

"Are going to kill me like Dock Baxter, or wait on the verdict to decide?"

Ray Elliott reached further on the grip of the pistol. "A dead man should stay dead. Wouldn't you agree it's the most expedient solution? Eleanor wouldn't have to fear you taking Walt and Elly or being skewered by your rapier lawyer in one of these trials. Martha would have the family land for her and the grandkids. And I could step on a fast train to anywhere."

Richard Watersong said, "You don't want to step on a train. There is a hope in your eyes today. You are foolishly believing in absolution. There is no salvation for men like you and I. You're not a believer in anything: not God, and certainly not justice. It's why you shot Dock Baxter. There is no God but ourselves. We protect people from the consequences of believing in fairy tales."

"I am trying to keep a promise to a man who knew better than to make a deal with the Devil. After I heard Denzel testify, I realized your offer was as fair as any. What if we turn it around? Denzel already has some royalty money in the registry of the court. Martha buys you out on the terms you offered her. You don't claim Walt and Elly. You don't want them, anyway."

Ray Elliott paused and satisfied himself he still had Richard Watersong's interest. "Financially, you are better off dead. You may take half of everything Eleanor has amassed in thirty years, but I bet if she can locate your true assets, her wealth isn't a drop in the bucket to what she could take from you."

Richard Watersong added, "And you get my wife."

Involuntarily, Ray Elliott slid the tips of his fingers along the hilt of the Colt in his holster before stopping himself. "Can you honestly tell me, from the moment you married her, there was ever a day, even a genuine minute, when you treated her like a wife?"

Richard Watersong looked at the semi-automatic pistol on Ray Elliott's hip. "No, I can't tell you I ever appreciated Eleanor for a minute. I will tell you I cheated myself out of the opportunity for any happiness with her; worse, I cheated her. If I walk away from your offer, will I be staring down the barrel of your forty-five sooner or later?"

Ray Elliott raised his empty gun hand. "No, we both know I have enough on my conscience. I won't kill another man."

"You are right. My death is expedient. As far as I am concerned, I died chasing Lukas Halten's killer. I heard it from a Texas Ranger Captain. Everybody knows Texas Rangers don't lie." Richard Watersong extended his hand. Ray Elliott took it.

Wesley Toben and Judge R.T. Brown were quite pleased with the agreement. Both were too well versed in settlement to show their elation, lest the deal come unraveled. Both attorneys had seen a wink, a smile from one litigant to the opposing party sink a fair deal many times.

Martha was satisfied she had honored her late husband's wishes. She beamed with pride that in his death, he had provided the opportunity he'd so desperately prayed for for his family.

However, Richie had changed his mind. He counseled against any settlement. Several times, he blustered and stormed over some inconsequential term. However, he eventually obeyed his mother's orders.

The jury was discharged without returning a verdict. There was relief on their faces. Ray Elliott took Martha into the County Clerk's Office. Martha was flanked by her daughter and son-in-law.

"Martha, this is a deed to you and Cecil's farm." Ray Elliott handed her the document.

Martha said, "Cecil would want you to have something for all of this."

Ray Elliott looked from Martha to Junior, then to Brother Alton Silver. "Cecil has given me far more than anything I've done for him."

Brother Alton Silver said, "You know it's Wednesday. All of Mount Hope is going to give thanks to God and be praying for you tonight."

Ray Elliott touched the pastor's arm. "You tell them thank you for their prayers."

Brother Alton Silver didn't exaggerate. That night, the congregation was alive with joy. There was singing, praise dancing, and an inspired Alton Silver preached the sermon of his life.

He stretched his arms to heaven, calling for a confession of sins and a public profession of faith. When he looked down at the railing before him, there was Ray Elliott, head bowed, kneeling at the altar.

CHAPTER 44: TIMING

Ray Elliott was dressed in his best suit with his freshly brushed hat when he walked through Sheriff Gault's door. "Is the invasion over?"

Sheriff Gault answered, "The devil in me is truly enjoying it. Hot oilers have concreted well controls open, bribed anyone with a handout, run pipe crossways every which a way between wells, and built houses over well heads. Soldier boys can't handle it. The more they try to close the spigot, the wider it opens."

Ray Elliott removed his gun belt and wrapped it around the holster of his 1911 pistol. "I want you to have my gun."

"I can't take your pistol. I have never shot an automatic. If you're giving it up, hang it on the wall."

Ray Elliott placed the belt and holster on Sheriff Gault's desk. The well-oiled leather gave the small office a pleasant aroma. "I can empty the magazine in a target before even an expert like you can get two aimed shots off from your old single action. I'll feel better knowing you carry it."

Sheriff Gault picked up the rig pulling, the Colt semi-automatic from the holster. "So, you're really retiring this time?"

Ray Elliott produced a badge and a letter from his inside breast pocket. "Will you give these to Ranger Gonzallas? He will get them to the right place. I decided I wouldn't give the general the opportunity to refuse this time."

"What will you do with yourself?"

Ray Elliott looked at his watch. "In about an hour I am stepping on a fast train. James Denzel has formed an association of independent producers. He has asked me to join him in Austin to convince the governor there are good alternatives to martial law."

"I had hoped you were going to ask me to drive you to Nacogdoches."

Ray Elliott looked down at the image inside the watch case. "Time passes. She doesn't care for me."

Sheriff Gault raised his hands like he was catching something with them. "How do you think you got Richie to strut with Mr. Fancy lawyer Toben until you could get the case worked out for Martha? Eleanor got nothing out of the settlement and Richie's soul is eaten up with hatred. Course, it's none of my business."

Ray Elliott said, "There is always a 'but' behind the phrase, 'It's none of my business.'"

"Since you asked. Seems to me she has done and done for you without much return. That's hard on a person's pride, especially a fine lady like Eleanor. She is too proud to say she needs you. Worse, she's embarrassed she was ever married to Richard Watersong. You're too bull headed to go to her with your hat in your hand."

"You figured all of this out on your own, did you?"

Sheriff Gault extended his hand. "Somebody 'round here has to think through these things. What's it going to be: the train depot or Nacogdoches? How close are you to the train leaving?"

Ray Elliott looked again at his watch and then he closed it.

CHAPTER 45:
A New Creature

Eleanor started her day checking on the children. She hugged Elly and told her she loved her, then did the same to Walt. Eleanor was slow and deliberately sounded each word out, as she had for months. She could never be sure how much Walt understood.

She walked to the kitchen. Yolonda had already started percolating coffee. Eleanor soon took over. She made bacon, fried eggs, and heated biscuits.

Yolonda's night had been difficult. "I done outlived my time, outlived my people. Woman shouldn't outlive her family."

Eleanor looked at her like she was scolding a child. "Foolishness, we are your family. I won't hear foolishness in this house."

"You know I am nothing but trouble to you."

Eleanor gave her the same cross look, only staring longer. She lifted the pan of biscuits out of the stove using her apron edge to protect her hand. "Do we still have juice in the icebox?"

Yolonda said, "I believe Elly drank it all yesterday."

"No matter, milk is–"

Walt came flying into Eleanor, grabbing around her apron strings. Eleanor kneeled down to him. "Walt, what is–"

Walt pushed his hand to his heart like he had seen Eleanor do so many times. "I." Then he moved his hand to Eleanor's heart. "L-o-v-e y-o-u."

Elly was standing behind Walt. “He has been trying for a long time. I told him to come show you. Why aren’t you happy?”

Eleanor wiped her tears aside. “I am ecstatic. Ecstatic means very happy. This is the greatest day in my life.” Eleanor’s eyes released her tears.

The three were hugging when Yolonda walked over and put her hand on Eleanor’s shoulder. “The Good Lord can surely take me now. I have not seen this house so happy since your father was alive.”

Eleanor chided her again. This time, she did so with a smile. “I told you, I won’t hear such talk in this house.”

Someone was rapping the brass knocker at the door. Eleanor said, “Probably Richie. He told me yesterday he had a case in Lufkin and would stop if he could.” She hugged Walt and Elly and then rose to walk to the door.

On the other side of the door was Ray Elliott, looking down, holding his big, wide-brimmed hat next to his chest. The morning sun was shining from behind him.

His face lifted, and he looked into Elanor’s still tearful eyes. “Preacher says I’m supposed to be a new creature in Christ. I can’t be sure he’s right. What I do know is if you will have me, I want to be a help to you and the children. Course, I know you know the worst of me.”

Ellie looked at him. Her hazel eyes caught the blue from her apron. She swung the door open wide. Ray Elliott walked into her home.